Praise for

THE TIGER MOM'S TALE

"*The Tiger Mom's Tale* is a heartfelt, delightful read. Lyn Liao Butler's story of Taiwanese and American identity had me turning pages and laughing (and drooling over the delicious descriptions of food)."

—Charles Yu, author of *Interior Chinatown*, winner of the 2020 National Book Award

"Sharp and humorous, *The Tiger Mom's Tale* is a scenic debut novel with a cast of complicated characters sure to bring laughter and discussion to your next book club. I can't wait to read what Lyn Liao Butler writes next!"

—Tif Marcelo, *USA Today* bestselling author of *The Key to Happily Ever After*

"*The Tiger Mom's Tale* is a breathtaking debut from a compelling new voice in women's fiction. With captivating characters and vivid descriptions of mouthwatering meals, Lyn Liao Butler whisks us from the bright lights of New York City to the bustle of Taichung. A story of belonging, betrayal, and the bonds between family that can never be broken, *The Tiger Mom's Tale* is a deeply emotional and satisfying read." —Kristin Rockaway, author of *She's Faking It*

"*The Tiger Mom's Tale* has it all—family drama, scorching love, vivid transcontinental settings, and culinary scenes that made me drool. A charming, engrossing debut from Lyn Liao Butler."

—Kimmery Martin, author of *The Antidote for Everything*

TITLES BY LYN LIAO BUTLER

The Tiger Mom's Tale
Red Thread of Fate

RED THREAD OF FATE

LYN LIAO BUTLER

Berkley
New York

BERKLEY
An imprint of Penguin Random House LLC
penguinrandomhouse.com

Copyright © 2022 by Lyn Liao Butler
Readers Guide copyright © 2022 by Lyn Liao Butler
Penguin Random House supports copyright. Copyright fuels creativity, encourages diverse voices, promotes free speech, and creates a vibrant culture. Thank you for buying an authorized edition of this book and for complying with copyright laws by not reproducing, scanning, or distributing any part of it in any form without permission. You are supporting writers and allowing Penguin Random House to continue to publish books for every reader.

BERKLEY and the BERKLEY & B colophon are registered trademarks of
Penguin Random House LLC.

Library of Congress Cataloging-in-Publication Data

Names: Butler, Lyn Liao, author.
Title: Red thread of fate / Lyn Liao Butler.
Description: First edition. | New York: Berkley, 2022.
Identifiers: LCCN 2021031053 (print) | LCCN 2021031054 (ebook) |
ISBN 9780593198742 (trade paperback) | ISBN 9780593198759 (ebook)
Classification: LCC PS3602.U8757 R44 2022 (print) | LCC PS3602.U8757 (ebook) |
DDC 813/.6—dc23
LC record available at https://lccn.loc.gov/2021031053
LC ebook record available at https://lccn.loc.gov/2021031054

First Edition: February 2022

Printed in the United States of America
1st Printing

Book design by Alison Cnockaert

To Lakon
Fate brought us together

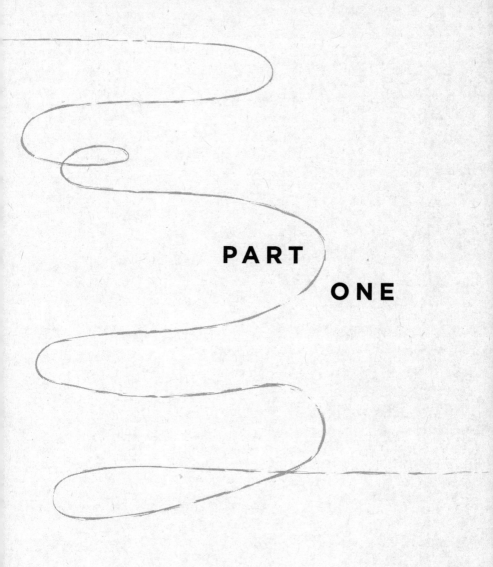

PART ONE

1

SHE WAS ON the phone with her husband when he died.

Tamlei Kwan leaned against a wall outside the elementary school during her lunch break, phone tucked between her ear and shoulder. She balanced on one foot and slipped her other foot out of her taupe pumps. Ah, much better. The shoes felt like prisons after a summer of flip-flops.

"Did we get it?" Tony's brusque voice greeted her. They were anxiously awaiting their letter of acceptance for the little boy they were adopting from China. But still. He couldn't bother to say hello first?

Tam stuck her tongue out at the phone. "No, I haven't heard anything. Will you be home for dinner?" Two days back at school and she was already acting like her young charges. "I could cook." But seriously, why was she even offering? He sounded so distant, as if he had better things to do than take her call.

"Sure, that sounds good. I shouldn't be home late. Thanks,

Tam." Tony's voice softened on her name, and just like that, she was glad she had made the effort. She knew she wasn't being fair. He *had* been doing a lot lately and she shouldn't be so prickly.

A sudden cacophony of traffic noises made her hold the phone away from her ear.

"What's going on?"

"Nothing . . . a lot of traffic." She could barely hear his voice.

"You going to the deli on Amsterdam?" she yelled.

"Yes . . . hang on a sec." She could hear Tony's muffled voice before he came back on the line. "I'm grabbing lunch before my afternoon class. Let me know if you hear from Sandra, okay?" Their caseworker, Sandra, had told them their dossier had gone through review and was in match mode, which meant they should be getting that letter any day now.

"Okay." Tam chewed on her bottom lip. "Um, what should I make?" She wished she didn't sound so wishy-washy. Why was she so confident in her mind, but the moment she opened her mouth, she sounded like a meek mouse?

"I don't care, whatever you . . . HOLY SHIT!" Tony's voice was cut off in the midst of a loud roaring sound that made Tam think of the old wooden roller coaster at Coney Island, which Tony had dragged her on once. Then, nothing. Silence.

"Tony? Tony! Hello?" Tam shouted. What the heck? She straightened off the wall, jamming her foot back in her shoe, all thoughts of her aching feet and wishy-washiness forgotten. She immediately redialed him, only to get his voicemail. His phone didn't even ring. She dialed again and again, her heart jumping into her throat. She finally decided to try his department at Columbia University, hoping someone could find him.

Her hands were shaking and she touched the wrong contact,

dialing Tony's Pizzeria instead of Tony's office. "Darn it," she muttered, stabbing her finger at the phone. "I don't want a freaking pizza." This time, she hit the right number and a colleague of Tony's in the Department of East Asian Languages and Cultures picked up, telling Tam that Tony had left for the day.

"What do you mean he left for the day?" Tam's voice rose with each word. "I just spoke to him and he said he was going to the deli on Amsterdam."

The woman on the phone was silent for a moment. "Uh, I saw Tony an hour ago and he was definitely leaving. He has a half day on Thursdays."

A half day? What was the daft woman talking about? Tony taught an afternoon class on Thursdays at Columbia this semester and then had office hours to meet with students, which was why he was sometimes late coming home. She started to explain but realized she was wasting her time. She hung up after making the woman promise to have Tony call her if she saw him.

Looking at the time, Tam knew she had to get back to her own class of first graders. She tried Tony one more time but still couldn't get through. She returned to her classroom, tamping down the panic that threatened to erupt.

Where was Tony? What had happened? Should she call the police? But if he had only dropped his phone and broken it, he wouldn't appreciate a police hunt for him. She had a bad feeling in the pit of her stomach and left her phone on her desk.

"Mrs. Kwan. Mrs. Kwan! I have a question about hot and cold." Tam looked up to see Steven Abrams waving his arm frantically. It was only the second day of school and already she knew this precocious little boy with the floppy brown hair would be a handful.

"Yes, Steven. What is it?"

"I heard my daddy talking to his friends about you. He said if you got rid of your glasses and unbuttoned your shirt, you'd be hot. But if you took off your shirt, wouldn't you be cold, not hot?" Steven tilted his head and looked up at her. His father was a single dad and so good-looking he had all the female teachers and some of the male ones fluttering about him.

"Oh, my." Tam knew she sounded like an eighteenth-century schoolmarm, but she was at a loss. Normally, she was quick on her feet with the children and could come up with a clever answer to the questions her students asked. But now she could only stare, her mouth open "like a nincompoop"—as Steven had so blithely called a fellow student yesterday—while the six-year-olds debated her hot-and coldness.

She tugged at the white shirtwaist dress she wore. When she'd pulled the dress out that morning, she'd debated against wearing it since it was a few days after Labor Day. But it was such a warm, sunny day, and she wanted to wear the dress one more time, despite the fact that it would probably get dirty from the children. It was buttoned to the top and a size too big. She hated clothes that dug into her skin. She dressed that way for school, but if she had to be honest, she dressed that way outside school too. She'd much rather be comfortable, even if it made her look like a shapeless blob.

When the bell finally rang and she saw her charges safely to the bus and pickup area, she huffed out a breath and rushed to her car. Tony hadn't called and she still couldn't get through. She threw her phone on the passenger seat in frustration. Driving the short distance to their home in Dobbs Ferry, she decided she would call the police when she got home. Maybe they could trace his cell.

But as she pulled into the dead-end street that led to their town house at the bottom of the hill, her heart sank. Sitting in front of their unit was a Dobbs Ferry police car. She knew then—something bad had happened.

She pulled into her parking spot and gripped the steering wheel hard to stop the tingling in her fingers. When her vision blackened, she squeezed her eyes shut and rested her head on the cool leather between her hands. She forced herself to breathe slower to stop the panic from taking over her body, not wanting to leave the safety of her car. She knew that the minute she got out, her life would change forever, and she wanted to hold on to her old life for as long as she could.

What happened next passed in a blur. Facing the sympathetic-looking officers as her legs turned to jelly, she heard only bits and pieces of what they said.

"Flushing police . . . accident . . ."

The officers' radios buzzed to life in a burst of static, and Tam turned toward the noise, her eyes glazed.

"Your husband . . . terrible . . ."

She turned back to the officers and they swam in front of her eyes. She swayed and would have fallen if one of them hadn't reached out to steady her, helping her inside and onto a chair. They continued to speak, but they might as well have been speaking Russian for all that she understood.

She looked down at her lap to avoid their gaze, grabbing fistfuls of her dress in her hands to keep from screaming. Then her eyes widened as she realized with dawning horror that she was wearing the symbolic color of death in China. Tony was more traditionally Chinese than she was and had commented this morning that she was dressed for a funeral. *Did I kill my husband by wearing white today?*

". . . call your family to come?"

She looked up, eyes wide with shock, and shook her head. The officers kept talking and she scrambled to understand, but her body refused to cooperate. She was frozen in her chair. Suddenly, something they said penetrated the fog that had descended over her brain.

"Flushing police? What do you mean? He was in Manhattan, at Columbia University, where he teaches."

The officers looked at each other and then at her. "Uh, no, ma'am. He was on the corner of Main and Roosevelt in Flushing, Queens."

Ma'am? She was a ma'am now? How'd that happen? She had an absurd urge to laugh and had to choke it down. "You're wrong. I was on the phone with him. He said he was going to the deli on Amsterdam Avenue." Tam pulled her phone out to show the officers, as if that would prove he was in Manhattan at the time of the accident. Maybe they had the wrong man, since her Tony was at Columbia where he belonged, and not miles away in Flushing, Queens.

The officers exchanged another look. The younger one asked if they could call a friend for her. Tam closed her eyes. She put her hands over her ears, knowing she was being childish, but she couldn't help it. She didn't want to hear any more. They were mistaken. They had the wrong man. She needed to make them stop, stop trying to ruin her life when she knew Tony was fine.

"His cousin was with him."

Her eyes flew open. She'd heard, even through her hands. Tony only had one cousin. "Mia? He was with Mia?"

One of the officers looked at his pad and said, "Mei Guo. She didn't survive either."

"Oh, no. That's her. She goes by Mia." Her head began to ache and she could feel every heartbeat in a vein in her temple. What was going on? Mia was dead too? Why would Tony tell her he was at work if he'd been with Mia? Hysterical laughter bubbled out of her and she was suddenly laughing even as tears streamed down her face and soaked her dress.

She gave in and let the police call her friend Abby Goldman. She was grateful to see her friend's familiar pouf of curly blond hair and sank into Abby's arms, the tears falling fast. She could finally let go and stop trying to piece together the events of the day, which made no sense.

Tam didn't remember driving with Abby to Flushing from their town in the suburbs of New York City or identifying the body. She didn't understand a word anyone said to her in the noisy police station except that one young officer thought it was incredible she had been on the phone with Tony when he died. She kept hearing him say, "That's so weird. She was on the phone with him!" until an older officer hit him on the side of the head and told him to shut up.

She let Abby take care of everything. All Tam wanted was to curl up in her warm, familiar bed with the blankets over her head, the smell of Tony lingering in the sheets. Her eyes were red and gritty and she was so tired, yet every time she closed her eyes, she heard again the last words he ever said to her, ringing like a giant gong echoing in a temple: "HOLY SHIT!" They rarely cursed, so for that to be his last word to her made her feel like . . . well, shit.

When they finally, finally got home, Abby helped her upstairs to her bed.

"Here, take this." Abby handed her a round pill. "It'll help you sleep."

Tam took it and gulped it down with the water Abby handed her, eager for the pill to work and take her away from this nightmare. She pulled off her clothes and put on one of Tony's T-shirts. Crawling into bed, she longed for sleep to stop the spinning of her mind and the questions she refused to acknowledge. But before the darkness finally took her, one thought broke through her defenses. What was Tony doing with Mia in Flushing when she knew they were no longer speaking?

2

THE NEXT AFTERNOON, Tam sat at her dining room table, her mom busy in the kitchen. Her parents had arrived in New York that morning on the red-eye from California.

"I made your favorite," Tam's mom said in Taiwanese and came around the breakfast bar, which separated the kitchen from the dining area. She placed a bowl in front of Tam. "Abby, you want some?" she called in accented English to Abby, who sat in the living room making the calls Tam should have been taking care of.

Abby nodded and held up a hand, signaling she'd be done soon.

"I'm not hungry." Tam still spoke Taiwanese with her parents because their English was limited, despite their living in the States for almost forty years.

"You have to eat something." Zhong-Ying nudged the bowl closer to her. Without a word, Tam took the spoon and chopsticks her mom handed her and started eating the *rou gen* soup. The black vinegar and white pepper flavors were rich on her tongue, and the warmth of the thick soup spread through her body, as if hugging her from the inside.

"You first had this soup when we went to Taiwan for Ah-Gong's funeral, remember?" Zhong-Ying asked.

Tam nodded. Her first and only brush with death before Tony's accident was her maternal grandfather's passing when she was ten. She guessed she was blessed that no one close to her had ever died until now. But, wow, what a way to make up for it.

Trying to think of happier times, Tam said, "Remember how Ah-Gong used to let us sip the foam off his beer? You and all the aunties got so mad." She and her cousins had had so much fun with their ah-gong. The pranks they'd played on their grandfather! Tam's laugh suddenly turned to tears when she realized she'd never drink foam from Ah-Gong's beer again (never mind that he'd been dead for twenty-seven years and she thought beer foam was disgusting). And then the tears turned into sobs when she realized anew she'd never see Tony again.

"Tam . . ." Her mom fussed at her and used a napkin to brush at the tears on Tam's face. Tam took a shuddering breath and waved her mother's hand away. She hated crying in front of people. It always made her feel naked somehow. She stared fiercely at her soup until the tears stopped, and that was when she realized she was holding a pair of unfamiliar chopsticks.

She turned them around in her hand. "Where'd these come from?"

"I brought them," Zhong-Ying said. "I can't believe you don't own chopsticks."

"Tony only wanted to use forks at home." Tam's bottom lip trembled and she clamped her lips together. Tony was so traditionally Chinese in some ways and so American in others. She'd resented not having chopsticks, but instead of telling him that, she'd simmered silently, shooting him spiteful looks that used to make him look at her in bewilderment. Now self-loathing filled her heart. Tony would never use a fork again. Why had she been so mean about it? It was just silverware, after all. What had she thought she would gain by punishing Tony the way she had these last few years?

A sob escaped again, and Tam covered her mouth. Her mom got up and ladled a bowl for herself, giving Tam a moment to control herself. There was silence except for Abby's soft voice on the phone while they ate their soup. Tam's father had gone upstairs to shower, and despite her rocky relationship with her mom, Tam was glad to have her here.

"You know, I never really liked Mia," her mom said. "She always seemed so needy and grabby. Especially when she lived with you when she first came to America."

Tam looked up. "Mom." Really? Her mom was going to bash someone who'd just died? Although she did know what her mom meant; Mia had been needy. But at the same time, Mia had stood by her during all her miscarriages. She'd become like a sister to her.

Her mom held up her hands. "I know, I know. But she wanted too much from you and Tony. You know their kind is different from us."

Tam gave a tired sigh and pressed her fingers to her eyes. "Mom. Not this again."

Tony and Mia were both born on mainland China. Tam's parents had a bias against the mainland, always proclaiming that Taiwan was better—the people, the food, the products. They were against the unification of Taiwan and China into a single sovereign state. Tam had once made the mistake of asking why Taiwan was better and had suffered through a long rant from her parents, none of which made sense to her. "We are Taiwanese, not Chinese" was drummed into Tam's and her brother Wei's heads from the time they were old enough to understand.

"What?" Her mom turned up her hands. "I warned you about marrying a man from China. Not to speak ill of the dead, and Tony was a good boy, but you know a Taiwanese boy would have been so much better for you. Understand you better."

Ugh. Why was her mom so judgmental? When Tam first told her parents she was dating Tony, Zhong-Ying had exclaimed, "*Aiya! No good*," and clicked her tongue so loud Tam had to hold the phone away from her ears.

"You're so prejudiced." Tam looked up at her mom, feeling a need to defend Tony and his family. "It wasn't like Tony's family was happy about him going out with me either. His father was horrified his son was dating someone from Taiwan." Even though the younger generations of Taiwanese and Chinese were more accepting of one another, often finding common ground, the older generations on both sides still held grudges. This all dated back to the tensions between China and Taiwan from the end of World War II. Tam and Tony had known their families would object, but they'd been in love and weren't going to let some age-old dispute keep them apart.

Zhong-Ying harrumphed, muttering under her breath, "He should have been jumping for joy to have such a smart and beautiful woman dating his son."

Tam gave a small smile at her mom's rare compliment. Zhong-Ying tended to criticize more than praise. "Tony's father did come around. And his mother was always welcoming."

Tam's mom sniffed. "Well. Your brother married a Taiwanese girl. But no! A nice Taiwanese boy is not good enough for you."

Tam snorted. "Yeah, right. Like the one who asked me if I was open to a threesome?"

"A what?" Tam's mom's forehead wrinkled in confusion.

"Never mind." Tam rolled her eyes. Her mom could be so dense sometimes.

Zhong-Ying clicked her tongue loudly, and Tam jumped. Her mom hated it when she rolled her eyes at her. Even in her grief, Tam was still a champion at needling her.

"Will you change your name back to Lin?"

"Mom!" Was she for real? "We've been married almost nine years."

Her father walked down the stairs at that moment. "Zhong-Ying, be quiet. Stop giving her a hard time."

"What? Lin is a nice Taiwanese name . . ." Her mom fell silent when her father shot her a look.

Her father turned to Tam. "Wei and his family will be here tomorrow." Tam's parents and her older brother and his family all lived in Torrance, California, where she'd grown up.

Tam nodded. It would be good to see Wei. She started eating again, letting the familiar flavors of the soup soothe her nerves. Her mom had added shiitake mushrooms, Chinese white cabbage, and bamboo shoots to the soup, and her eyes stung again, but this time with nostalgia for her childhood and a time when her biggest worry was trying to get her father to let her date.

Abby hung up the phone and walked over to the table. "I just talked to the lawyer for the beverage company that owns the truck that ran over Tony and Mia." Tam shuddered, thinking about the truck that had mowed them down. Before she could imagine the horror of Tony's last moments again, Abby continued. "I think they're afraid you're going to sue. The news is really running with the story that you were on the phone with Tony when he . . ." Her voice drifted off. "Anyways, I told them you're contacting an attorney."

Tam stopped eating. "I'm not going to sue anyone."

"I know that, but they don't. I think they might offer you a settlement. You're going to need all the money you can get now that Tony is no longer here. They owe you."

"Oh." Tam's shoulders slumped forward and her shoulder-length hair swung in her face. She didn't want to think about a life without Tony. Even if she had been imagining just that kind of life. Wracked with guilt, Tam wrapped her arms around herself and rocked.

Abby turned away and studied her notebook. "Are you sure you want Tony cremated and his remains sent back to China? You only want a service and not a funeral?"

Tam nodded, squeezing her eyes shut. Tony's father had died three years ago and Tam thought Tony would have wanted to be laid to rest near him. She didn't want to have to think about these details. Tony was too young! He wasn't even thirty-eight yet. They'd both said they wanted to be cremated, but that was a lighthearted conversation from when they first started dating. Now the reality of actually burning Tony's body made her cringe, and she said out loud, "But what if he isn't really dead and they burn him alive?"

Abby stopped checking things off her list and looked at Tam, her brown eyes brimming with sympathy. "Oh, Tam."

Tam gave a grunt, disgusted at her thoughts. She needed to stop being a baby and get off her butt. Why was she letting Abby do all the work while she lounged around crying like a spoiled brat? But she couldn't. Her body felt like it was weighted down with bricks.

"Okay, well." Abby looked back down at her list. "I know you spoke to Fei-Yin Wang in Beijing, and she said she'd have Tony's remains laid to rest with his father in their family plot."

"Fei-Yin?" Tam's father asked. "The woman taking care of Tony's mother?" Tony's mother had been diagnosed with dementia a few years ago and Tony had flown back to China to move his mother in with Fei-Yin and her husband.

Tam nodded and used her napkin to blow her nose. "I guess it's a blessing that Tony's mother didn't understand when Fei-Yin told her Tony and Mia are dead."

"Poor woman." Tam's father shook his head. "Better she doesn't know she lost both her children." Mia's parents had died when she was a teenager and she'd gone to live with Tony's family. Tam was under the impression that Mia was more like a second cousin rather than Tony's first cousin, but Tony had been vague about the exact relationship. Mia had always said Tony's mother was like a mother to her.

Zhong-Ying tilted her head. "That Fei-Yin is an angel. I still don't understand how she could take on such a big responsibility when they're not even related."

"Tony said she owes her whole life to his mother." Tam could feel all three sets of eyes staring at her with interest. She shrugged. "He never told me why." Just another secret between them. Why hadn't she spoken up and asked? Why had she been so afraid to talk to Tony?

Abby handed a piece of paper and Tam's phone to her. She'd been fielding phone calls for Tam. "This woman keeps calling and insists on talking to you. She said she's Mia's boss." Tam glanced at the paper. She recognized the name—Jenny Chao. She had given Mia a job when she first came over from China. "I think you should call her now. She'll just call again later."

Tam sighed. The last thing she wanted to do was talk to someone she barely knew. But as if on cue, her phone rang and Abby said, "That's Jenny again."

Tam grimaced but picked up the call.

"Tam? Is that you?"

"Yes."

"I'm so sorry about your husband and Mia. It's such a shock," Jenny said in Mandarin.

Tam didn't answer and closed her eyes.

"I'm calling to see if you'll arrange the funeral for Mia."

Tam's eyes snapped open. "No!" Her adamant reply in English made her parents and Abby turn to her. "No," she said again, quietly. "It's not my place."

"But you her family," Jenny said in accented English.

"No. She was Tony's cousin. And they weren't talking anymore." But then why had they been together at the time of the accident? Guilt rose in Tam when she thought of the money Jenny would have to spend on Mia's funeral, money that she probably didn't have, and she said, "I'll give you money for the funeral, but I can't arrange it myself."

Jenny was quiet for a moment. "Okay, I do it. But you need come to Flushing."

"Why?" An overwhelming tiredness descended on Tam, and she suddenly felt as if she couldn't hold herself up anymore.

"I need talk to you. It's important."

"What?" Tam slumped in her chair, shivering as a sudden awareness flooded her body, and she suddenly knew what Jenny was going to say before she spoke.

"It's about her daughter, Angela."

3

*Four Months
before the Accident*

"MAMA! I MADE you a card. Happy Mother's Day!"

Angela took a flying leap and landed on top of Mia on the bed, forcing Mia to let out a whoosh of breath. Mia grabbed Angela around the middle and tickled her. She was rewarded with a burst of giggles from Angela.

"Let me see, Angel." They spoke in Mandarin to each other at home, although Mia tried to speak English everywhere else to practice. She hated the way her broken English sounded. She'd made so much progress when Tam had worked with her, but in the years since she'd moved out of Tony and Tam's home, she'd backslid. Mia pursed her lips, her brows furrowing. Damn, but she missed Tam.

"Do you like it?"

Mia pushed herself to sit up in the bed and reached for the card Angela was waving in the air. "It's beautiful. You made this all by yourself?"

Angela nodded, sitting up to snuggle at her mother's side. "Lily and I made it at the nail salon yesterday."

Mia admired the card, smiling wryly at the use of nail polish instead of markers to color in the flowers. That's what kids who spent so much time in a nail salon did. Seriously, how the hell had they ended up like this? She wanted so much more for Angela than to grow up thinking picking gunk out from under people's toenails was normal. Gross. How she wished she had studied with Madame Zheng longer in China and learned acupuncture from her. Her mentor had started to teach her, and Mia had been great at the practical, hands-on part. But when Madame Zheng handed Mia all the charts and materials she had to study, Mia couldn't process them. It was like being back in school again, and she was the dunce who understood nothing. Mia shook her head to clear her mind of that godawful time when she'd always felt so stupid at school.

"I have to work today, but we'll go out to dinner as a treat. We have money in the jar." Mia saved some of her tips in a jar they kept in a kitchen cabinet for special days like today.

Angela squealed with delight and clapped her hands. "Can we go to the hot-pot place?"

Mia smiled, but her eyes pooled with unshed tears. "Yes, baby. I know it's your favorite." Tam was the one who'd introduced Mia to hot pot—a simmering pot of stock served at the dining room table, where everyone cooked their own meats, vegetables, and other ingredients, much like a fondue pot. She couldn't seem to stop thinking of Tam today. Why in the world was Tam flooding her thoughts and making her drown in regret?

Mia pushed the covers aside, determined to banish Tam from her thoughts, and got out of bed. "Let's get dressed." Angela tumbled out after her and ran to her dresser, tucked in a corner of their small studio, one flight above Jenny's apartment. Mia hadn't wanted to live on the fourth floor, since "four" in Chinese sounded like the word for "death." But she'd had no choice. It was the only apartment available and she'd been desperate.

Mia straightened the bed she shared with Angela and looked around their studio. It was tiny ("cozy," the fat, greasy landlord had said, eyeing Mia's generous chest greedily and licking his lips, making Mia's own lips curl in disgust), barely three hundred square feet. But it was her first real home that she paid for all by herself, and as long as she avoided the landlord after that encounter when she convinced him to lower the rent, she was fine. *Gross.* Mia shuddered. What a shit show her life had been reduced to. She might as well have stayed in China.

She and Angela had hung colorful tapestries over walls that were the color of old white socks washed too many times. Mia found lantern lampshades in the back of a dusty store, and they cast a warm glow over the room. There was a small altar with the statue of Guan Yin, the goddess of mercy, that Xing Xing Ayi gave her when she left China. Mia prayed to the statue every morning and replenished the water or tea and the fruits she left as an offering, just like Xing Xing had taught her.

They'd painted the wooden table and chairs Mia found on the curbside white, and that's where they ate and drew and worked on projects. She'd found the metal-frame bed on Craigslist for only ten dollars. The mattress she bought new with money she'd saved from working, and it was such a treat compared to those scratchy pallets and hard surfaces she used to sleep on in China.

She sighed, thinking of all the things she'd done to get here, and then squared her shoulders. She wouldn't wallow in the what-ifs of the past. She would focus on her future and finding a better life for her precious Angel.

When a little voice whispered in her ear, *But you won't live long enough to see Angela grown,* she hissed at it and said out loud, "Shut up. Leave me alone."

Angela looked up. "Who're you talking to, Mama?"

Mia forced a smile onto her face and turned to her daughter. "No one. Just talking to myself." Angela turned back to getting dressed, and Mia pulled on her uniform of white shirt and black pants that she wore at the salon. She knew she should start that journal for Angela soon. If the gods were right and she wouldn't see Angela grow up, she wanted her daughter to know about her past.

THREE HOURS LATER, Jenny came up to Mia in the salon and asked, "What's wrong?"

Mia was staring at her work-reddened hands, thinking she needed to use more lotion on them at night. Her hands were cracked, and they ached from all the massages she gave and from submerging her hands in hot water for the pedicures. She'd been working in Jenny and her husband Neil's salon for almost seven years now and should know better.

"Nothing." But she heaved a sigh like someone who'd just been sentenced to life in prison.

Jenny watched as Mia eyed the woman she had just given a pedicure to. The older woman looked plucked and preened to within an inch of her life and was dripping in gold jewelry. She was talking on her phone as if she owned the world, which she probably did. *That's what money and privilege did for you,* Mia thought with a surge of envy.

The overplucked woman spoke with a Cantonese accent, much like Mia's own from Guangdong. How then did she have so much while Mia had so little?

Jenny placed a hand on Mia's shoulder. "Don't be jealous," she said in Cantonese. "I heard her husband is a fucking pig and she has to wash his feet and kiss each toe every night."

They giggled together, and Mia snorted at the thought of kissing hairy toes. The woman gave them a quizzical look, causing the laughter to start again.

They sat together at the back of the salon, where they could see the kids in the back room but also keep an eye on the door if a new customer walked in.

"So, what's on your mind?" Jenny asked again.

Mia heaved out a breath. "I guess I'm tired of people asking if I give happy endings when I tell them I work as a masseuse in Flushing." They laughed again, knowing it was a hazard of their job. And so what if Mia had given a happy ending or two here and there? Jenny didn't have to know, and Mia needed the money to give Angela treats, like going to dinner tonight. It wasn't as if she had sex with those men. At least not anymore.

"I know doing nails and giving massages isn't your life's dream. But it's honest work, right?"

"Yes." Mia smiled, not wanting to offend Jenny, since this was her life. "I just wish I could go back to China and study with Madame Zheng, then bring it back to New York and start my own practice."

Jenny raised her eyebrows at Mia. Madame Zheng was the one who had connected Mia to Jenny. When Mia had decided to move to New York, Madame Zheng had given her Jenny's contact info. Jenny knew Mia had overstayed her visa and was in the United

States illegally. She couldn't go back to China unless it was for good. Even Xiao Cici, the woman who had helped her get her visa, couldn't help her this time.

Mia sighed again when she heard Angela's peal of laughter from the back room. She had to come up with a plan soon. That foreboding feeling that was ever present in her life had reared its ugly head again recently. She knew she had to make sure her daughter was taken care of if anything happened to Mia. She would do anything to give her daughter a better life.

Even if it meant finally telling *him* the truth.

4

TWO DAYS AFTER the accident, Tam found herself in the third-floor hallway of an apartment building in Flushing, Queens. Abby had driven her here because Tam hated driving in the city. All the traffic and the cabs with no regard for road rules terrified her. Abby was waiting for her in a coffee shop downstairs.

She didn't want to be here. The hall was musty with the odor of stale sweat and the greasy smoke of barbecued meats from the restaurant downstairs. Tam stood in front of the apartment she was looking for. A baby cried inside, competing with a Chinese soap opera from next door and the honking traffic on the street.

Taking a deep breath, she finally pressed the doorbell. They'd only met a few times, but when Jenny opened the door with a crying baby in one arm, she greeted her like an old friend.

"*Lai, lai,*" Jenny said in Mandarin and gestured for her to come in. She led Tam to an old gray couch. "You want something to drink? Sorry place such mess. We have four kids, hard to keep clean." Jenny had switched to her accented English because Tam had told her on the phone that her Mandarin wasn't great. Tam spoke Taiwanese better, which might as well be a completely different language.

Tam declined a drink and Jenny put a pacifier in the baby's mouth, quieting him. "I know was family fight and you no longer speaking with Mia, but she always said good of you." Her eyes filled. "I can't believe Mia gone—and your husband. He was good man."

Tam perched on the couch, spine straight, steeling herself against whatever was about to unfold. Her eyes focused on a red diagonal square on the wall with the Chinese character for *fu*, good fortune, written in gold, and wondered briefly why it was upside down. She finally brought her gaze back to Jenny. "Thank you. But what did you need to tell me?"

Jenny wiped her eyes on an old tissue and said, "It's Angela. I told Mia, you need to make will. In case something happen . . ." She paused and blew her nose. "Anyways, she put you and your husband as, uh, how you say . . . to watch over Angela."

Tam felt like someone had ripped her brains out. She wasn't computing. "What?"

"You know, um, take over her care. What's the word?"

Tam's mind scrambled to catch up with Jenny. "You mean . . . guardians?"

Jenny nodded. "Since Tony died with Mia, you now Angela's guardian." Tam stared at Jenny in shock as Jenny continued to talk. Tam tuned her out and thought of the conversation she'd had with Mia right after Angela had been born.

She'd been Mia's labor coach and had been in the delivery room with her. After the nurse had taken Angela away, Mia had grabbed Tam's hand and drawn her close.

"Promise me you'll always take care of my baby." There was a brightness in Mia's eyes that made Tam wonder if she had a fever. "If something should happen to me, promise me you'll take her."

Tam laughed. "Nothing's going to happen to you, silly."

But Mia squeezed her hand so hard she left fingernail marks in Tam's hand. "Promise me, Tam."

Tam realized Mia was serious. She stared at her in shock, wondering what could cause a new mother to think such morbid thoughts.

"What are you thinking?" Mia asked her. When Tam didn't answer, Mia pressed her. "You always hold back. Just say it. Say whatever is on your mind."

"Shitballs." Tam was surprised at what came out of her mouth. She rarely cursed. But it seemed to sum up the situation.

Mia laughed and her eyes cleared. "I love it! Shitballs."

Tam had laughed with her, and it was only later, after she'd gone home, that she realized she'd never promised Mia.

"TAM?"

Tam blinked and found Jenny staring at her.

"You okay?"

Tam nodded, still thinking about Mia.

Jenny raised her voice. "Lily! Angela! Come here." Then in her normal voice she said to Tam, "Angela and my Lily same age and best friends. Mia and Angela lived upstairs. Angela very sad her mama gone."

Two little girls came into the room holding hands. Tam knew immediately which one was Angela, even though she hadn't seen her since she was a few months old. She remembered those serious brown eyes staring up at her from her crib. Angela let go of Lily's hand and walked to Tam, her heart-shaped face solemn. In Mandarin she said, "I know you."

Jenny laughed and answered in Mandarin. "Oh, honey, no, you don't. This is your aunt Tam. She's your mama's cousin Tony's wife."

Angela studied Tam and then said, "You're the princess." Jenny laughed again, saying something about big imaginations, but Tam's attention was on Angela, who didn't say another word. Lily grabbed Angela's hand and asked if they could go back to her room.

"I don't believe this. Are you sure she named us the guardians? Why not you?" Tam asked after the children left the room.

Jenny gestured around her apartment. "No room." She jiggled the baby on her lap. "I know this big shock, so I keep Angela for now. Mia paid the rent for this month, so I have time to pack it up, see what Angela needs, and get rid of the rest. But you take her soon?"

"What if I don't want her?" Tam exclaimed. Jenny's mouth dropped open, and Tam tried to backtrack. "I'm sorry, that came out wrong."

Jenny looked at Tam with wariness. "You have take her. She your family."

"I can't. I just lost my husband." Even to her own ears, Tam's voice sounded pitiful.

"She needs you."

They stared at each other and then Tam dropped her face into her hands, unable to face Jenny any longer. There was no way she could be responsible for Mia's child. Not after what she'd done.

5

TAM SPRAWLED ON her bed, an arm thrown over her face. She could hear Abby talking to her parents downstairs, their voices floating up the stairwell and in through her open door.

"It's so strange . . ." Her mother's voice drifted up the stairs. She heard her father's voice murmur something unintelligible in reply. *What was strange?* They were talking about the accident. She held still, straining to catch their words. She knew Tony had been standing on a street corner in Flushing with Mia, waiting to cross and talking on the phone with Tam, when a beverage-distribution truck ran a red light, jumped the curb, and plowed right into them.

She wondered again why Tony had been in Flushing with Mia, whom he hadn't spoken to in almost five years, as far as she knew. *You know why,* a little voice inside her head said. "No!" she said out loud. "I don't." She put both hands on either side of her head and pressed, as if she could physically push the thought out. She refused to acknowledge it.

She couldn't stop watching the news coverage of the accident, which she'd recorded on DVR. She felt like a drug addict; she knew it probably wasn't good for her, but she couldn't curb her craving to watch any details of the accident over and over. She needed to see where Tony had been, needed to see with her own eyes the truck crashed up on the sidewalk and the police tape cordoning off the area.

"*Aiya*, so violent," she heard her mom say. Tam pushed off the bed and tiptoed to hover at the landing, ducking down so they couldn't see her from the living room below. "Tony was pinned under a wheel of the truck?"

"I know, it's awful," Abby said. "That's why I didn't want to tell Tam. She's got enough going on without hearing the gory details. They said pieces of Mia's head . . ." At this point, Tam stuck her fingers in her ears and scrunched her face up tight. Okay, maybe she didn't want to hear the grisly details. But curiosity got the better of her and she unplugged one ear.

". . . was decapitated." Tam's mouth dropped open in horror. Mia had lost her head? Literally? She stuffed her fists into her mouth to stifle a scream. Poor Mia. As mad at her as Tam was, she wouldn't have wished that on Mia. They'd been the best of friends once.

Tam turned and crawled back to her room and into bed, pulling the covers over her head. She would stay here forever. It was safe and she didn't have to deal with Tony's and Mia's deaths and all the unspoken words left between them. Why had she been so annoyed with Tony during her last conversation with him? Was she being punished? And she'd never talk to Mia again. Even though she'd meant it when she told Mia she never wanted to speak to her again, a part of her had hoped to reconcile with her one day. But now they were both gone and there was nothing she could do about it. She hugged Tony's pillow to her body as the tears flowed, and she wished she could turn back the clock and do it over again.

THE DAY AFTER Tony's service, her father and her brother, his wife, and their two kids flew back to California. After the shuttle picked them up to take them to the airport, Tam once again sat at her dining table with her mom and Abby. Her mom had made her famous wonton soup in a clear broth. It smelled so heavenly from the roasted garlic that Tam's stomach growled despite her lack of appetite.

"Thanks, Mom." She reached over her soup bowl to squeeze her mom's hand. Times like this, she wished they lived closer. But most of the time, the two of them bickered like politicians taking cheap shots at each other.

"This is delicious." Abby bit into a homemade wonton and almost purred in appreciation. "I could get used to this home cooking. I usually just microwave something."

Zhong-Ying smiled in satisfaction. "Microwave so bad for you." She shook a finger at Abby. "So, Abby. How long you know Tam? She don't tell me nothing about her friends."

Tam growled in exasperation. She hated when her mom tried to butt into her life.

"What?" Zhong-Ying shot Tam a look and turned to Abby. "She so shy. Never made friends when she little. I had to step in. Force her to play with my friends' kids."

"Mom!" Why did her mom have to make her sound like some mutant antisocial misfit? So what if she had been? Still was, come to think of it. But her mom didn't need to embarrass her by telling Abby.

"We've known each other for years." Abby put down her spoon. "We used to teach at the same school in Astoria when I lived in Queens. Before I moved here."

"Abby got me the interview at our school here when there was an opening," Tam said.

"What a nice friend." Zhong-Ying nodded in approval. "Abby Goldman. You Jewish?"

Tam groaned inwardly. She hoped her mom wasn't going to make some racist comment by accident. Zhong-Ying could be so blunt sometimes, not realizing she was being insensitive.

When Abby nodded, Zhong-Ying said, "That's good. The Jewish, they have same values as us Taiwanese. Study hard, work hard, respect family."

Abby caught Tam's eye and smiled. Thank goodness her mom wasn't going to embarrass her.

"What about you?" Abby asked. "What does your family do in Torrance? Something about computers?"

Zhong-Ying nodded. "My siblings started computer software business in Torrance in late seventies. My husband and I, we move there from Taiwan to work with them. Wei and Tam born there. Now Wei and all his cousins work there too." Her mom turned to give Tam a frown. "All except this one."

Tam narrowed her eyes at her mom. "Yeah, Mom didn't speak to me for a month when I told her I was staying in New York after college and not joining the family business."

Abby laughed and Zhong-Ying said, "Why you keep Abby a secret, Tam? She such good friend to you, but you never mention her."

Thanks for putting me on the spot, Mom. But it was true. Tam had always kept Abby at a distance, even though she was probably the closest friend she had.

"Oh, it's not Tam's fault. Tony didn't like me too much." Abby gave a throaty laugh and Tam looked at her, startled.

"That's not . . . true." But it was true; Tam had always suspected Tony hadn't liked Abby. He'd never said so, but it was in the way his face changed when she talked about Abby, or how he'd disappear into the basement if she invited Abby over.

Abby waved a hand at her. "Don't worry, I'm not offended. He probably didn't want you to be led into a life of sin by hanging out with a single divorcée like me." She dropped her voice and whispered to Zhong-Ying, "Less temptation, right?" Abby was forty-two, five years older than Tam, and had gotten divorced a year before Tam met her. In all the time she'd known her, Abby had never had a serious boyfriend.

Tam glanced at her mother, thinking she'd be appalled. But her mom was smiling. "Ha ha, you so right. When I was living in Taiwan, I used to be—"

Tam cut her off. "Okay, Mom. Abby doesn't want to listen to your old stories."

Zhong-Ying pressed her lips together, and Tam knew she'd offended her mom. But really? Her mom could go on and on about the olden days, and she didn't want her to embarrass herself in front of Abby.

"I don't mind," Abby started to say, but just then, Tam's cell rang. Abby picked up the phone and looked at the caller ID. "It's someone named Sandra?"

"Oh, gosh. We've been waiting for this phone call!" Tam dropped her spoon with a clatter. But there was no *we* anymore. It was just *her*.

A fresh surge of grief overtook her, and she wrapped her arms around her middle.

"Do you want me to get that?" Abby asked.

"No," Tam cried. She stared at her phone until the voicemail alert dinged and then she played the message on speakerphone.

"Hi, Tam. This is Sandra. Your letter of acceptance just appeared on the China Center for Children's Welfare and Adoption site. Call me back as soon as you can."

Tam sucked in her breath and clutched her hands over her heart. It had finally happened! Tony would be so happy. She had to call him right away. And then she remembered.

"What is it? More bad news?" Abby looked concerned as tears streamed down Tam's cheeks unchecked.

Tam shook her head and smiled through her tears. "No, it's good news. Great news." And she burst into loud sobs, stunning Abby into silence.

"Who's Sandra?" Abby finally asked.

"Their caseworker," Tam's mom answered for her.

Tam nodded, unable to speak. She didn't know if she was weeping from happiness that they, *she*, was one step closer to bringing their son home, or sadness that Tony wasn't here.

"What?" Abby looked at Tam in confusion.

Tam took a breath. "It's for the little boy we're adopting from China."

"You're adopting a little boy?" Abby's voice was incredulous. "You never told me."

"I . . . didn't tell anyone. Except my family." Tam grabbed a napkin and mopped her face.

"That's amazing. I'm so happy for you." Abby got up and hugged her. "What's the letter of acceptance?"

"It's China's formal invitation for us to accept the child we're matched with. We'll be able to travel to China in the next couple of months to pick him up." Tam dropped her face into her hands and her tears turned to hysterical laughter. "Except," she gasped out between chortles of mirth, "joke's on me. It's just me now. There's no 'we.' I'm going to be a single mom." And she cackled like a hyena while her mother and Abby stared at her as if she'd lost her mind.

6

Four Months
before the Accident

MIA'S CELL PHONE rang while she was trying to find a clean plate to hold the *cheung fan*—the steamed rice noodle rolls—and the fish balls she'd bought from her favorite food stall. The tea eggs and the dried tofu pieces sprinkled with scallions she was serving right out of the container they came in. She'd even bought a small bag of egg tarts, her favorite treat since Tony first bought one for her when she was six. Mia paused, her mind going back to all those years ago, when the sight of these bright yellow egg custards with the crimped edges used to make her squeal with delight.

The continuous ringing of her phone brought her back to her studio.

"Can you answer the phone for me, Angel?"

"Okay, Mama." Angela picked up the phone and shouted with joy when she realized who it was. "Auntie Fei-Yin! Guess what Lily and I did today!"

Mia surveyed the spread she'd put on the table for their dinner and shrugged. She wasn't much of a cook. She used to help Tam when Tam cooked for them, chopping and stirring, but when she was left to her own devices, it was easier to pick something up on the way home. Who had the stomach to cook when she'd been slaving over people's stinky, dirty feet or rubbing hairy backs all day?

She listened to Angela chattering to Fei-Yin, and, damn it, there was that shot of regret again. She missed Tam. They'd once been so close, and Mia missed her like she'd miss an arm if it were cut off.

"Here, Mama. Auntie Fei-Yin wants to speak to you." Angela shoved the phone at Mia and went back to the tea party she was having with her dolls and stuffed animals.

"Mei." Fei-Yin called her by her Chinese name. Mia had changed her name long before she moved to New York. Fei-Yin's voice was quiet, and her tone made Mia's heart stop. Had something happened to Xing Xing?

"Fan Fan died in a fire last night."

Mia let out a sigh of relief at the same time a stab of pain hit her heart. Fan Fan, her sweet friend with spina bifida. They were about the same age, but their lives had taken different turns. The last time Mia saw her was right before Mia left for America seven years ago. She'd gone to visit Fan Fan in the building where the adults with special needs were kept, locked away and out of sight. Fan Fan had looked as if the life had been drained out of her. She didn't sit up straight in her wheelchair like she used to, and her mouth didn't turn up in her usual smile.

"What happened?"

"There was a fire in her room at her brother's house. Fan Fan and the woman who helps her were sleeping. Her brother tried to get to them, but the fire was too big."

Mia clapped a hand to her mouth to keep the bile from rising to her throat. She felt sick to her stomach. Just a few months ago, Fei-Yin had finally managed to find Fan Fan's younger brother, after years of searching and dead ends. He'd never known about the older sister who had been sent away because of her disability, but also to make room for a son to be born into the family. He was grown now, and married, and had decided to bring Fan Fan to his home to live with them. Fei-Yin and Mia had wept tears of joy that Fan Fan was finally getting a chance at a better life. She'd escaped institutional life only to die in a fire a few months later.

They talked about Fan Fan, which brought back echoes of Mia's horrible childhood. They fell silent, each lost in her own thoughts, and Mia fought to keep down her guilt that she hadn't done more for Fan Fan and the others. She'd sent presents and letters at first, but those had dwindled in the last few years when she'd moved out on her own and no longer had Tony and Tam to lean on.

"How's Xing Xing?" Mia asked.

Fei-Yin sighed. "Not good. She's getting worse. Ever since Shushu died, her mind's been deteriorating. More rapidly lately, it seems. She asks for you sometimes. You and Tony."

"Shitballs," Mia cursed, immediately thinking of Tam. A cloak of sadness enveloped her. "I wish I could see Xing Xing."

"Why don't you, then?" Fei-Yin asked boldly. "What's keeping you in America? Bring Angela and come back to China. I'll help you raise her."

"I can't. You know why."

"When are you going to realize you're chasing after a little girl's dream? You need to let it go, Mei." Fei-Yin's huff of exasperation made Mia's hackles rise. They'd been friends since they were young and had no one else to count on. But Fei-Yin had never understood what was in Mia's heart.

"It's not that."

"Then what is it? You complain about your job and how hard it is in New York raising Angela by yourself. You're not even talking to Tony and Tam anymore, so what's keeping you there? Come back to me. Xing Xing needs you."

"I know. Stop trying to make me feel bad. And I am talking to Tony again. We made up."

"What?" Mia could hear Fei-Yin's shock all the way down the phone line.

"I called him. Recently. He was still so mad at me, but—" Mia broke off and brought a hand to her cheek. "I told him."

"*Wo de tian!* My God! What did he say? How'd he take it?"

"He was so angry. He hung up on me. But he called me back a few days later. I don't think he'll ever forgive me, but it's not about me." Mia's eyes cut to Angela talking to her stuffed animals. It was about Angela. Mia shivered as a tingling sensation ran down her spine, as if someone had walked on her grave. "If anything ever happens to me, Angela's going to need her family."

"If you come back to China, she'd have me and Bolin and Xing Xing."

"I know. I do consider you family, but . . ." Mia trailed off.

"But I'm not the family you want," Fei-Yin finished for her. She let out a sigh of resignation.

"That's not it."

"You know they have every right to be mad at you."

"I know." It was Mia's turn to sigh. "But they're my family. The only one I have."

Fei-Yin started to ask questions, but Mia cut her off. She didn't want to talk about it anymore. "Anyways, I feel guilty that you're the one taking care of Xing Xing when I'm the one she took in. I should be taking care of her." Mia sat down at the table, looked at the piti-ful dinner she'd put together, and lost her appetite. Little girls needed fresh fruits and vegetables, yet she never had time to shop, and when she did, the produce sat in the fridge and rotted because she didn't have the energy to make anything. Was Fei-Yin right? Would life be easier if she went back to China with Angela?

"I'm sorry." Fei-Yin's voice was contrite. "I'm not trying to make you feel guilty. You know Bolin and I are happy to have Xing Xing live with us. I just miss you."

"Me too." Mia smiled, thinking of the boy Fei-Yin had fallen in love with when she'd gone to university. She'd tried to set Mia up with one of Bolin's friends, but Mia had refused. She knew where her heart lay, and it wasn't with carefree university boys. "It's just that Xing Xing is the only mother I've ever known. I wish . . ." She trailed off. She wished so many things. But she didn't seem closer to getting any of them.

"Well, you know you can always come here to Beijing if you decide to."

"Thank you. I'll figure something out. I swear, I will come back to China somehow and see Xing Xing again. I just have to be able to come back to New York." And how was she going to do that? Even if she married an American, she'd have to go back to China and apply for a green card, which could take years.

Fei-Yin didn't answer, but Mia knew she'd never understand.

"Hey," Mia said to change the subject. "Remember how the ayis always said I was a *yao zhe* baby?"

Fei-Yin made a noise in her throat. "What did they know? You didn't die young like they predicted. You're alive, aren't you?" Fei-Yin's voice held a hint of laughter. "Don't worry about what those cows said."

Mia laughed out loud. God, it felt so good to laugh with her friend. She'd missed the closeness she'd had with Tam and, before her, Fei-Yin. Jenny was great, but they were mostly work friends. They didn't tell each other their deep, dark secrets.

But then her laughter died as she looked at her beautiful little girl, who was singing to her stuffed bear. "I've been getting a feeling lately—*yu gan*—that something's going to happen to me. It's getting stronger every day."

Fei-Yin was quiet and didn't try to discount what Mia was saying, like Jenny had. Jenny had told her to draw up a will if she felt that way. But Fei-Yin and Mia both believed in Chinese superstitions. "That's terrible, Mei."

"I want Angela to know about my past, about how we grew up. I need to write it all down in case something happens to me." She'd been thinking about this for a while now, and hearing about Fan Fan's death made her realize anything could happen at any time.

"That's a good idea, whether you think you're going anywhere or not. But take care of yourself. I want to see you again. Soon."

"I will. I'm not planning on going anywhere." Mia stood and beckoned to Angela. "I've got to feed Angela. It's getting late."

They said good-bye and Mia hung up. Angela came running over and they sat down to eat, just the two of them. Mia had once prayed for a family of her own, and she finally had it. When Angela had been born, Mia had taken one look at her and known they were connected by the red thread of fate. Mia had once thought she was connected to *him* by the red thread, the invisible red cord that bound two people who were destined to be together. But she was wrong. Her red thread tied her forever to Angela, her precious daughter.

She gazed at her daughter's face as Angela peeled a tea egg and started eating with gusto. She would start that journal tonight. She needed Angela to understand about her past and why she'd done the things she had. In case she didn't make it and Angela ever found out the truth, she didn't want her daughter to grow up hating her.

7

ABBY HAD A lot of questions about the adoption. Tam's mom
had gone for a walk after Tam returned Sandra's call, leaving them
to talk alone.

"I'm surprised you're adopting a boy. I thought there were only
girls available from China because of the one-child policy."

"That policy was recently lifted." Tam twisted her fingers together. She didn't want to talk about this. But her mom had just
called her an antisocial wallflower who didn't know how to make
friends. Her childish desire to prove her mom wrong won out over
her reluctance to talk about personal issues. "There was a surplus of
abandoned baby girls starting in the 1990s, and that's when foreign-
ers, a lot of them Americans, started adopting them. But recently,
there was a surge in domestic adoptions, resulting in the dropping
number of healthy children in the orphanages."

"Does that mean your little boy has a medical condition?" Abby
asked.

"Yes." Tam took a breath and continued. "Tony's mother worked in an orphanage in China for years. When we decided to adopt, we contacted his mom's friend Cecilia Armstrong, who had volunteered at the same orphanage. She's now the director of the China program at an adoption agency in California." Tam swallowed, remembering her disappointment when Cecilia had told them they'd most likely get a boy, one with special needs. "Cecilia told us the wait for a healthy baby girl now can be as long as five to seven years."

"That long?"

Tam nodded. "But there are many kids in the Waiting Child program, kids who are either older or have a minor to severe medical condition. China has no social security for the disabled, so many of the kids born with a special need are abandoned because the parents can't care for them or they want a healthy child."

"What's wrong with your little boy?"

"He has something called cerebral dysplasia, and he's very small for a three-year-old. He's lived in the orphanage his whole life." She'd wanted a girl, but when she saw the little boy's picture, her heart had been captured.

Abby placed a hand on her chest. "That's so sad. But cerebral dysplasia?"

"The international adoption doctor we consulted said it means he has brain seizures, but there's no indication he's ever had one or an MRI, which is the only way to diagnose it." Tam placed the picture of the little boy in front of Abby. "I took one look at his photo and forgot about his diagnosis."

Abby studied the picture of a scared little boy with huge eyes peering out of a thin face and grasping a toy in his hand. "He's precious."

Tam took the picture back and studied the boy she and Tony had named Charlie. "I know. And now things are starting to happen for his adoption and Tony's not here." The photo blurred and she quickly moved it out of the way before her tears could ruin it.

"How long have you waited for him?" Abby asked.

"It's been eight months. We estimated about a year from the time we submitted the application until we'd travel to get him, but now it might be longer. Sandra said I'll have to redo my home study and refile some paperwork, since I'm now adopting as a single woman."

"What if you decide not to continue with the adoption?"

Tam whirled to look at her friend, her eyes wide. "How could I not?"

Abby held up a hand. "I just think it's a lot for you to be taking on right now—Tony's death, Angela, and now this."

"Oh." Tam's face crumpled in anguish.

"You need something to relax you." Abby thought for a minute and then grinned. "I know just the thing."

"Abby! I'm not having sex with another man. It's too soon."

Abby laughed. "I wasn't talking about sex. I was talking about yoga. But sex works too."

"Oh." Tam blushed. Jeez, why had her mind jumped to sex?

"Why don't you come to class with me next weekend?"

"Maybe." Maybe she should. And then she thought about the kids again and buried her face in her hands. "What am I going to do?"

"Are you going to take Angela?"

Tam shrugged, but inside she was screaming, *No! You can't make me!*

Before she could say anything, Zhong-Ying walked in the front door.

"Tam-ah. You should go for walk. Nice day out."

Tam walked to the kitchen window and stared out at the sunshine. Somehow the cheerful bright day seemed to be mocking her. How dare the sun still shine when her life had been torn apart? How was she going to cope when her mother went home, leaving her all alone in this suddenly too-big town house? And what was she going to do about two children who needed her at a time in her life when she was least able to take care of even a cactus?

". . . poor little thing. She's lost the only parent she knew. What happened to her father?" Abby's voice brought her back and she realized her mom and Abby were talking about Angela.

"He was Mia's ex-boyfriend, right?" Zhong-Ying asked.

Tam shrugged, her back to them.

"Mia never told him he was the father?" Tam stared out the window and didn't answer her mother.

"Shouldn't someone tell him he has a daughter, especially now that Mia is dead?" Abby asked.

"He knows." Tam turned to face them. "It's a complicated situation. Let's just say Kenny doesn't want her."

"I feel so bad for Angela," Abby said.

"Me too," Zhong-Ying said, walking to the sink. "But isn't there anyone else who can take her?"

Tam looked at her mom, who was now washing the dishes. That woman could never let a dirty dish languish in the sink in peace. "No. You know Mia's parents are dead. The only relative she has left is Tony's mom."

"How exactly is Mia related to Tony?" Abby asked.

"She was his cousin." Tam paused. "But you know, now that I think about it, I'm not sure how. His father was an only child and Tony once told me his mom was estranged from the rest of her family. Maybe she was his second cousin, not first."

Either way, she knew Mia had no other living relatives. So really, the only person who could possibly take Angela was Tam. *But I can't*, she argued with herself. *You have to*, a little voice said inside her head. *You owe her. You have to make it up to her.*

"Shut up, shut up, shut up!" Tam didn't realize she'd spoken out loud until she found Abby and her mom staring at her. She squeezed her eyes shut as the voice inside her head gnawed at Tam's conscience until she couldn't take the guilt she'd been harboring for years anymore.

"Fine! I'll take her!" The words burst out of Tam's mouth, shocking not just her but her friend and mother.

Her mom shut off the water. "What? Are you sure?"

"I don't know." Tam leaned against the kitchen counter, suddenly too tired to stand up straight. "But I owe it to Angela. It's the right thing to do." And with those words, it felt like a weight was lifted off her shoulders. "It's not her fault all of this happened. I feel like I've been given a second chance."

"What you mean?"

Tam lifted her shoulders. "I just . . . never mind." She knew they were waiting for an answer, but she had none to give.

"It not going to be easy," her mom said. "Raising someone else's child, all the grief of her mama die that way."

"I know."

"What about Charlie?" Abby asked. Hearing his name made Tam want to weep again. Tony would never get to meet the little boy he'd fought so hard for and was so looking forward to bringing home.

"I don't know. I don't know what to do." Tam slumped forward, her elbows on the blue granite countertop that Tony had been so proud of. She dropped her head into her hands.

Her mom came to her and Tam leaned into her side, breathing

in the familiar scent of Ivory soap and the Nivea cream her mom used. She took her glasses off and put them on the counter. One minute she thought she was fine, and the next, she felt as if she'd explode from all the pent-up feelings inside her.

"It's okay," her mom said, putting an arm around her. "I know how you feel, though it was different for me. Years ago, when I live in Taiwan—"

"Mom, please." Tam cut her off. She wasn't in the mood for one of her mom's stories right now.

Zhong-Ying stiffened at her side, but Tam's own misery crowded in until she couldn't think of anyone else's feelings.

"Well, I think someone should find Angela's father. Maybe he'll want to take her now that Mia isn't here." Tam knew Abby was trying to change the subject, and she gave her friend a grateful smile.

"I don't think so," Tam said, but then she froze. Something niggled at the back of her mind, but she couldn't bring it into focus. Something about Mia's ex Kenny . . . What was it? Her face puckered in concentration as she tried to recall a thought that had come to her in the fog of her grief those first few days after the accident. She almost had it, but then the memory melted away and she shook her head in frustration.

She forced herself to smile at Abby and her mom as they discussed Angela, but she continued to rack her brain, trying to make the thought come back. Somehow, she knew it was important. But what was it?

8

TAM DIPPED A toe into the bathwater, and finding it hot enough, she lowered herself into the tub. She sighed as the warm water enveloped her like a cocoon, and she sank into its depth, wanting to burrow away from the world. She was glad for her mother's and Abby's company, but her head ached from putting on a brave front for them. Here, in the privacy of the bath, she could let go. Her face slackened in grief and she closed her eyes, letting her head fall against the tub.

She missed Tony. As much as their marriage had been on the rocks, they had been trying to come back to each other. Why, oh, why, then, had he been taken away before they'd completely reconciled? Her face screwed up in pain as the grief of having him suddenly gone hit her again, this time a physical blow, as if someone had punched her in the stomach. They'd finally bonded again over something they both wanted. Adopting a child. And now she was close to being able to bring Charlie home, and Tony was no longer here.

They'd both wanted a family right away, so Tam had stopped using birth control on their honeymoon. It had taken them two years to get pregnant, and when it finally happened, they were giddy with glee and full of plans for their new baby. Tam didn't even mind being violently sick because everyone told her it meant a healthy baby.

At their nine-week checkup though, the doctor couldn't find a heartbeat. How could that be? Just two weeks ago, they'd heard the heartbeat, strong and sure as a drum. Tam grabbed Tony's hand and turned to him in desperation when the doctor talked about performing a D&C that afternoon. He had to stop her. The doctor was wrong, her equipment faulty, her technique flawed. The baby was fine.

But Tony did nothing, and later that same day, she was home on their couch in Astoria, minus a baby in her stomach and a piece of her heart. And then she suffered from a rare reaction to the D&C, a blood clot the size of a grapefruit in her uterus. Mia had just moved in with them a few months earlier, and it was Mia who found her, pale and shaking from nausea at the kitchen table a few days after the D&C.

"You look awful," Mia said. Tam made a face but didn't reply. She hadn't been happy when the younger girl came to live with them in their spare room, and it didn't help when she felt criticized by her. But Mia was family, a young girl of only twenty, alone in this country, and they had to open their home to her.

Tam stood, wanting to get away from Mia, but waves of nausea bombarded her, and Mia rushed to her side.

It was Mia who accompanied her to the doctor, since Tony was in a lecture and couldn't be reached. It was Mia's hand she clutched when the doctors decided to suction out the clot without putting her under.

"It's going to feel like a bee sting," the male doctor who was assisting her doctor warned, before they gave her a shot in her cervix to numb the area.

"How would he know?" Mia whispered in Tam's ear. "Has he ever had a bee sting him in his whoo-whoo?"

Tam giggled despite her pain and discomfort, but then the laughter died when they began the procedure. It literally felt like they were trying to vacuum out her insides. She'd ended up with scarring on her uterus and needed surgery.

Mia took over Tam's care when she came home from the hospital. Mia had apprenticed with a traditional Chinese doctor in China before she came to New York, and she put together remedies filled with herbs like goji berries, *si wu tang*, and dong quai to help Tam's body heal and grow stronger. Tam held her nose and downed the mixture as fast as she could, because it smelled like boiled socks and tasted like hot rubbing alcohol with a bitter aftertaste.

She healed but endured two more miscarriages after that, the third resulting in another blood clot. The doctor gave her the abortion pill this time, afraid of more scarring. Mia shooed Tony out the door, telling him this was "women's business" and promising to take care of Tam.

But Tam stared after Tony, who'd been reluctant to go. It was Tony's arms she wanted around her as she lay doubled over on the floor, writhing in pain as the cramps ripped through her with unrelenting fury. It was Tony's hands she wanted to feel massaging her lower back after she crawled off the toilet, where she'd passed clumps and clots of blood and matter, so much that she'd had to flush again and again, wondering how it was possible that all of this came from her body. It was Tony's presence she wanted by her side as she wept bitter tears, saddened by this third loss and grieving for the babies she'd never know.

Then in the New Year, only two months after her third miscarriage, Tam got pregnant again. When she told Mia the news, Mia hesitated a beat too long and then broke into a big smile. "I wasn't going to tell you yet, but guess what! I'm pregnant too. We'll be pregnant together!"

"What?" Tam was surprised. "Was it an accident? I thought you were going to break up with Kenny." Tam and Mia had grown close in the last few months, and Mia had told Tam she'd been trying to break up with her boyfriend.

Mia shrugged carelessly. "It was an accident. I did break up with him. I don't want Kenny to have anything to do with the baby."

Tam would have spoken to Mia more about her decision not to tell Kenny he was the father, but then a few days later, she woke up bleeding. Despite her best effort to keep the baby in by lying down and clamping her legs together, the spotting turned to a heavy stream of blood that flowed freely out of her, along with her dreams for this baby.

Tony held her while she cried, and then he said, "No more pregnancies." He placed his lips on the side of her head. "I'd rather have you than a biological child."

And that's when he told her he wanted to adopt a child from a Chinese orphanage. Tam warmed to the idea right away, and they contacted Tony's mother's friend Cecilia Armstrong.

By then, Mia's bump had become noticeable. Tony said to Tam, "I'm going to help Mia find a place of her own. She's lived with us for a year and a half already."

Tam hadn't been happy when the girl had first moved in with them, but now she stood up for Mia. "How can you think of asking her to move when she's about to have a baby? She needs us more than ever now."

Tony looked torn. "But won't her having a baby make you feel bad?" He looked at her with such tenderness that she had to swallow not to cry.

"We can't ask her to leave," Tam said. Tony was quiet, and nothing more was said about Mia moving. She stayed with them for another ten months, until the big argument that had blown apart all their lives.

After Mia left, their lives felt like the aftermath of a war, bloody hearts and bombed-out bodies left standing with nothing inside. It was as if both she and Tony were holding their breaths, waiting to see which way the wind would blow. Would they stay together and try to make their marriage work? Would they drift apart, like two parts of a boat that had once been melded closely and broken apart by a storm? *Hurricane Mia*, Tam thought with a bitter laugh.

Over the next four years, without consciously meaning to, she'd started her silent campaign against Tony. She'd nursed her anger and hurt, refusing to continue with the adoption process just to spite him. She'd stare at him in resentment as they ate their meals in silence, conveniently forgetting about her own part in the fiasco.

Things had only started getting better eight months before the accident, because after dinner one night, Tony had said, "Enough. I can't live like this anymore. Either we start over and maybe start the adoption process again, or we end this now."

She'd looked into Tony's eyes and wanted so desperately for the past few years not to have happened. She realized she still loved him under all the anger, and so she'd nodded, and they'd called Cecilia that very night. At the look of joy on Tony's face as he talked to Cecilia, the cold, icy band that had been squeezing around Tam's heart for the last few years began to melt.

"TAM?" HER MOM tapped on the bathroom door, jolting Tam back to her bathtub in her town house. "You in there so long. You okay?"

"I'm fine," she called out, and then submerged herself underwater so that she didn't have to hear her mom's reply or the echoes of the past in her head.

When she came up for breath and heard no sound outside the door, she sighed and filled the tub with more hot water. She loved this town house; she really did. She and Tony had moved here four years ago from Astoria. Tam couldn't stand to live in the Astoria apartment after what happened. She had thought starting over in Dobbs Ferry would bring them back to each other.

"Aaaggghhhh." She let out a scream, wishing she could stay in this bathtub forever.

"Tam? You need something?" her mom yelled from outside.

"I'm fine!" Tam hollered. "Leave me alone."

"Okay. Jeez," Tam heard her mother mutter.

Darn it to hell, now she'd annoyed her mother, and Zhong-Ying was going to give *her* hell when she got out. Her mom was going home tomorrow, two weeks after Tony's accident. Tam wanted to beg her to stay even as she knew they'd just get on each other's nerves.

The water grew cold and she knew she should get out of the tub. But she didn't move, her grief rendering her immobile even as her skin puckered and a chill passed over her body. Tony was gone, just when it felt as if their marriage was back on track. And in his place, there was an orphaned little girl who needed a home, as well as a little boy far away in an orphanage who was waiting for her to come and get him.

THE NEXT DAY, she helped her mom bring her suitcase out to Abby's car. Abby had volunteered to drive them to the airport.

"Got everything?" Abby asked. She turned to pop her trunk and then cursed when she saw the Poland Spring water truck parked behind her car, blocking her way.

Tam looked up, and seeing the truck suddenly made her remember what it was that had been bothering her. She dropped her mom's suitcase on the sidewalk and ran inside, clicking on the TV. She scrolled through the taped segments of the accident, looking for the scene that had set off alarm bells in her head. She found the section she was looking for and squinted at the TV.

"What's the matter?" Abby and Zhong-Ying had followed her in.

"I thought I saw him," Tam muttered. She rewound the segment and turned to her mom and Abby.

"They said there were two men in the truck. I think this one is Kenny, Mia's old boyfriend," she said, pointing to one of the men wearing the beverage company's shirt.

"What? Angela's father?" her mom asked.

"Yes. I'm pretty sure he worked for that company. Look—there's another shot of him." She turned to them, a horrified look on her face. "Is that possible? He ran over Mia and Tony?"

"I'm calling the police." Abby pulled out her cell phone. Tam didn't hear a word Abby said on the phone because she was too busy studying the segment. When Abby hung up, she shook her head. "Well, Tam, you were right. The two men in the truck were Joe Walsh and Kenny Wong."

Tam's mouth thinned into a grim line. "Mia's ex-boyfriend."

9

*Three Months
before the Accident*

"MIA."

Mia nearly jumped a mile when the voice drifted out from behind her as she left the nail salon. One hand flew to her heart as the other closed on the keys in her hand, ready to attack if needed. But when the shape in the shadows stepped out and she realized it was Kenny, she relaxed a bit. Kenny might be annoying, but he was harmless. Mostly.

"Seriously, Kenny? Not this shit again." She spoke in Mandarin and started walking away from the salon, putting on a brave front that she didn't quite feel.

He'd been calling her on and off ever since they broke up years ago. She knew he was still in love with her. Sometimes when things were desperate and she barely made enough in tips and had to beg at the kitchen door of the hole-in-the-wall restaurant downstairs for leftovers, or when she and Angela had to huddle under a mound of blankets to stay warm because she couldn't pay the electricity bill, or she'd let her fucking pig of a landlord grope her breasts, which she'd always lamented were too big for her body but were now allowing her out of a month's rent as long as she let him come all over them, she'd wonder why she hadn't married Kenny like he wanted. She'd loved him once.

"Happy birthday."

"Thanks," she tossed over her shoulder, "for reminding me I'm twenty-seven today."

"Can I take you out?"

She stopped and shot him a look filled with disbelief. "Are you kidding? What makes you think I want to go out with you?"

"Come on, Mia." Kenny reached out and placed a large hand on her arm. "You know we were good together. We shouldn't have broken up."

"You threw a chair at me." Mia poked him hard in the chest. Although it had been her fault that he'd thrown the chair.

"I didn't throw it at you. And it was only the one time. You wouldn't marry me." Kenny sounded so pitiful that for just one moment, Mia's heart softened. But only for a moment.

She pulled her arm away and started walking, hoping he'd leave her alone.

"Mia. Please. We loved each other once."

Exactly what she'd been thinking a moment ago. She stopped again and turned to face him. They used to do this all the time—have the same thought at the same moment. She gazed at his familiar figure. He was stocky but tall, with well-muscled arms from working manual labor all his life, and wearing his usual uniform of jeans and a T-shirt. He had a tattoo of the word "love" in Chinese on his forearm, and his crew cut gave him a street-smart, rough look that complemented a childhood growing up on the streets of Flushing.

She'd fallen for him on their first date, when he'd told her how his white mother had run away with their plumber when he was seven, leaving him with his Chinese father. She'd been drawn to the vulnerable, naked look in his eyes and thought, *He's just like me. We're both broken.* She'd held him in her arms that night after he made rough love to her and felt such tenderness for this big, awkward man when he buried his face between her breasts and wept. She'd wanted to shelter him like no one had sheltered her when she was a child.

But over the years, Kenny's temper started to get to her. The first time she saw him mad at a co-worker from the beverage-distribution company, she'd been shocked by the possessed look in his eyes as he started ranting and raving about killing that motherfucker. She was the only one who could calm him down, but she got tired of constantly soothing his temper away.

"Kenny, it's done. We're over. You have to stop following me and showing up out of the blue." *And scaring the crap out of me.*

"Why wouldn't you marry me? You broke my father's heart too."

Mia sighed, a long exhalation that echoed in the street. "I love your father. But I can't marry you because of him." Kenny's father was a gentle Chinese man who spoke very little English and worked hard in the kitchen of a Chinese restaurant. He'd raised Kenny by himself after Kenny's mother left them. He was the exact opposite of Kenny.

"But you love me."

"Not anymore, Kenny. I told you that."

"You'll change your mind." He reached out to take her arm again and she sidestepped out of his reach.

"Kenny." She held both hands up in front of her to ward him off. "Showing up at my apartment, pounding on my door, and yelling and crying that you love me is not going to make me change my mind. And neither is calling me and leaving long ranting voicemails asking me why I'm torturing you. You've got to stop this. You keep appearing and disappearing over the years and I'm sick of it. I never know when you're going to pop up."

"I love you, Mia."

"It's over, okay?" She dropped her hands and swallowed. "I'm not being mean. I'm just telling it like it is."

Kenny stood on the sidewalk, a big man frozen in the middle of a busy city street, as kids ran shrieking around him and people rushed about, eager to get home and have dinner with their families. For just a moment, Mia felt sorry for him and wondered again if she could marry him and give both herself and Angela a better life. It wasn't that she had a problem using someone to get what she wanted. After the childhood she'd had, she'd learned that in order to get anywhere in life, you had to be willing to fight for it, no matter who you stepped on to get it.

But then she thought of being stuck with him for the rest of her life just to get her citizenship (which could take years and require her to go back to China) and give Angela a father, and she knew she couldn't do it. Just thinking about it made her feel like someone had stuffed a wet rag down her throat, and she gulped for breath. He might look sad and contrite now, but she knew within days, he'd act like he owned her. If she married him, he'd never let her go.

"I can wait." Kenny finally moved again, as if awakening from a dream. "I'll wait for you forever, Mia."

"Don't." She gave a tired shake of her head and turned away. "Bye, Kenny. I hope you find a girl who deserves your love." She waved over her shoulder and headed home again, toward her baby girl, who'd gone home with Jenny and her brood earlier to plan a surprise party for Mia.

But her heart stopped when Kenny shouted after her, "You're mine, Mia. I'll never let you go." She shuddered, her body suddenly filled with dread, before she shook it off and squared her shoulders. She wasn't going to let Kenny intimidate her.

10

TAM AND ABBY stood in front of the upside-down *fu* sign in Jenny's apartment, waiting for Angela and Lily to come out of Lily's room. Tam had been grateful that Abby had offered to drive her to get Angela. There was no way she could have faced the city traffic. Tam had asked Abby if she was starting to feel like Tam's driver, but Abby had laughed and said that was what friends were for, making Tam feel guilty again for not being a better friend to Abby.

It was hot for late September, and the small apartment was stifling. They'd already loaded Abby's car with the boxes that Jenny had packed of things Angela would need. Jenny hadn't had a chance to completely clean out Mia and Angela's apartment but would have to get anything else she thought Angela might need by the end of the week. The furniture, she was either giving away or throwing out.

Tam lifted her hair off her neck and pointed to the sign.

"Why do you hang that upside down?" Tam asked.

"It's supposed to be good luck," Jenny said. "The pronunciation for 'upside down' is like that for 'to arrive.' Means 'good luck arrives.'"

"Huh." Tam understood basic Mandarin but couldn't read or write it.

As if reading her mind, Jenny asked, "You didn't study Mandarin?"

"I quit Chinese school in middle school. I didn't think I'd ever use it."

Jenny gave her a funny look. "But you're Chinese."

Tam laughed. "That's what my brother, Wei, said. Or rather, he said we're Taiwanese. And I said I'm American."

"You're both," Abby said.

Tam raised her eyebrows but didn't answer. Wei had said the same thing.

"Everything okay with lawyer about Angela?" Jenny asked.

"I think so. I didn't understand most of what Mia's lawyer said. Something about having to wait until the will was probated, and then I have to appear in court." Tam shrugged. "He said he'd take care of everything."

"That good." Jenny nodded. "Have you heard anything else about the police investigation?"

Tam shook her head.

Abby said, "So who was driving that truck? Mia's ex or his coworker?"

Tam sat on the couch and shrugged. "Kenny said he was driving, but eyewitnesses said it was the guy with blond hair who was driving."

"That's weird." Abby crossed her arms over her chest. "Was it an accident?"

"I don't know." Tam frowned. "It's too much of a coincidence to be an accident. But what was his motive? Why would he want to kill Mia and Tony?"

"Kenny was so in love with Mia," Jenny said. "Almost obsessed."

"Obsessed could be bad though," Abby said.

"The police are confused by the conflicting eyewitness reports." Tam made a face. "Some said it looked like the blond guy, Joe, purposely drove the truck into them, while others said the Chinese guy looked like he was fighting with the blond guy. And then Kenny said he was driving and that the brakes were stuck."

"Stranger and stranger." Abby pursed her lips.

"Oh!" Jenny exclaimed, making Tam and Abby turn toward her. "I forgot to tell you. At Mia's funeral, this man, Chris, he come talk to me. I try set Mia up with him but she go on one date and tell me he not for her. But Chris tell me they been going out for months."

Tam stared at Jenny. "Mia had a boyfriend?"

Jenny raised a shoulder. "I guess."

"Maybe Kenny found out and was jealous?" Abby asked.

Just then, Angela and Lily walked into the room, bringing a halt to the conversation. Angela looked so much like a miniature Mia it was eerie. She was petite like Mia had been, with the same heart-shaped face and double-lidded eyes. Her black hair was tied into two braids and she held a wrapped present in her hand.

"It's Angela's birthday today," Lily announced. "She's five."

"Oh, no. I'm such an idiot." Tam brought her hands to her face. "I can't believe I forgot." It had been years since Angela had lived with them, but when she was born, Tam had thought she'd never forget the date. "Happy birthday." Tam gave Angela an awkward hug. "We'll pick up a cake on the way home to celebrate, okay?"

Angela turned away without answering, and Tam stood back,

feeling useless as Angela said a tearful good-bye to Lily. Angela then followed Tam and Abby silently out of the apartment.

Tam and Angela's first night together was a disaster, the silence in the town house deafening. Tam sat stiffly next to Angela on the couch after dinner. She wanted to talk about Mia, find out from her daughter how Mia had been the last few years. But to Angela, Tam was a stranger she was now forced to live with. She had no idea Tam had loved her like her own once.

"How 'bout we watch TV?" Tam blurted in a burst of inspiration. She turned on the TV, but after fifteen frustrating moments of looking for PBS Kids or Nick Jr. or anything that was goddamn kid-friendly (Weren't there like a million channels for kids? Why couldn't she find one when she needed one?), Angela finally spoke up.

"I'd like to take a bath, please."

"Oh, sure! Yes, we bathe here." *Duh, Tam.* She sounded idiotic. No wonder Angela was staring at her as if she had two heads. Tam led Angela up the stairs to the bathroom between the two bedrooms.

"Do you want me to help?" Tam asked.

"No, thank you," Angela said, so Tam retreated to her own room, only to come back and hover outside the partially open bathroom door, unsure if she should leave a five-year-old in the bathtub by herself. Why didn't she know these things? She was an elementary school teacher, for God's sake. But her students went home at the end of the school day. She didn't have experience with the day-to-day living of a young child. Tony was supposed to be here with her, getting ready to bring their son home. They would have figured out this parenting thing together. And now here she was, all alone, and she didn't even have any friends with kids whom she could turn to. How was she going to manage two kids under the age of five if she didn't even know if she should let a five-year-old bathe herself?

When Angela emerged clean with teeth brushed, Tam let out a sigh of relief and helped her into the full-size bed.

"Do you want me to read you a story?"

Angela shook her head. "My mama always told me a story she made up."

Tam sat on the edge of the bed. "I can make up a story. It probably won't be as good as your mama's, but I can try."

Angela stared at Tam. Then, to Tam's surprise, she reached out a small hand and laid it on Tam's cheek. "It's okay. You don't have to. You were the princess in the stories my mama told me. You got to live happily ever after with the prince."

Tam felt the emotion behind her eyes and swallowed hard.

Angela took her hand away and turned on her side. "I want to dream about my mama."

Tam kissed her on the cheek and slipped out, breathing a sigh of relief. But Angela woke screaming from a nightmare an hour later and couldn't be consoled. Tam spent most of the night in Angela's bed with her, soothing and rocking the little girl, knowing she'd made a mistake. Angela didn't sleep through the night for the first week, so Tam didn't either. Tam was exhausted and dragged through the days in a fog. How did single parents like Steven Abrams's father do it? He approached her before school on her first day back to teaching. The extremely handsome single father grabbed her hands and squeezed.

"I'm so sorry for your loss," Jeff Abrams said. Tam blushed, remembering what Steven had said about his father thinking she would be hot if she unbuttoned her shirt. She was uncomfortable to have such a gorgeous man holding her hands, but when she met his dark eyes, a look of understanding passed between them. His was a look of compassion, not of a lecherous man thinking about undressing her. She knew his wife had died two years ago from an illness.

"It'll get easier," he said.

She nodded, unable to respond. She'd always been painfully shy and found it difficult to talk to people she didn't know.

"I heard you have your niece living with you?" Jeff asked. Tam nodded again, not correcting him on the niece part. "Why don't we arrange a playdate with Steven? He went through a lot when his mother passed away and he might be able to help her."

Tam finally found her voice. "That would be really nice. Thank you."

Her little first graders were just as sweet. They crowded around her, handing her cards they'd made. Steven Abrams said with a serious expression on his face, "I'm sorry your husband went to the same place that my mommy went. But my daddy said they're safe up there and are looking down on us." He paused and sucked on the side of his finger. "I hope they didn't see that I peed in the bathtub at Jimmy's birthday party this weekend."

Tam stifled a laugh. It was so good to be back with her kids, to get away from the depressing reality of her life without Tony. They didn't know she was incompetent as a parent. Her kids loved her and looked up to her. They didn't know she was a fraud. Because the truth was, having Angela live with her was proving right a suspicion she'd had since her miscarriages. She wasn't cut out to be a mother.

11

BREATHING HARD, TAM slowed her pace to a walk and stretched her arms overhead. The sun filtered through the leaves of the trees surrounding the Old Croton Aqueduct Trail, which ran behind her town house. She reached out of habit to push her glasses back up her nose before remembering she'd put on contacts for the run. Instead, she pulled the rubber band out of her stubby ponytail and ran her fingers through her shoulder-length hair.

It was so nice to have this time alone. Angela had been living with her for only two weeks, and Tam was strung up as tight as a violin string about to break. She'd enrolled Angela in kindergarten at the same public school where she taught first grade. When they weren't at school, Angela stuck to her like glue. She wouldn't even let Tam use the bathroom in peace, and no wonder. She was scared out of her mind and grieving for her mama.

Thank goodness Jeff Abrams had invited Angela for a playdate today. Abby was going to pick Angela up at the Abramses' house and bring her back later.

A little black-and-tan dachshund dashed up to Tam on the trail with his leash dragging and plopped down in front of her. The dog smiled as he panted up at her. Tam bent to pet him and he flopped to the ground and rolled over, belly up for a tummy scratch. As Tam obliged, the dog's owner came puffing up.

"Monte! How many times do I have to tell you not to beg for a tummy rub?" The woman scolded the little dog as two other dachshunds danced around her on their leashes.

"It's okay, Bee," Tam said. "Monte knows I love him." She smiled at the older woman, who was about the same height as Tam at five feet four inches, but who was almost as round as she was tall. She was beaming at Tam and wearing one of her trademark loud Hawaiian-print shirts and flip-flops, even though the fall air was starting to get nippy. Her dark brown hair, peppered with gray, was pulled back in a long braid down her back.

Standing up, Tam grabbed Monte's leash and continued to walk with Bee back toward her town house. As they came up the path leading to the complex, Tam could see Abby and Angela sitting on the stoop in front of her unit. When Angela saw Tam holding the dachshund's leash, she ran over and squatted down in front of Monte.

"He's so cute!"

"Bee, meet Angela. She's come to live with me. Angela, this is Bee. She lives in one of the single-family houses over there." Tam pointed up the hill.

"It's very nice to meet you," Bee said. "How old are you?"

Angela stuck out all five fingers of one hand. "Can I pet him?"

She waited for Bee to say yes before reaching a hand out for

Monte to sniff. "My mama told me always to ask before petting a dog 'cause you never know if they'll bite you." She looked up at Tam and Bee with tears swimming in her eyes before bringing her attention back to the dog. She swiped away her tears and broke into a smile when the dog licked her face.

Tam and Abby exchanged a look over Angela's head. This was the first real smile Tam had seen from Angela since they had brought her here. She was glad the dachshunds were making the girl happy. Tam was convinced Angela knew Tam was defective as a parental figure.

"Are they all yours?" Angela asked.

"Well, Monte is mine, and I have another one named Oscar back at the house, but these two here are fosters."

"What are fosters?"

"I work with a dachshund rescue group, and we take in dachshunds that are homeless and try to find new homes for them. Foster means that some of them come and live with me until they get adopted and go to their forever home."

Angela looked up from the dogs. "Kind of like me. I was homeless and then Auntie Tam took me in."

The adults looked at one another before Tam said, "But, Angela, you'll stay with me forever."

One of the foster dachshunds was licking Angela's face with enthusiasm. She giggled. "I'm staying with you forever? I'm not going somewhere else?"

Tam crouched down next to Angela. "Is that what you've been thinking? That I was going to send you away?"

Angela nodded, not meeting her eyes. "I heard you tell Jenny Ayi that first day that you didn't want me. So I thought I was only staying with you until someone else wants me."

Oh, shitballs. Tam's heart ached when she heard those words. She'd blurted that out without thinking, and all this time, Angela had been living in fear that Tam would send her away. She really was a failure at this whole parenting thing.

Bee caught her eye over Angela's head and gathered up her dachshunds. "I've got to get these three back to the house so I can walk the others. Angela, come over anytime you want and play with them."

Abby stood also. "And I've got to go." She leaned down and kissed Angela, catching Tam's eyes over Angela's head. She was grinning broadly and mouthed something that Tam couldn't decipher. Tam tilted her head in question but Abby blew her a kiss and was gone.

Tam and Angela sat on the front stoop. Angela scooted away from Tam and hugged her legs to her chest. The little girl acted like Tam had cooties or something. How was she going to fix this?

"Did you have fun with Steven?" Tam asked, stalling.

"Yes. He has a Jack Russell terrier named Bandit." Angela spoke into her arms.

"That's nice." Tam scooted closer to Angela when the little girl didn't answer. "Listen, I know you heard me say I didn't want you, but I didn't mean it. Tony had just died and I was very sad. But once I was able to think clearly, I knew I wanted you to live with me. You're family."

Angela held herself stiffly. "I'm very sad my mama died. And I'm sad Uncle Tony died too. I miss them so much."

Tam pulled back to look down at Angela. "You knew Tony? When did you meet him?"

The little girl buried her face in her knees. When she didn't answer, Tam asked again, "When did you see Tony?"

"I wasn't supposed to tell anyone that Uncle Tony comes to visit sometimes," Angela whispered, lifting her face. "Am I in trouble?" Her chin wobbled and Tam's heart ached again at the pitiful look on her face.

"No, sweetie, you're not in trouble." Tam decided to let it go for now. "And you're not going anywhere. I promise. I know things are hard right now, but you're my family and we'll make this work."

Angela's face filled with hope. "Really? I can stay with you?" When Tam nodded, Angela let out a big sigh and leaned into Tam's side. "Maybe I can play with Steven again? He's nice. He told me about his mommy."

Tam swallowed the lump in her throat, grateful Angela had a friend who understood. Angela sighed and Tam put an arm around her. They stayed that way for a long time, as Tam wondered when Tony had started visiting Mia and Angela and what it all meant.

12

*Three Months
before the Accident*

MIA AND ANGELA sat in a booth at the back of a tea shop off Roosevelt Avenue, an untouched tea on the table. Angela was coloring in her book while Mia drummed her fingertips on the table, her eyes fixed on the front door. As soon as Tony walked in, her hand stilled and she stood.

He looked older and his face was thinner. It'd been four and a half years since they'd seen each other, and she searched his face for any indication of forgiveness. But he gave nothing away, only a small nod, and waited for Angela to notice him.

"Angela, this is your uncle Tony. You don't remember, but we used to live with him and his wife, Tam."

Angela looked up and smiled at Tony. "Want to see my unicorn?" She held up her book to show him the unicorn she was coloring in rainbow colors. "Me and Lily love unicorns. We want to be unicorns for Halloween this year, but Mama says that's too hard to make." She scooted over so Tony could sit next to her. "Lily's my bestest friend. We play together when our mamas paint people's fingers and toes and rub their backs."

Tony caught Mia's eye and smiled at Angela's description of Mia's work. It broke the ice, and as Angela chattered on, Tony said quietly, "You look well."

"You too." Mia was the first to break eye contact. Her heart was pounding out of control and she had to stop herself from hyperventilating. He hadn't wanted to come here today. He'd been so angry when she called, telling her she'd promised she wouldn't contact them ever again. But she had to get Tony and Tam to forgive her. For Angela's sake.

Mia let Angela do most of the talking. She needed Angela to trust Tony and for Tony to see what a great little girl she was. He and Tam were the only family besides her that Angela had in this country. She could see Tony thawing with each laugh the little girl coaxed out of him and with each smile she beamed his way.

When there was a lull in the conversation, Mia asked, "How's Tam? Does she know you're here?"

Tony's face immediately shut down, as if someone had pulled the shades over a window. Mia knew that was the wrong thing to ask even before he said, "Tam is none of your business. Leave her out of this. I will tell her when I'm ready."

Mia couldn't believe the hurt she felt that Tony was treating her like the enemy when once they'd been as close as siblings. She pulled her phone out and put *Dora the Explorer* on and gave it to Angela. She very rarely let Angela use her phone, and Angela snapped it up eagerly.

Once Angela's attention was diverted, Mia said, "I'm sorry. I didn't mean to hurt her. Or you." She could feel tears gathering and fought to keep them in. She knew Tony would think she was using tears to manipulate him if she let them fall. "Do you think Tam will ever forgive me?"

Tony sighed as if she'd just asked him if there would ever be world peace. "Mia, I don't know. This is all so complicated."

"I miss spending time with her when you used to go back to China every winter break. We had such good times. I'd give her makeovers and she'd cook for us. She practiced her Mandarin while I practiced my English. I miss her." She couldn't keep the wistfulness out of her voice and looked at him with a pleading expression, willing him to understand how much she needed them back in her life.

But Tony's face only hardened. "Maybe you should have thought of that before you betrayed us."

Heat rushed through her at the unfairness of his accusation. "It wasn't all on me. You . . ."

Tony jumped up and moved out into the aisle. "Don't make this my fault. You were the one who overstepped." He raked a hand through his hair. "I knew it was a mistake to meet you today." His eyes turned to Angela, who was absorbed in *Dora*, and his expression softened. "I only came because of Angela."

Mia scooted to the edge of the bench so that she was next to Tony. "I'm sorry. Please, for Angela's sake. She needs you, both of you. Can we try to work this out?"

Tony stood still, his jaw convulsing. Mia held her breath. She needed Tony to agree. She needed his help in making things up with Tam. When he gave a short nod, she exhaled a breath of relief.

He reached across the table and placed a hand on Angela's arm. "It's nice to meet you, Angela."

She looked up and smiled at him. "You too, Uncle Tony. See you again soon?"

He reached to give her a hug. "I'd like that." He turned to Mia and gave her a short nod. "I'll be in touch."

Mia watched him walk away to Dora yelling, "The map, the map!" Tony hadn't been warm, but it was a start. It was the first step in getting Tony and Tam to let her back into their lives.

13

TAM POKED HER head out the front door. "Angela." The little girl was supposed to be playing in front of their unit with Steven. Her toys were there under the tree, but they weren't. Tam shouted, louder this time, "Angela! Steven! Where are you?"

Out of the corner of her eye, she saw the door of the apartment next door open. Before she could retreat, the man who came out caught her eye and raised a hand in greeting. She groaned inwardly. She liked her neighbors a lot. The Hoopers were an older couple and had welcomed her and Tony when they moved in. But their son Marcus made Tam slightly uncomfortable whenever she ran into him. He lived in Manhattan and sometimes came home to see them on the weekends. She wasn't attracted to him, God no, but he had a tendency to stare at her that made Tony tease that Marcus had a crush on her. He was tall and thin, good-looking in a nerdy kind of way.

Now he stood on his parents' front stoop and flipped his brown hair out of his eyes. He looked slightly unkempt, as if he'd been up all night studying.

"I'm sorry to hear about your husband."

"Thank you." Tam looked around for the kids as an excuse not to meet his eyes.

"My parents told me your niece is living with you?"

"Yes. Have you seen Angela and her friend?" She had thought it was safe to let them play out front, since they lived at the end of a cul-de-sac and she knew all their neighbors in the small town house complex.

Marcus walked over to Tam. "Maybe they're playing with the McMahons' little girl on the corner?"

She shook her head. "They're in the same class, but they didn't click." She had asked Angela's teacher if Angela was drawn to any of the kids, but so far, Angela mostly kept to herself. Her only friend was Steven Abrams.

Tam slipped back inside to put her shoes on, and just as she came out again, she heard someone calling her name. Bee stood in front of her redbrick house halfway up the hill, waving. Tam ran toward Bee's house with Marcus trailing after her.

Bee yelled, "I have Angela and Steven."

Tam let out a breath and slowed her pace. She arrived at Bee's driveway just as Angela burst out of Bee's door. "Auntie Tam, come see the puppies. They're so cute!"

"Angela! Don't ever leave our place without telling me. I had no idea where you went. I thought someone took you," Tam let out all in one breath.

Angela's smile fell from her face and she looked down. "I'm sorry."

Tam crouched in front of her and pulled her into a hug. "I'm sorry for yelling, but it's not safe for you and Steven to wander away by yourselves. You have to tell me where you're going." Tam looked up at Bee. "And you're lucky Bee's a nice person."

"I'm sorry," Angela said again. "But I saw her going into her house with the puppies. She left her door open. She said I could come over anytime. Steven wanted to see the puppies."

Bee patted her on the head. "Yes, dear, I did say that, and you are welcome anytime, but you have to tell Tam first, okay?"

Angela nodded so hard her pigtails shook. "Okay, promise. Now can we show Auntie Tam the puppies?"

Tam got off the ground and Angela pulled her inside. Tam looked back to see Marcus standing outside Bee's front door. He cleared his throat. "I'm glad you found her."

"Thanks, Marcus," she called as Steven ran toward them, two puppies following at his heels. It was nice of Marcus to help her look for the kids.

Angela was excited, hopping from one foot to the other in front of the puppies. Tam had never seen her so animated before. In the few weeks since they'd had their talk and Tam reassured her she wasn't going anywhere, Angela was slowly opening up. But she still woke up crying every night. She'd call out for her mama, looking confused when she found Tam sitting next to her. She'd rub her eyes, and the look on her face when she realized again that her mama was gone broke Tam's heart every time. Her anguish exhausted Tam on a physical and mental level. Tam felt wrung out, like an old dishrag, unsure of how to help her.

Bee picked up one of the puppies and put it on Angela's lap, where it scrambled around and wagged its tail like a metronome. She showed Angela and Steven how to hold a dachshund. "Because they're so long," Bee explained, "you have to support their backs."

Tam let them play with the puppies for a few more minutes. "We've got to go back. Steven's dad will be here soon."

Angela stood with reluctance. She looked at the puppies and then down at her feet. "I wish I had a dog."

Steven piped up, "Yes! Angela needs a dog. Like my Bandit."

The longing on Angela's face was apparent and hard to ignore, but Tam couldn't commit to adopting a dog right now. She knew she would have to tell Angela about Charlie soon. Her caseworker, Sandra, had checked in with her once, and even though she hadn't pushed, Tam knew she couldn't keep the fate of an innocent little boy dangling.

She took Angela's hand and gave it a squeeze but didn't say anything about her wish for a dog. At the door, Bee said, "Why don't you have Angela come over for a couple of hours twice a week after school? You look like you could use a break and I don't mind watching her."

"I can't impose on you like that," Tam said. But the truth was, she would give anything for a couple of hours to herself.

"No imposition at all," Bee said. "We get on well, don't we, Angela?" Bee smiled. "Besides, I could use the help with the new puppies. I'll watch her, and in return, she helps me."

"Please?" Angela's eyes pleaded.

Tam relented and it was decided they would try out this arrangement tomorrow. Angela and Steven chattered the whole way home. As they reached their front door, Marcus came outside.

"Everything okay?"

"Yes."

"I bet those puppies were cute, huh, Angela?" Marcus asked. Angela only stared. Tam couldn't believe how quickly she changed from a chattering, excited girl to one with absolutely no expression on her face.

Just then, Jeff Abrams pulled into the parking lot and parked next to them.

"Daddy!" Steven ran toward the car. "We saw some weenies!"

Jeff got out of the car and walked over to them. "Thanks for having him." Jeff reached out to kiss Tam on the cheek. Tam blushed, knowing Marcus was watching.

Angela waved as they drove off and then went to pick up her toys.

"Don't you want to tell Marcus about the puppies?" Tam encouraged her, trying to dispel the awkwardness in the air. Angela shook her head and disappeared into their unit.

Tam's eyebrows shot up at Angela's rudeness, but Marcus appeared to have something else on his mind. "Are you seeing him?" His face reddened and he kicked at a stone on the ground.

"Jeff? God no. I mean, I didn't mean it like that." Tam's hands fluttered in the air. "He's just a friend."

"Well, if you ever need someone to talk to, I'm . . . I'm here." Marcus scuffed the ground with his shoe.

"Um . . . thanks."

"I just thought maybe you were lonely without Tony . . ." His words trailed off.

"Oh. That's nice of you." Tam couldn't meet Marcus's eyes. He was standing so close that she could feel the heat radiating off his body. Her face warmed and she said abruptly, "I have to go." She opened her front door and then shut it firmly, leaning her back into the door. She closed her eyes and took a deep breath.

If she didn't know any better, she would have thought Marcus was interested in her. But her husband had just died. Marcus couldn't have meant to be anything other than friendly, right? She wasn't good around men and wasn't sure if she'd read his signals wrong. She'd only had one serious boyfriend before she met Tony, a sweet

Korean man named Jiho at NYU. He was as shy as she was and they'd bonded over the horrors of having to give a presentation in their communications class. They'd dated for two years after college and she still remembered the Korean breakfasts, complete with *ban-chan*—the small side dishes of kimchi, bean sprouts and spinach, pickled radishes, and thin pancakes with scallions—that he used to make for her on the weekends, and the notes he'd slip into her purse so that she'd find them during the day.

"He's still standing in front of our door," Angela said from where she was crouched under the kitchen window, breaking into Tam's thoughts about Jiho and her sadness when he had moved back to Korea.

Tam's eyes flew open. "Jesus Christ, you scared the crap out of me!" Then she clapped a hand over her mouth and said, "Sorry. Didn't mean to curse."

"That's not cursing," Angela said. "I've heard a lot worse."

"You have?"

"Yes, at the nail salon. The women who go in the back room to have their private parts cleaned up. They shout out bad words."

Tam bit back a smile at Angela's description of a bikini wax. "What are you doing under the window like that?"

"I was watching him. I don't like him."

Walking over to Angela, she pulled the girl off the floor. "Why don't you like him? He's nice."

Angela didn't say anything, and instead ran up the stairs to her room. Tam wondered if Angela was being protective of her. She seemed to sense, as Tam did, that Marcus was interested in her.

14

TAM SAT ON the floor in front of Tony's closet and stared at its contents. She'd thought she would clean it out this Sunday morning while Angela was walking the dogs with Bee, but she found she couldn't. She'd been sitting here for over an hour. Every item she pulled out, she found an excuse why she couldn't get rid of it, until she realized she wasn't ready to give away his clothes yet. It was too soon.

Wei used to tease her and say she was too sentimental. As if on cue, her phone dinged with a text from her older brother.

> Ma wants me to check on you to see if
> you're okay.

Tam smiled and shook her head. Nice, big brother. You're such a suck-up.

Not sucking up. Ma just likes me better.

You've always been a brownnoser.

He'd married a nice Taiwanese girl from the neighborhood whom their parents approved of and gone to work in the family business. Wei's son and daughter were the lights of their parents' hearts, and Tam knew her mom loved having them only fifteen minutes away.

Who's brownnosing? I don't do things to
please the parentals. I only do what I want.

And there was the difference between them. Wei had always done what he wanted, whereas Tam tried to fit in with everyone around her. He was the calm one. He never got upset when the non-Asian kids at school made fun of them. When she was in middle school, he'd once found Tam in tears because some of the popular kids had called her a Chink. He said to Tam, "Why do you let them upset you? They're ignorant. Doesn't make them better than us." She said, "But I'm not a Chink! I was born here. I'm just as American as they are!"

She felt split in half between her Taiwanese self and her American self, never completely comfortable with either. But Wei never had that problem. He had a group of Asian friends but also had other friends from his math club and science team and never cared if they were cool or not. Whereas Tam was ashamed of her Taiwanese heritage and tried to avoid being grouped with the many Asian kids at their school. She wanted to be like the American girls and was embarrassed by the braised pork rice or the sticky rice balls her mom packed her for lunch.

What are you doing?

Trying to pack up Tony's clothes.

Her phone rang a moment later, and she picked up.

"Are you alone?"

"Yes, Wei."

"You shouldn't be doing that by yourself. You need someone there. You're too sentimental—you'll never throw anything out."

"I am not sentimental."

"You are. Remember that dried-up old flower I found you mooning over in high school?"

He'd walked into her room without knocking and found her staring at an old corsage. She shoved the dried flower under her book. "Have you ever heard of knocking?" She pushed Wei out of her room and closed the door with a bang before retrieving the flower to make sure she hadn't damaged it.

"I wasn't mooning. I just wanted to keep it as a souvenir."

Wei snorted. "Yeah, a souvenir from that jerk-off. What was his name again? Eric something? He took you to the junior prom but then dumped you for that Jennifer Lee."

"Eric Klein, and he didn't dump me. We weren't going out. Baba wouldn't let me date in high school."

She'd begged her parents to let her go when Eric had asked her to the prom. Her father had said no, especially because Eric was white. She'd run into her room, slamming the door behind her, and thrown herself facedown on the bed. It was so unfair. All her friends were going to the prom, some of them with their boyfriends. Why did her father have to be so traditionally Taiwanese? They lived in

America! What was wrong with dating a white boy, or any boy for that matter? And it was just the prom.

Her mom had come into her room and sat at the edge of her bed. Tam held still, hoping she'd go away. "Tam-ah," her mom said. "I know how much this means to you. Let me talk to your baba."

Tam flipped onto her back, surprised. "You'll let me go?"

Her mom sighed. "I know it's not easy for you, being Taiwanese but living in the States. Your baba, he just wants to protect you. We both think a Taiwanese boy will be better for you, when you're old enough to date. He'll understand your culture better than a *wai guo ren*." Her mom paused. "You like this boy?"

"Not really." Tam shrugged. "But all my friends are going to the prom." She liked Eric well enough. He was kind of cute, but it was the prom she cared more about.

"If you want to go to the prom, why don't you ask one of the nice Taiwanese boys from the neighborhood?" Tam pretended to shove a finger down her throat, earning a swipe from her mom.

In the end, her mom had talked her father into letting her go. She'd had a great time with Eric, and he'd even kissed her. He'd asked her out again, but she'd had to tell him no. Her father was serious about her not dating until she was eighteen. But she'd kept the corsage, taking it out sometimes to relive her one and only kiss so far in her life. She'd only thrown it away in senior year when Eric started going out with that ice queen Jennifer Lee.

"Whatever." Wei's derisive voice brought Tam back to her bedroom and she realized she'd missed most of what he was saying. "But seriously, Tam, don't go through Tony's stuff by yourself. Call a friend."

"I don't have any friends." Mia had been the closest friend she had.

"What about that Abby I met who was helping you?"

"She's done so much already. I don't want to impose." Tam put extra cheer in her voice. "I can do this myself."

"Okay, well, call me if you need me to talk you out of keeping everything." His voice turned serious. "It's good you're doing that. It'll help you move on."

"Thanks, Wei." She hung up and reached over to pull one of Tony's sweaters off the shelf. She held it up to her nose but only smelled the detergent they used. Despite what she'd said to Wei, she wasn't ready to let go of his things. Just like she couldn't imagine moving to a new place, like her mom suggested, or at least changing her bed, as Abby suggested. It comforted her to be in the house and bed where she and Tony had started coming back to each other.

She kissed the sweater, put it back on the shelf, and closed the door just as her phone rang. Thinking it was Wei again, she pulled open the closet as if he could see and said in an impatient voice, "What now?"

There was a pause and then her mother said, "So rude! Is that how you answer the phone?"

"Sorry, Mom." She sighed. "Did Wei tell you to call me?"

"He said you were cleaning out Tony's closet."

Tam rolled her eyes in exasperation. Did her whole family think she was incompetent and unable to do a simple task like this? Granted, she had been about to give up, but still . . .

"What's going on with the police investigation? Have they figured out what happened?" her mom asked.

"No. Kenny keeps claiming he was driving and that there was something wrong with his brakes. But everyone they interviewed was positive that the other guy, Joe, was driving."

"I don't get it," Zhong-Ying said. "Why would Kenny say he was driving if he wasn't? But why would Joe want to kill Mia and Tony?"

"I don't know." Tam rubbed her forehead. Thinking about Kenny was giving her a headache. She'd met him numerous times when Mia was dating him and always thought he was the dark and brooding type, but she'd never thought he was dangerous. And yet . . . was he capable of running them over on purpose? But then why did witnesses say he wasn't driving the truck?

"How's Angela going to feel when she grows up and finds out her father killed her mother? And that he didn't want to have anything to do with her?"

Tam sighed. "We don't know that he killed them on purpose. Maybe it really was an accident." But was it really just a coincidence that Mia's ex-boyfriend just happened to be in the truck that ended her life? What a mess.

She didn't tell her mom that the police had gotten Kenny's phone records, and a few days before the accident, he had repeatedly called Mia. Kenny claimed Mia had lost her phone and he was helping her find it by dialing it over and over again while she searched. But Jenny said she wasn't even aware that Mia was talking to Kenny again.

"Something's not right," her mom said.

"I know." Tam stood and closed the closet door again. She couldn't face it. For the first time since their estrangement, she wished she was still friends with Mia. Mia would have made quick work of getting rid of Tony's stuff. She didn't have a sentimental bone in her body and would have taken a no-nonsense approach to it. But then she remembered. Mia was dead too.

And somehow, Kenny was involved in their deaths.

15

*Two Months
before the Accident*

"THANKS FOR THE drinks," Mia said, twirling the rose Chris had bought her. Chris was a second-generation Chinese whose family was originally from Shanghai. Jenny had set them up, claiming they were perfect for each other. Chris was only a few inches taller than her, which wasn't very tall. But he had an open face and his eyes shone with kindness and interest.

"I had a good time. Let's do it again soon?" Chris had taken her hand when they'd left the bar of the Chinese BBQ joint where they'd met for drinks. He was walking her home through the busy streets of Flushing, which were filled with Saturday night revelers. The fluorescent lights of restaurants and bars shone brightly, lighting up the streets, and the hustle and bustle reminded Mia of Guangzhou.

She smiled at him as they turned down the street where she lived. He was a nice enough man, but she wasn't really interested, despite Jenny's claim that he was perfect for her. She was about to tell him she didn't think it was a good idea to go out again when a shape emerged from the shadows, causing her to jump.

"Mia." The shape moved into the light.

"Jesus, Kenny! You've got to stop scaring me like this." She went to drop Chris's hand, but he held on tighter and pushed her behind him.

Mia blew out a breath. The scene would be funny if her heart wasn't galloping like a racehorse and she wasn't battling her annoyance at Kenny for following her again. Chris was so much smaller than Kenny, and he looked almost scrawny next to Kenny's heft. But the look on Chris's face was fierce as he stared down Kenny as if he meant to fight him to protect Mia.

"Chris, it's okay. I know him." She introduced them and felt Chris's grasp on her hand loosen slightly. To her surprise, she missed the intense pressure of his hand. Could it be possible that she might like him more than she thought, especially given his show of protectiveness?

"Where were you?" Kenny asked, breaking into her thoughts.

This time, she did take her hand back from Chris and crossed her arms over her chest. "It's none of your business where we were. Why are you lurking on my street again?"

Kenny's face hardened like a stone statue, and he squinted at her with a cold look in his eyes, causing goose bumps to break out on her arms. "I'm not lurking. I went to your place to see if you wanted to take me up on that drink. But you weren't home, so I waited for you."

Mia could feel Chris staring at her, his face full of questions, and she wanted to shut Kenny down as soon as possible.

"I never agreed to have a drink with you. Leave me the fuck

alone, Kenny. Okay?" With that, she took Chris's hand and walked toward her apartment, literally dragging Chris behind her.

They were almost in front of her building when she heard, "Mia!" It was a cry of anguish. She halted and turned back. Kenny stood in the middle of the sidewalk with both hands on either side of his head as he stared after her. Mia had the absurd thought that he looked like a parody of a scene from *A Streetcar Named Desire*.

Despite her resolve, she could feel herself softening toward him. He infuriated her, but there was something about him. They understood each other on a deep, spiritual level. He had treated her like the most precious person in the world when they were together. And despite her annoyance at his following her, she understood why he did. They were bound in some way to each other. Even though she knew they weren't good for each other, she felt sorry for him.

"Kenny, go home." She turned away, steeling her heart, and pulled Chris with her inside the front door of her building, when only moments before, she'd been prepared to say good-bye to him for good.

"Who's that?" Chris had a deep voice that was incongruous with his slight frame. But right now, the richness of his voice was like a balm to her raw nerves.

"An ex. He hasn't quite gotten the message that we're over, even though it's been years." She rolled her eyes to show her exasperation.

Chris nodded, lifting his eyebrows. "Ah, got it. I could see he wasn't happy to see you holding hands with me."

"Forget about him."

"So." Chris stepped closer to her. "Does this mean you'll go out with me again?"

She hesitated. She hadn't wanted to go out with him in the first place. She'd been annoyed at Jenny when Jenny told her she'd given Mia's number to her husband's brother's friend. Mia loved Jenny, she really did. Jenny had given her a chance and a job when she first moved to New York and had found her this apartment when Tam kicked her out. But when she got her mind set on something, she was like a dog with a bone. She wouldn't let go until she got her way. So she'd bullied Mia into going out with Chris tonight, but now, suddenly, Mia was glad. Not that she would tell Jenny that. If she did decide to go out with Chris again, she wouldn't tell Jenny.

She gave him a slow smile, the one that always made men melt like putty. She'd put that smile and her ample bosom to good use when she first came to New York from China and had no money. Back then, she'd slept around in a desperate attempt to ease her broken heart and also to get a good meal, since the tips she earned back then were almost nonexistent.

Now she aimed that smile at Chris and watched his gaze slide down to her cleavage, where her breasts were on proud display, thanks to the push-up bra she wore. She placed a finger under his chin and made him look up. Locking eyes with him, she leaned in slowly and settled her mouth over his. And when his body melded to hers and he pushed her gently until she was up against the foyer wall, she knew she could have him if she chose. Maybe he was the answer to all her problems.

16

"MARCUS ASKED ME out," Tam said casually at the beginning of yoga class.

Abby sat up on her yoga mat. "Who?"

"Marcus. My next-door neighbors' son. I saw him yesterday." Tam looked around the yoga studio to avoid Abby's curious stare.

"You have a date? That's great!"

"No, it's not. It's too soon for me to be dating." Tam was surprised to see so many men in the class. The man on her left was there with his wife or girlfriend, a stunningly gorgeous brunette with long wavy hair who texted rapidly on her phone even as the instructor walked into the studio and welcomed them to the class. The man smiled at Tam and she thought of the Marlboro Man. Sandy hair and rugged good looks, but without the cigarette: a health-conscious Marlboro Man.

Abby poked her in the arm. "You should go," she whispered. "I've got a date too."

"You think?" And then, "Wait, what? With who?" Abby winked and put her finger to her lips, pointing to the teacher.

Tam stared hard at Abby, who ignored her. She rolled down to lie on her mat, catching the Marlboro Man's eyes. He shrugged and pointed to his wife, who was still texting away. They shared another smile before he turned to his wife. Tam watched the gentle way he took his wife's phone out of her hands. A pang of longing went through her; she no longer had anyone to watch out for her like this man was doing for his wife. Maybe she should consider going out with Marcus. What could it hurt? Tony had been gone for almost two months. She was tired of feeling mopey and depressed. She wanted to smile and laugh again.

TWO HOURS LATER, Tam sat at a small table with Abby at Sushi Mike's restaurant. It was a Friday night and the small, popular restaurant was crowded.

"I'm so glad Bee offered to babysit Angela so we could take yoga and have dinner." Tam had only accepted once Bee agreed to take payment for her time.

"Me too." Abby took a sip of her sauvignon blanc. "So, did you like yoga?"

"Yes. The teacher's great," Tam replied, not saying out loud that she'd enjoyed the view too. She couldn't help but be aware of the Marlboro Man next to her, who was surprisingly limber and moved with a grace she envied.

"Great, then we can make it a weekly thing."

"I don't know." Tam frowned. "I had a hard time getting Angela to let go."

"I thought she loves going to Bee's."

"She does. But she's gotten clingy lately. She doesn't want to be away from me for long. Even at school, I have to check up on her or she gets anxious." Tam looked around the restaurant, her heart catching when she caught sight of the familiar table in the corner. She blew out a breath.

"What's wrong?" Abby asked.

"Nothing. It's just, the last time I was here was with Tony, about a week before the accident."

"Oh, I'm sorry. We could have gone somewhere else."

"It's fine. We were sitting over there." Tam pointed to the table in the corner. "We always sit there if it's free." She stuck her bottom lip out and gave Abby a sad smile. "I was teasing him about his love for sushi." Tam rested her chin on her hand. That had been a good night for the two of them.

The waitress approached their table, and as she gave them the specials, Tam's thoughts drifted back to that night with Tony.

"Sushi isn't American, you know," she'd said to him. "I thought you wanted to be as American as possible."

Tony picked up a piece of tuna with his chopsticks and dunked it in the wasabi soy sauce before expertly popping the whole piece in his mouth. After he swallowed, he said, "Sushi is so popular in the States now, it's almost as American as pizza and hot dogs. That's what makes America so great. It's a melting pot of all different nationalities and cuisines." And he ate another piece of American sushi with his chopsticks.

Tam couldn't resist teasing him more. "Why are you using chopsticks when you refuse to own any at home?"

"It's okay to use them when eating an American meal out."

"I don't get why you embrace all things American, yet hold fast to your Chinese way of thinking."

"I guess I'm like yin and yang. One part of me will always be Chinese, but the other part is American. I wouldn't exist without both parts."

"But which is Chinese—the yin or the yang?"

Tony ignored her teasing and reached for her hand, interlacing their fingers together. It'd been a while since they'd held hands in public. "We're like yin and yang too. 'When two things are balanced, they are equal but still separate. In a relationship of harmony, the two energies blend into one seamless whole.' That's us; one can't exist without the other." Tony squeezed her hand. "I feel like we've been split into two for a while now, and it upset the equilibrium of our wholeness." He looked at her. "But I think we've been coming back together the last few months and finding a new balance."

Tam nodded. This was the Tony she fell in love with.

But if things between her and Tony had been getting better, then why had he not told her he'd made up with Mia and was visiting her and Angela?

Abby brought her out of her reverie when the waitress left. "Hey, have you done anything about the adoption yet?"

Tam shook her head. She'd stared at the three photos and one short video of Charlie they'd been given, wondering how she could possibly not bring him home. The orphanage had named him Jia Li, and they'd planned to keep his Chinese name as his middle name.

"Realistically, I should stop the adoption. It's been so much harder than I thought with Angela."

Abby nodded. "No one would blame you if you don't go through with the adoption."

"But then I think about Charlie in that orphanage. My heart just won't let me pick up the phone and tell Sandra I'm stopping the adoption." Tam played with her chopsticks. "I can't explain it, but I feel as if he was meant to be in my life. At the same time, how can I possibly raise two kids by myself?"

"You've got Bee now. And me."

"I know. Thank goodness."

"Did the adoption agency give you a deadline?"

"No. I almost wish they would. Then I'd be forced to finally get off my butt and do something."

"I can't even imagine the pressure you're under right now. You've had a hard couple of months." Abby tilted her head. "How're you doing?"

"A bit better." Tam averted her eyes. She didn't say out loud that there'd been moments when she wished she'd died with Tony. The rational part of her brain knew she hadn't caused his death, but mentally, she couldn't help but blame herself. How many times in the last few years had she hated him so much that she wished he were dead? Her mother had always told her, *Be careful what you wish for.* If only she'd confronted him instead of smoldering in silent resentment and hurt.

"Sometimes it feels like a bad dream." She wanted to tell Abby how she really felt, but years of holding back kept her from saying more. The last friend she'd trusted and told all her secrets to had been Mia. And look what Mia had done with her trust.

Abby made a sympathetic sound, but the waitress approached to take their order before she could say anything.

While they were eating, Abby asked, "Do you want me to pick Angela up from the Abramses' tomorrow? She told me she has a playdate with Steven."

"You don't have to do that."

"I don't mind." Abby's tone was light. "It'd be my pleasure."

Something about Abby's voice made Tam look up. Abby had a big smile on her face. "Why are you smiling like that?"

Abby bit her bottom lip and gave Tam a wink. "No reason." Before Tam could dig in deeper, Abby asked, "So, have you told Angela about the adoption?"

"No." All thoughts of Abby's odd behavior left Tam's mind.

"I think you need to. It'd be better for her if you presented it as something the two of you decide on together, rather than a done deal that you spring on her."

Tam sighed. "I know. You're right."

"I'm always right. Trust your instincts, Tam." Abby gave a satisfied nod. "And go out with Marcus. You need something fun to take your mind off your life."

"Maybe." Tam put a piece of salmon sushi in her mouth and chewed slowly. She'd think about Marcus's invitation later. For now, she knew she needed to quit stalling. There was no question in her mind that she had to bring Charlie home. It was the last thing she and Tony had been doing together, and it was important to her to complete it. Now she just had to figure out how to tell Angela.

17

"AUNTIE TAM! WHERE are you? Hurry, come here!" Tam had told Angela to just call her Tam, but the little girl still called her Auntie.

Tam ran down the stairs of the town house at Angela's urgent calling. She halted when she saw Angela waiting at the bottom with Bee, who was wearing a bright orange Hawaiian shirt. Angela held the leash of a red short-haired dachshund.

"You scared me." Tam placed put a hand to her chest. "I thought something was wrong."

Angela bent down to pet the dachshund. "This is Stella. Can she stay here today so that Lily can meet her?" Jenny was finally bringing Lily to visit. "Bee says she trusts me to take really good care of her 'cause I've been doing so good with all the dogs."

"Okay."

Angela cheered, taking off Stella's harness and turning on her *Frozen* video while Tam walked Bee to the door.

"Just bring Stella back later today," Bee said. "It'll be good for Stella to interact with children."

Tam nodded, closed the door, and turned to look at Angela, sprawled on the couch. Tam picked Stella up and placed her on the couch next to Angela, then paused the video with the remote.

"Hey! I was watching that." Tam smiled at the indignant tone of Angela's voice. She sounded so . . . normal. Maybe they were finally breaking down the walls between them.

"There's something I want to talk to you about before Lily and Jenny get here." Tam sat on the couch next to Angela.

"Okay." Angela looked at Tam with so much trust that Tam swallowed. What if Angela freaked out?

"Before the accident, Tony and I were going to adopt a little boy from China."

"My mama was born in China." Angela's eyes welled, but no tears fell. "You mean 'dopt like the way Bee 'dopts out the dogs she fosters?"

"Yes, like that." Tam was suddenly grateful for Bee and her dogs, giving Angela something to relate the adoption to. "We were approved to adopt as a couple, but now it's just me. Good news is, the little boy is considered Special Focus, so a single woman can adopt him."

Tam watched as Angela tried to process everything. "What is Special Focus?"

"It means he has a special need, either medical or developmental. Or is older." Tam looked at Angela, wondering why she was having a hard time explaining things to her, when she was a first-grade teacher. Somehow, talking to other people's children was easier than talking to one in her charge. "Do you understand any of this?"

"No." Angela cocked her head to the side. "So where is he? What's his name?"

"Tony and I named him Charlie, and he's in an orphanage in China."

Angela looked horrified. "He's living in an orph'nage? Like I would have been?"

"You wouldn't have gone to an orphanage. I think you would have gone into a foster home." At the worried look on Angela's face, Tam quickly added, "But don't worry. You'll always stay with me."

"I wish my mama and Uncle Tony were still alive," Angela whispered.

"I know," Tam said. "But since they're not, I'm glad you're here with me."

Angela looked down and Stella took that moment to lick Angela's face. A tiny giggle escaped, and Angela turned her head to avoid the puppy's tongue.

"My mama told me all about the orph'nages in China. She said they were awful places. One time, when I was really bad, she told me she would send me to one if I didn't behave."

Tam was taken aback. "Really? I'm sure your mama didn't mean it."

Stella settled next to Angela. "I know, she said she was sorry."

"What did she say about the orphanages?"

"That it wasn't a nice place and was really smelly and the kids were always hungry and they had no one to give them hugs and kisses. It made me sad. That's why I was so scared when Mama died. I thought I was gonna be sent there."

Tam had no idea Mia had been inside the orphanages. Maybe Tony's mom had taken her. She knew that after Mia's parents died when she was a teenager, she had lived with Tony's parents for a few years. She was ten years younger than Tony, and Tony was already in the States for school, but he would see her when he went home to China for his monthlong visit at the winter break. Tam knew Mia was really close to Tony's mother, and Mia always spoke of her with great respect and gratitude. Tam had once asked Mia why she seemed so grateful to her, and Mia had given her a look and said, "She took me in when I had no one. Isn't that enough to be grateful for?" To which Tam had no response, since she didn't know what it was like to lose her parents or be alone.

Angela tugged on her sleeve. "What are we going to do about the little boy?"

"Well, that's why I wanted to talk to you. What do you think we should do?" Tam stopped when the video suddenly started playing again, with Elsa belting out "Let It Go." She reached to turn it off. She was starting to hate that song. Angela watched the video so much that Tam found herself singing "Let It Go" in her head at the most inopportune times.

"How old is he?" Angela asked.

"He turned three recently."

Angela pursed her lips and her brow crinkled, as if she was thinking hard. "I think we should bring him here."

"You do?"

Angela nodded. "He shouldn't have to live in an orph'nage. Mama told me she hated living there."

Wait, what? "Mia lived in an orphanage?" Tam asked with surprise.

"Yes." Angela's face scrunched up. "I mean no. She told me stories." Angela looked concerned. "But she didn't really live in one, right?"

"No," Tam said. "She lived with Tony's family." But now Tam was confused. What had Mia been telling Angela? "So, you think we should adopt Charlie?"

Angela nodded and hugged Stella.

Tam let out a breath of relief. "I'm glad you feel that way. Sometimes I think I should let him go and give him a chance with a family that has both a mommy and a daddy. But I can't seem to just forget about him. It's hard to explain."

Angela looked at Tam. "Is that why you're keeping me? 'Cause something's not letting you just forget about me?"

When had Angela gotten so intuitive? Or had she always been like that? Tam wished she could ask Mia. "Yes. I just couldn't say no. I had to bring you home." That, and her guilt over what she'd done to them when Angela was a baby. She wondered if the little girl would forgive her if she ever found out the truth.

Angela turned her attention back to Stella. "Then I guess we have to bring him home."

"I'm glad you're okay with this." Tam flopped back on the couch. "I must be out of my mind to think about raising two kids by myself."

"Where'd your mind go?" Angela looked confused.

Tam laughed. "Never mind." She picked up the remote and turned Elsa back on. "Oh, and that would mean you're going to have to travel to China with me. Do you know if you have a passport?"

Angela's eyes were already glued to the TV. She shrugged. "I dunno. What's that?"

"Never mind. I can ask Jenny when they get here."

Later that day, after they'd feasted on Angela's favorite scallion pancakes wrapped around a *you tiao*—a long Chinese doughnut—and the soybean milk to dunk it in that Jenny had brought, Tam asked

Jenny if Angela had a passport. Angela and Lily were in the finished basement with Stella. Tam and Tony had used the basement as a guest room and office.

"No," Jenny said. "You know Mia not legal here, right? She had no any visa."

"What?" Tam asked. "I thought Tony got her a green card, sponsored her."

"No," Jenny said. "He was trying but it not go through. Something about a cousin can't sponsor you? She had only visitor's visa."

Tam was shocked. "I had no idea."

"Angela is citizen, 'cause she born here. But they could go no anywhere since Mia not able to come back to States, so Mia never got passport. Why you ask?"

"If I decide to adopt Charlie, then I'm going to have to get Angela a passport. She'll have to travel to China with me."

"How long you be there?"

"About two weeks. I want to stop in California to see my parents first. And I'd like to visit Tony's mother in Beijing," Tam said. "Do you know where her birth certificate is?"

"It probably in box of papers I cleaned out from Mia's apartment. I saving it for you, for next time you come to Flushing with car. But I look this week."

"That would be great. This way we're prepared. Thanks, Jenny."

Tam looked at the other woman and could see how tired she was. There were circles under her eyes and her hair was in a messy ponytail. Her hands looked red and raw, probably as a result of all the work she did in the nail salon. Yet she'd brought Lily to visit Angela and even remembered to bring Tam the stinky tofu she liked from Flushing.

Tam took a deep breath and decided to ask Jenny the question that'd been weighing on her mind.

"Jenny, Angela told me Tony used to visit them. Do you know when this started and when they made up?"

Jenny shifted on the couch. She said in Mandarin, "Mia didn't really share with me. One day, a few months ago, she told me they made up. I only saw him once, but Angela told Lily he visited more." Jenny tended to switch to Mandarin when she had trouble finding the English words, and Tam would answer her in English. She'd found she understood more Mandarin than she thought, even though she had a hard time speaking it.

"Oh." Tam was quiet for a moment. When she didn't say anything else, Jenny asked, "You didn't know Tony was visiting Angela and Mia?"

Tam shook her head. She was sorry she had started this conversation. She was embarrassed to admit Tony never told her.

"It's good they made up, right? Family shouldn't fight, even second cousins. They need to stick together."

Tam nodded. "You're right. Family shouldn't fight. But I thought Mia was his first cousin."

Jenny frowned. "Mia told me they were second cousins."

"Hmm." Tam's forehead furrowed. This was getting weird, combined with what Angela had said earlier. "Oh, and did you hear about Kenny's phone records?"

"Yes, so strange." Jenny's forehead wrinkled. "I don't think he did it on purpose. He was crazy about Mia." She stopped. "Unless he saw her with Chris? Maybe he jealous?" She shook her head. "But she said she didn't like Chris and only went out with him once. But he came to the funeral . . ."

Tam shook her head, confused. The girls chose that moment to thunder up the stairs from the basement.

"Can we take Stella for a walk?" both girls asked at the same time.

Tam stopped thinking about the past in the flurry that ensued. It wasn't until later, when Jenny and Lily had gone home and Stella was back with Bee and Angela was sleeping in her bed, that Tam allowed the thoughts that were bothering her to enter her mind.

She'd been trying to convince herself it didn't mean anything that Tony hadn't told her he'd made up with Mia. But hearing Jenny confirm that he had been visiting the past few months without telling her, Tam wondered if Mia had told Tony the truth, and about Tam's own part in the deception. How she wished they'd all sat down and talked and worked this out, instead of letting it fester in silence. And now it was too late. They were dead and Tam would never find out what really happened.

18

MIA LOOKED UP from the black-and-white composition note-book she'd been writing in when the front door opened and Angela came running in, slamming the door behind her. She threw herself on the couch.

"Angela. Shoes off."

The little girl kicked off her shoes and let them fly so they landed somewhere near the front door. Mia was about to say something when she noticed Angela's face was bright red and she looked like she was about to cry.

Mia closed her notebook and walked over to the couch, sitting next to her daughter. "What's wrong, Angel?"

Angela shook her head but didn't speak.

"Was someone mean to you? Why aren't you with Lily? I thought her baba was taking you to the park."

Angela shook her head again, this time more violently. "I don't want to go to the park with them."

"What's wrong?"

Angela was quiet for so long that Mia thought she wouldn't an-swer. But then she sat up and turned eyes so sad to Mia that Mia felt her heart crack. "Why doesn't my baba want to take me to the park? Why doesn't he come see me?"

Oh. Mia's heart sank. Angela was upset about her father. Mia had known she'd have to tell Angela something besides the fairy tales she'd been making up for her, especially since Angela had started asking about her father last month on Father's Day. Where was he? Why didn't he live with them like Neil lived with Lily and her family? Did he not like them?

Mia looked at her daughter and wished with all her might she could take her hurt away. She didn't know how to answer her ques-tions. Angela wasn't old enough to understand. Mia reached out and smoothed the hair away from Angela's face. "It's complicated, Angel. But it doesn't mean he doesn't love you. You're such a smart, funny, beautiful little girl."

"Is he dead?" Angela's voice was small.

"What? Who told you that?"

"Lily. She said maybe he was dead and you didn't want to tell me. Since he never comes to see me. She said she couldn't imagine her baba not wanting to see her if he wasn't dead."

Mia prayed for strength. Maybe she should have just told Angela her father was dead. It would have been easier, but she couldn't lie to her daughter like that.

She reached out and pulled Angela onto her lap and buried her face in her little girl's hair. She loved the way her daughter smelled, a combination of little girl and Angela's own sweet scent. Her arms tightened around her daughter.

"Your father does want to see you," Mia finally said, her voice muffled in Angela's hair. "But the evil witch who cast a spell on him won't let him go. He's working very hard to escape and come to you." Mia fell back on the fairy tale she'd been telling Angela from the time she could understand. She'd made up a whole story about how her father was a prince who had to marry a princess because an evil witch had cast a spell on him.

"With the princess?" Angela asked.

Mia squeezed her eyes shut. "Yes, hopefully with the princess. He has to figure out how to escape with her too and not leave her behind with the evil witch. That's why it's taking so long."

"My baba is very brave." Angela turned so that she could see Mia. "He's going to save the princess and come back to us. Will they both live with us?"

"Um . . ." Oh, God, this fairy tale was getting out of control. Mia was starting to mix up what was real and what was made up. "I don't know," she finally said. At least that was the truth. She had no fucking clue what she was doing. Her daughter deserved the truth and Mia was doing everything she could to fix the situation. But it wasn't fast enough for Angela's questions.

As Angela continued her interrogation (Do you think the princess will like me? Will my baba play with me like Neil plays with Lily and give me piggyback rides? Will he come home every day from work to us when he finally gets away from the evil witch?), Mia rocked Angela on her lap. She closed her eyes, trying to absorb her daughter into her being. She would do anything for her. She'd thought she was protecting Angela back then, but now she was starting to have second thoughts. Should she have told the truth from the very beginning?

A sense of urgency hit her and she held her daughter tighter, stifling a sob. She'd write more in her journal after she put Angela to bed. She had to get her story out, had to leave the truth with Angela so she could read it when she was older and could understand. The feeling that something was going to happen to her was growing stronger every day. She needed to get everything down on paper before it was too late.

19

TWO WEEKS BEFORE Thanksgiving, Tam took Angela for
a meet and greet with a pediatrician recommended by one of her
fellow teachers. Angela spent the car ride telling Tam about Steven's
dog, Bandit, who had learned a new trick.

She was still talking about Bandit when they got to the building.
"He can jump so high. But Bee told me Stella shouldn't jump like
that 'cause of her back." Angela tripped when the automatic doors
slid open, and she sprawled to the ground. Before Tam could move,
someone from behind her rushed forward and got the little girl off
the floor and out of the way. Angela had split her lip when she
hit the floor, and her mouth was bleeding. Tam grabbed a tissue out
of her purse and held it to Angela's lip.

"Angela, are you okay?" Tam did a visual scan, looking for other
injuries. The little girl nodded, and Tam was impressed she wasn't
crying.

"Thank you so much for helping us," Tam said to the man who had come to their aid.

"No problem." He followed as Tam helped Angela to a bench.

"Your name's Angela?" the man asked. She nodded. The man turned to Tam. "My office is just down the hall. Why don't you come with me and I'll get her an ice pack and clean off her lip. Which doctor are you seeing?"

Tam looked at him for the first time and realized he looked familiar. Before she could figure out why, he said, "Hey, I know you. We take yoga together."

It was the health-conscious Marlboro Man. The man she'd noticed taking class with his wife that first time she went with Abby. She'd been to class every week since, and while she hadn't seen his wife again, she'd found herself next to him the last two weeks. They both liked the back wall. They'd exchanged smiles and once a grimace when the instructor was demonstrating crow pose, but they'd never talked.

"Oh, right. I didn't recognize you in clothes," Tam said. "I mean, not that you were naked . . . Oh, dear." *Shut up, Tam. Just shut up.*

His eyes crinkled and he laughed, making her look at him. In the darkened yoga room, she hadn't noticed he had the lightest brown eyes she'd ever seen. There were little wrinkles in the corners of his eyes and he had a square jaw, something she found appealing. She was suddenly glad she wasn't wearing her glasses and that the dress she'd worn to school today was a pretty shade of blue and fit her well.

Then she caught herself. What was wrong with her? Why was she thinking like this? He had a wife, a gorgeous one at that. She was a grieving widow and should be more concerned about Angela and not how strong she remembered his forearms and triceps looked in chaturanga. She shivered.

He looked at her with a quizzical expression, and she quickly smiled. Oh, my Lord, what was wrong with her? Why was she attracted to this man when she knew he was off-limits?

"Sorry. Um, I don't know if we're in the right building." She looked down to avoid his gaze, afraid he could read her mind. "We're looking for the pediatrician, Dr. Morgan?"

"Well, you've found him. I'm Dr. Adam Morgan, but the kids call me Dr. Adam."

"Oh." No way. This man who was giving her goose bumps was going to be Angela and Charlie's doctor? No. No frigging way. "Um, we're early."

"That's fine." He smiled and Tam's insides turned to liquid. He gestured down the hall. "Let's get Angela cleaned up before the appointment." Angela slid off the bench and, looking at Dr. Adam with trust, followed him into his office, with Tam trailing behind them, mentally slapping herself across the face to stop her fantasizing.

Once Tam cleaned the blood off her face, Angela spoke up. "Are you going to be my doctor? And we're 'dopting a little boy from China, so Tam said we have to give you some papers too."

It took Tam a moment to realize Angela had just called her Tam and not Auntie Tam. Maybe Angela was finally starting to feel comfortable with her.

"That's wonderful! Tam's not your mommy?"

Angela shook her head. "My mama died and left me all alone, and Uncle Tony died and left Tam all alone, so now we live together," Angela said.

Adam sat down next to Angela. "I'm sorry your mama died." He turned to Tam. "And was Tony your . . ." He trailed off with a questioning look on his face.

"Tony was my husband. He and his cousin, who was Angela's mama, were killed in an accident recently."

Angela piped up, "They got hit by a drink truck and died instantly." Tam and Jenny had been careful to keep the details of the accident from Angela, only telling her that Tony and Mia had died instantly and didn't feel a thing.

"A drink truck?" Adam asked, one eyebrow rising in question.

Tam stared at it in fascination. How did he do that? Adam quirked his eyebrow again and Tam shook her head. "Um, she means a beverage-distribution truck. It ran a red light and hit them."

"I remember seeing something like that in the news. Wasn't there some confusion as to who was driving?" he asked.

Tam looked down but didn't answer. She'd forgotten how much the news had made of the accident at the time, and that she'd been on the phone with Tony when he was hit.

"I'm so sorry about your husband and his cousin," Adam said.

"Thank you."

Adam gave her a look oozing with so much compassion that she wanted to drown herself in it. "When do you go get your little boy?"

"Probably in late March," Tam said. "I had to redo my home study and refile the I-800A form now that I'm adopting him as a single woman. Because of the change in status of my household—'cause it's just me now . . ." Tam trailed off and could feel her face burning at the mention of being a single woman. Why was she babbling about I-800A forms? She was acting like a silly schoolgirl with a crush on the teacher.

"Yeah, and also 'cause she has me now," Angela chimed in.

"Congratulations. That must be very exciting for both of you," Adam said. Angela beamed at him. Tam, meanwhile, was finding it hard to breathe. Since college, she tended to gravitate toward slim, neat, and compact Asian men who had very little body hair. And while Adam didn't look like a hairy beast, she could see chest hair peeking out of his collar, and he was more muscular and broader than Tony. She wondered what it would be like to run a hand under his shirt and over his muscular chest and hard abs . . . *Gah!*

She brought both hands to her flaming cheeks. Seriously, what was wrong with her? Why was this *married* man having this effect on her? Marcus had been calling and they'd made a date for the day before Thanksgiving. She'd imagined what it would be like to kiss Marcus, but at least he was single. Adam was a married man!

"Tam, why is your face so red? Are you sick?" Angela studied her with worry.

"Uh . . ." Great, now she sounded like Beavis and Butt-Head. She couldn't put together a coherent sentence to save her life. She handed Charlie's file to Adam instead. He studied it, giving her time to compose herself, and then he confirmed what the international adoption doctor had said.

"It looks like Charlie has severe failure to thrive, but otherwise, he seems healthy despite his diagnosis of cerebral dysplasia."

Tam finally found her voice, glad to drag her mind out of the gutter. "Our adoption agency told us they think Charlie was born prematurely. It seems a lot of preemies are labeled with cerebral dysplasia for some reason. Maybe a mix-up in translation."

"That would make sense." Adam nodded slowly, flipping through the paperwork. "When you have your travel date, make an appointment to bring him in when you return to New York. I'd like to see him in the first few days home. And you'll have to bring this pretty young lady in for some shots before you go to China." He winked at Angela.

When they were getting ready to leave, Adam said, "See you in yoga class?"

She nodded, rendered speechless again.

"Bye, Dr. Adam! I can't wait to see you again, even though I have to get shots." Angela made a face and Adam laughed.

He walked them out to the waiting room, and, conscious of him watching them, Tam tripped over her own feet. Throwing out her arms, she caught herself and kept walking, crossing one foot in front of the other, trying to be smooth and not act like a klutz. Angela asked in a loud voice, "Do you have to pee, Tam? Why are you crossing your legs like that?" Sneaking a peek over her shoulder, Tam saw by the way Adam was chuckling that he'd heard. He gave her a wave, and she turned around, her face burning. She grabbed Angela's hand and practically ran for the car, drowning in her embarrassment.

20

"SO, ABBY WAS right. The beverage company is offering you a settlement," Zhong-Ying said with a satisfied air. It was the day before Thanksgiving and her mother had called for an update.

"Yes. And it's a lot of money." Tam looked at Angela, who had latched herself to Tam's arm. "The school's also giving me maternity leave for a few months after I bring Charlie home."

Her mom's next words were lost when Angela tugged so hard the phone fell out of Tam's hand. "Angela, stop pulling on me." Tam picked up the phone and could hear her mom's voice squawking. "Sorry, Mom. What were you saying?"

"Why don't you move back here? We can help and you can finally join the business."

"You know I'm not interested in computers and software."

"*Aiya*, why do you always say that? It's our family business." Her mother sniffed. "Your ah-gong made sure all us kids, even the girls, had the best education. Unlike most men of his generation, he thought women were equal to men. That's why he was so mad when I . . ."

Tam cut her off. "I know he was a good man, blah, blah, blah."

"What is this blah, blah, blah?" Her mom's voice rose. "So disrespectful. So rude."

"Sorry." Tam rolled her eyes.

"You'd have free babysitting anytime. Even though you are an ungrateful daughter."

Before Tam could answer, Angela pulled on Tam's arm again. "Why do you have to go out with Marcus tonight?" Angela whined.

"Mom, I have to go." Tam hung up to her mom's exaggerated sigh.

"I don't like Marcus." Angela stamped her foot for emphasis. "Stay home with me." She was cranky because Bee had told her someone wanted to adopt Stella.

"I thought you love going to Bee's."

Angela flung herself on the couch and kicked it with her feet. "She's giving Stella away!"

Tam was glad Angela was finally letting down her guard. Too bad it was in the form of a temper tantrum. "Please don't yell or kick. Bee fosters them until they find their forever home."

Angela's legs stilled and tears leaked out of her eyes. "But I love Stella."

Tam sat on the couch next to her. "Maybe it's not a good idea for you to work with the dogs if you're getting so attached."

"I'm not. Just to Stella. I was okay when the two puppies left for their forever homes." Her eyes pleaded with Tam, making her feel like the ogre in the princess story they had read.

The doorbell rang and Angela sprang off the couch toward the front door. Tam followed and passed Angela to open the door to Marcus.

"Wow, thanks." Tam took the bouquet of flowers Marcus was proffering. "They're beautiful." She could literally feel Angela bristling with indignation when Marcus leaned down to kiss Tam's cheek. He smelled good, but so unlike Tony that a tinge of unease went through her. Was she really ready to be dating another man?

Angela glared at Marcus. "I thought you said this wasn't a date."

"It's not. We're just friends." Tam turned away to put the flowers in water.

"That's not what my mama said. She said a gentleman always brings flowers on a first date. That's how you know if he's interested."

Marcus blushed. "We should go. I made reservations at Red Hat," he said, making Tam's pulse jump. She and Tony had gone to Red Hat for special occasions only.

As Tam struggled to get over her discomfort at going with someone else to her and Tony's special place, Angela ran out the front door. "Stop right there," Tam shouted. Angela froze and Tam quickly gathered her coat and purse. "Okay, let's get you to Bee's."

Bee opened her door in a multicolored Hawaiian shirt, and Angela rushed in without saying good-bye. Bee lifted her eyebrows and Tam said, "She's really upset about Stella."

"Are you sure you can't adopt Stella?" Bee asked. "Angela's so attached." At the look of dismay on Tam's face, Bee held up a hand. "I'm sorry. I know you've got a lot on your plate."

"Thanks for watching her." Tam gave a small smile. "We won't be home late."

Tam couldn't shake the feeling that the whole evening was a

mistake. She sat awkwardly across the table from Marcus as he told her about his job as an event promoter. Tam tried hard to contribute to the conversation, but making small talk had always had as much appeal to her as driving nails into her forehead. She gulped at her wine, drinking as if she was dying of thirst, and Marcus gave her a strange look. Great. Now he probably thought she had a drinking problem.

By the time their main courses arrived, Marcus had run out of words, and they ate their meal in silence. Tam shoved grilled salmon into her mouth because she had nothing to say. Why couldn't she behave like a normal human being? Why was she so shy that it made a night out so awkward? Desperate, she cast about in her mind, and what came out was, "I like your pants."

I like your pants? WTF? Where had that come from? Granted, he was wearing nice khakis, but who says that? She blushed when he said with a hint of laughter, "Um, thanks?"

She squeezed her eyes shut. He must think she was such a moron.

"Are you okay?" She opened her eyes to find Marcus staring at her in concern.

"Um . . ." She blotted her mouth with a napkin. "I'm just . . . I'm not ready for this."

"What? Eating dinner?" Marcus joked, but Tam only stared. "I'm sorry." He pushed his plate away. "This was too much for our first date. I should have taken you for beer and pizza."

"It's not that." Tam paused and decided to be truthful. "It's not that I don't appreciate it . . . I just . . ." She shrugged. "I don't think I'm ready. It's too soon. I'm sorry."

"It's okay." Marcus held up a hand. "You don't have to explain. Do you want to go?"

Tam nodded, and Marcus hailed the waiter. As they drove back to the complex, Marcus said, "I'll wait while you get Angela and I'll drive you both down."

"You don't have to do that. We can walk. It's not far."

Marcus pulled up in front of Bee's house. "Please. I know this didn't go well, but the least I can do is see you home safely. And maybe we can try this again later on, when you're ready?"

Tam smiled at him. "Okay."

She had just opened the car door when Bee's front door banged open and Angela ran out in tears. She threw herself at Tam. "Bee's giving Stella away this week!"

Bee rushed out behind her. "Angela, I'm not giving her away." She clasped her hands together and gave Tam a worried look.

Tam sighed. "Angela, we talked about this. Let's go home and I'll read you a story."

Angela shook her head, her face flushed with anger. "No, I'm not leaving Stella."

"You can't stay at Bee's all night." *I'm sorry*, Tam mouthed at Bee.

"NO!" Angela shouted. "You're mean! I told you I didn't want you to go out with Marcus and you still left." She clenched her hands into tight fists at her sides. "If I leave Stella, Bee's going to give her away. I already lost my mama. I can't lose Stella too!" Her words ended in a wail and she turned and ran back into Bee's house.

Tam's heart ached. Angela had had fewer nightmares lately, and Tam sometimes forgot she had lost her mother only three months before. Her own grief for Tony seemed to have abated somewhat—it was still there but was no longer as raw as it had been those first few weeks.

Tam stood on the sidewalk between Marcus's car and Bee and knew what she had to do. She turned to Bee. "Do you mind if I come in and try to talk to her?"

"Of course not. I'll be inside," Bee said, leaving Tam to face Marcus alone.

She slid into the car and stared out the windshield. Marcus gave her a sad smile. "She didn't want you to go out with me, huh?"

"No." Tam finally dared to turn and look at Marcus. "I'm sorry. I need to focus on her right now."

He took his glasses off and rubbed his nose where they left a mark. "It's okay. I get it."

"Thanks, Marcus," Tam said, torn. Under other circumstances, she thought she would have liked to get to know him better. "I am sorry."

Marcus raised both arms in defeat. "Stop apologizing." He put his glasses back on. "You'll be okay getting home?"

She nodded and got out of the car and stood there in the night watching him drive down to the complex. She looked up at the stars and a wave of loneliness hit her. She wished Tony were here so they could figure out how to help Angela and mend her broken heart. But if Tony were here, then Angela wouldn't be living with her, since Mia would be alive too.

Tam brought her hands up to her face. What should she do? She didn't think she could handle one more responsibility, but at the same time, she knew she couldn't break the little girl's heart more by taking away the dog she was so attached to.

Dropping her arms, she turned to go comfort the little girl.

TAM LET ANGELA sleep in her bed after she finally calmed her down at Bee's house and coaxed her to come home.

"I love you. Sweet dreams." Tam slipped under the covers.

Angela sat up next to her. "You love me?"

"Yes, of course." Tam turned to look at her. "You didn't know?"

Angela shook her head. "You've never said," she whispered.

"Oh, Angela." Tam drew her close and kissed the top of her head. "I should have told you sooner. I love you. I've loved you from the moment you were born. Did you know I was there in the delivery room with your mama?"

Angela shook her head and snuggled next to Tam, her bright eyes fixed on Tam's face. "You were? You saw me borned?"

Tam smiled. "Yes. I was actually the first one to welcome you into the world. And I loved you from that first moment, when you were screaming your lungs out."

Angela smiled and Tam thought, *And I loved you even when I did the unthinkable to you.* She pushed down the thought and focused on Angela. "You're my family now."

Angela wanted to hear all about her life when she was a baby and had lived with Tam and Tony. They talked until Angela's eyes got heavy and she fell asleep.

The next morning, Tam woke before Angela and stared down at the little girl, thinking how peaceful Angela's face was in sleep. *May you always be this innocent and at peace. May your feelings for me not change when you find out the truth.*

Angela stirred and Tam leaned over to wake her. "Time to get up. We're going to Lily and Jenny's place for Thanksgiving, remember?"

Angela's eyes popped open and she was immediately awake. Oh, to be young again and able to wake instantly and so enthusiastically. Sometimes Tam felt like an eighty-year-old compared to Angela.

"Yay! I can't wait." Angela jumped out of bed and headed to her room to change. She stopped at the door and turned around. "And we're going to talk about maybe 'dopting Stella?"

"Yes. We'll talk. But I'm not making any promises. I'll call Bee and tell her to put off the prospective adopters until after Thanksgiving."

Tam and Angela took the train and then the subway to Jenny's apartment. It was a long trip, and Tam thought maybe she should get over her fear of city traffic and try driving in next time. But then she shuddered. She didn't think she'd ever get over her dislike of driving into the city. She'd rather take the train, even though it took so much longer.

Jenny and Neil's apartment was noisy and filled with the mouthwatering aroma of a Thanksgiving feast. Besides the traditional turkey and stuffing, they had prepared many Chinese dishes. There were homemade dumplings, plates of noodles stir-fried with thinly sliced beef and scallions, rice noodles with tofu and vegetables, and Angela's favorite, scallion pancakes. Tam listened to Angela speaking in Mandarin and English with Lily and her ten-year-old sister, Merry, and Lily's brother, Jeremy, aged seven. Jenny's family spoke Cantonese too, but Tam knew Mia had wanted Angela to learn Mandarin only. Tam realized she should probably put Angela in Chinese school so she wouldn't lose her first language.

Tam ate so much she was tempted to unbutton her pants when she sat on the couch with Jenny and baby Evan after the big meal. The kids were running around the apartment playing their own version of hide-and-seek. When Tam had first come here that awful day after the accident, she had hated the building. But Jenny kept her apartment neat and clean. It was small and run-down, and the neon signs on the outsides of the buildings cast an eerie glow inside, even with the curtains drawn. Jenny had made it a home, with photos of the kids all over, bright rugs on the floor, and colorful curtains on the windows.

Jenny handed Tam a folder. "I looked through the box I packed from Mia's apartment, and here's all the paperwork. Angela's doctor records, a copy of the will, the lease for her apartment, and bank statements, but no birth certificate."

Tam fanned through the paperwork. "Darn."

"You can look in the box if you want. There's a lot of other stuff that I didn't know if Angela wants. You probably won't be able to take it home on the train, but I can keep it until next time Abby drives you here." Jenny spoke in Mandarin.

"Thank you." Tam smiled at the other woman. It was nice to have someone on her side. She followed Jenny to where she had stashed the box in a corner of their bedroom and rifled through it. But Jenny was right; it looked like there were just some books, notebooks, and knickknacks in the box. Nothing that looked like a birth certificate.

"I'll go through this box closely when I have more time." Jenny sighed. "But I never seem to have time. Between the nail salon and my kids . . ." She shrugged, and Tam's heart went out to her. Jenny worked so hard to provide for her family.

Angela fell asleep on the train ride home. It was so rare to have a quiet moment these days, and Tam realized she was feeling optimistic. As she brushed Angela's hair off her face, her heart softened and she felt that familiar tug of longing she'd felt when Angela was first born. How she'd loved her then. She'd thought she would always be a part of Angela's life, never knowing that the storm that would blow through their lives and separate them was only a few months away.

But now she and Angela had created a little family of their own in just three months. Angela was hers now, and she no longer doubted her ability to love her. Fueled by that thought and the feeling of contentment this brought her, Tam made a decision and knew Angela would be overjoyed.

"Do you mean it?" Angela's eyes were wide when Tam told her the next day. "Really? I get to keep Stella?"

"What the heck. We're adopting both Charlie and Stella." Angela jumped off the couch and threw her arms around Tam's middle. "But you have to promise to help take care of her. Once Charlie gets here, I'm going to have my hands full."

Angela nodded against Tam's stomach. "Yes! I promise. And I'll help take care of Charlie too. Jenny Ayi sometimes let me feed and hold baby Evan. And I even helped her change a diaper once. Not the poopy one though." Angela let go and made a face.

Tam laughed. "Charlie is over three and they told me he's toilet trained. There shouldn't be any poopy diapers."

"Can Stella sleep in my bed?"

"Why not?" Tam threw up her hands. "Do you want to call Bee and tell her the news?"

Angela raced for the phone and let out a yell of such pure joy that Tam was glad she'd agreed. The weekend passed in a blur of excitement. Normally, they were supposed to go through an application process and phone interview with the dog's foster parents, as well as a home visit set up by the dachshund rescue. But since Bee already knew Angela and Tam, there was no need for all that. Once Tam submitted the application and paid the adoption fee, Stella was declared theirs and Angela was able to bring her home that Saturday.

Tam couldn't believe the change in Angela as soon as Stella came home. She acted more like a little girl than a small adult with the weight of the world on her shoulders. She started sleeping through the night with Stella curled up next to her and no longer woke Tam with nightmares and tears. Because she got to sleep through the night now that Angela was, Tam finally caught up on sleep. She was able to think clearly for the first time since Tony died.

With the extra steps Tam had to take care of before she could get her travel approval and make her travel plans, her caseworker, Sandra, estimated that she'd probably be getting Charlie in February or March. In spite of all her doubts and fears, Tam felt like she was doing the right thing. Charlie belonged with her as much as Angela and Stella.

21

*Two Months
before the Accident*

MIA AND TONY stood at the door of her apartment waiting for Angela to come out of the bathroom. Tony was taking Angela to the Queens Zoo, just the two of them. Mia had a date with Chris, but now she wished she was going with Tony and Angela instead. She hated the way Tony was watching her, as if she were a wild animal that he had to be wary of. She wanted the chance to show him she'd changed and that he could trust her again.

"What's Tam doing today?" Mia finally asked, unable to take the uncomfortable silence.

Tony looked at her, and at first she thought he wasn't going to answer. But then he sighed and said, "She's at a barbecue with Abby."

"Oh." Mia remembered Abby. She'd met her once, Abby of the wild blond hair and bold manners, so unlike Tam. Mia felt a frisson of jealousy. Had Abby replaced Mia in Tam's life?

"Does she know you're here?"

Tony sighed again, a long-suffering sound that made Mia want to strike him. "No, Mia."

"Why are you keeping this from her?"

He stared at her as the toilet flushed in the bathroom. "Because things are finally going well with Tam. I don't want anything to spoil it. I will tell her, soon." He took her by the arm as the bathroom door opened. "She needs time, Mia. Let me deal with it, okay?"

She nodded as Angela ran up to them.

"I'm ready, Uncle Tony! Let's go." Angela took Tony's hand and dragged him toward the front door, unaware of the tension between the adults.

Tony laughed, and his whole demeanor changed. He focused on Angela, his eyes lighting up when just seconds before they'd stared at Mia as if he wanted to bore a hole through her. She was so glad Angela was bonding with Tony.

After they left, she went to the statue of Guan Yin and the incense sticks she had stuck in a small cup filled with rice. They had burned down almost to the bottom, and Mia brought her hands together and bowed. She stood still, her hands in prayer touching her bowed forehead, and closed her eyes. She should get ready since Chris would be here soon, but she remained still, thinking of Tam.

Mia had first learned of Tam's existence the December Mia was seventeen. Tony had gone to New York for university and stayed on after graduating, eventually becoming an associate professor. But he always came home to China for a month during his winter break. When he came home that year, Mia had been happy to see him as always, but he was distracted and barely paid her any attention. He had a secret smile on his lips, and when she asked him what was so funny, he only smiled more and tweaked her nose.

That night, after they ate the dinner Mia had prepared, he sat back in his chair. "Ma. Baba. I have something to tell you."

They both leaned forward in anticipation, but Mia watched him with trepidation. She didn't like the sound of this.

"I've met a beautiful, wonderful girl, and I'm going to ask her to marry me."

His parents were happy for him, but Mia sat in stunned silence. Did this mean Tony was never coming back to China? Was he staying in New York with this American girl?

She barely listened as his parents asked him questions. Was she Chinese? Was she born in America? How did they meet? Had he met her parents?

"Yes, she's Chinese. Her parents are from Taiwan, but she was born in America. Her name is Tamlei Lin. We met at a Columbia University function, at a lecture I gave. And, yes, I met her parents when they came to visit her in New York."

"*Ayo!*" Tony's father said. "Her family is from Taiwan?" Mia took a small bit of pleasure in seeing the frown on his face. Like most of the people around Guangdong, they didn't think much of the Taiwanese, some even going as far as to hate them. "Does her family want independence from China? I don't understand thinking like that. Taiwan is part of China. Why do they want to be free from us? Bah."

"Hush," Tony's mom said and waved a hand at her husband. She was more tolerant than him, and Mia could see she didn't want Tony to get upset that his father didn't approve of the girl he wanted to marry. They all started talking at once: Tony, as he tried to defend the Taiwanese by saying that the Taiwanese and Chinese of his age had more common ground than people in his father's generation; his mom, as she tried to tell her husband it didn't matter Tam was from

Taiwan if she came from a good family; and his father, who muttered under his breath about the Taiwanese but knew better than to
voice his complaints out loud in front of his wife.

Mia hadn't said a word. She'd sat and listened as Tony said Tam
was a schoolteacher, and so good with little kids. He thought she
was beautiful, even though she didn't paint herself up and dress in
sexy clothing like the American women. She was shy, but once you
got to know her, you could see how smart and funny she was. He
couldn't wait to bring Tam to China to meet them.

"Aren't you moving back to China?" Mia asked Tony once his
parents had gone to bed in the tiny bedroom. Tony slept in the alcove of the main room, which had become Mia's area when he went
away but which she now gladly gave up to have Tony home. She slept
on the couch for the month he was home.

"No, Mei," he said. "I love New York. It's my home now. I'll always come back every year to see you all, but I'm staying in New
York." He paused and looked off into space, and Mia could tell he
was no longer there in their humble living room in China. "America
is so full of possibilities, not like here," he said. "Anyone can do
anything. The government doesn't restrict your thoughts and control
what information you get, how many kids you can have. You can
learn so much on the Internet." He turned and finally seemed to see
her. "You'd love it there, Mei."

"I'd love to see it." And in that moment, Mia knew she wanted
to go to America.

"Maybe one day." He reached out to ruffle Mia's hair. She really
hated it when he did that. She'd brushed her hair carefully that
morning and tried to tame the flyaway strands that stood up around
her face, and he was messing it up with his misguided gestures of
affection.

"Did you get an American name?" Mia was curious about his life in New York.

"My American name is Tony," he said. "When I become a citizen after I marry Tam, I'm going to legally change my name."

"You want to become a US citizen?" Mia was amazed. She could understand that he loved America and wanted to stay there, but to become a citizen when he was a Chinese first and foremost?

"Yes," he replied. "If I'm going to live there, I'd like to become a citizen." He turned to her. "You should have an American name too."

"I don't know any."

"Hmm . . . I think you look like a Mia. And it's close to your Chinese name."

"I love it." She was breathless. "Sounds so much more grown-up than Mei."

"Don't be in a hurry to grow up, Mia. Enjoy being a kid while you can." He ruffled her hair again and then got up to get into his bed, leaving her fuming in frustration.

She'd hated Tam at first for taking Tony away from her. But as she got to know her, Mia had come to care for her. Of the two of them, Tam was the good one. She hadn't deserved all those miscarriages. The irony wasn't lost on Mia. Tam should have had her babies with Tony, yet it was Mia, the one who didn't deserve it, who'd carried a baby to term. And because of what Mia had done, she'd lost Tam and Tony. Mia had tried to tell Tam the truth on that last day when everything erupted, but Tam wouldn't listen. She wouldn't even look at Mia. She'd told Mia she never wanted to speak to her again.

The doorbell rang, startling Mia. She smoothed a hand down her skintight black dress, which clung to every curve and showed off her cleavage to its best advantage. Tam would have said she was dressed like a ho. Mia stifled a sob. She wished so much that Tam was actually standing here, teasing her and telling her to put more clothes on.

Even after all these years, the shame of what she'd done to Tam and Tony washed over her again and struck her heart like someone had taken a hatchet and was carving it out, piece by piece. At the time, she'd been driven by her desires, what she wanted, and hadn't thought about anyone else. Now she was so sorry she'd acted like a selfish bitch. She vowed again that she'd make it right by them if it was the last thing she ever did.

22

"YOU COMING TO the New Year's Eve party with me?" Abby was facedown on her yoga mat, sinking her hips back into child's pose. "There's a guy I want to introduce you to."

"My parents and my brother and his family are flying in next week for Christmas and staying until the New Year." Tam glanced at the door to the studio.

"Perfect. Then Angela can stay with them and you can come to the party with me." Abby's voice was muffled.

"I promised Angela we'd spend it together. She's excited about staying up until midnight." Tam's pulse quickened when she saw Adam walk into the studio by himself. They'd seen each other every Friday at yoga class for the past month and had struck up a casual friendship.

"You'd rather stay home with a five-year-old than come to a party with me and possibly hook up with a nice guy?" Abby asked, flipping over to stare at Tam.

Adam set his mat down next to Tam and she gave him a shy smile, ducking her head so Abby couldn't see. Abby hadn't been to yoga lately, so she didn't know about Adam.

"Hi, Tam." He gave her a big smile.

Not wanting Abby to know about her new friendship, Tam did her best to appear normal. "Hey," she croaked, causing Abby to sit up and look at her. Tam cleared her throat and asked nonchalantly, because she was dying to know, "Your wife's not joining you today?"

He looked taken aback for a moment before his face cleared. "Oh, you mean Jessie? She's my girlfriend, not my wife. No, she's not coming. She's the one who dragged me to yoga, and then she stopped coming, saying she was too busy with work."

Before Tam could respond, Abby leaned over. "Hi, I'm Abby, Tam's friend."

"Nice to meet a friend of Tam's. I'm Adam Morgan." He turned to Tam and handed her a book. "Here's the book I told you about. I saw it in the bookstore and got it for you."

Tam ran a finger down the cover of the book by a child psychologist on how to understand and help traumatized children. She'd told him about her fear that she wouldn't know how to help Charlie once he came home, and he'd suggested this book.

"Thank you." She looked up and gave him a smile filled with gratitude.

"That's so nice of you," Abby said, shooting Tam looks that she ignored.

"I think it will help you prepare for Charlie's arrival." Adam looked up as the teacher entered the room and asked everyone to sit at the front of their mat. "We can talk more about it, maybe over coffee after class one day."

Tam gave a quick nod, then turned her attention to the yoga

teacher. She sat on her mat between Adam and Abby and closed her eyes. Her heart was elated. He wasn't married! He got her a present! Not that it meant anything. He was still taken and she'd never encroach on another woman's boyfriend. But she liked him, was starting to think of him as a friend, even if he made her pulse race every time she saw him.

Abby poked her and Tam opened her eyes. Abby mouthed, *He's hot.*

Tam swatted Abby's hand away. She didn't need a reminder that Adam was hot. She would not think of him that way. Tony hadn't been gone that long. There were still times when she'd wake in the middle of the night expecting to feel Tony next to her. Then her mind would remember and she'd lie there, sadness weighing down on her chest. In the daytime, she could almost get through the days now without that crushing grief hitting her at the most unexpected times, taking her breath away and making her wonder how she would survive it. But at night, nothing could stop the loneliness that pressed down on her like a heavy blanket.

"You going to ask him out?" Abby leaned over and whispered in Tam's ear.

"No! He's got a girlfriend. I saw her once and she's beautiful," Tam hissed back at Abby, causing the woman in front of her to turn and give her a gentle rebuke.

"We'll talk more after class," Abby whispered and focused back on the teacher.

Tam pursed her lips. She did not want to discuss Adam with Abby.

"SO, TELL ME everything!" Abby plopped onto her seat with her latte at the coffee shop next to the yoga studio after class.

"There's nothing to tell. He's going to be Angela's and Charlie's pediatrician." Tam squirmed on her seat, not comfortable with the topic of their conversation.

"He's so hot. You should sleep with him."

"Abby!" Tam's face flamed. That was one thing Abby had in common with Mia. They both talked openly about sex, making Tam fidget because . . . ugh. She didn't think sex should be discussed like that. It was something sacred to be cherished and thought about in the privacy of one's own mind. "We're just friends. I'm not ready to date. Look what happened with Marcus." It had been so awkward when she'd run into Marcus the other day.

"What? Tony's been gone for over three months now. You haven't had sex in all that time. It's a natural, healthy thing." Abby took a sip of her latte and settled back in her chair.

Tam shook her head, refusing to engage if Abby persisted on this line of talk. She changed the subject. "Anyways, he has a gorgeous girlfriend. He wouldn't want frumpy old me."

"Don't sell yourself short. You, my friend, have your own beauty, and it's not just on the outside. It comes from the inside and from here." Abby thumped a hand over her heart.

Tam suddenly remembered something. "By the way, have you been seeing someone? You mentioned you had a date before Thanksgiving, but you never told me with who." Tam had forgotten about Abby's offhand comment from a few weeks ago.

Abby gave her an enigmatic smile but didn't answer.

"Come on, tell me. Is it someone I know?"

"Yes." Abby gave her a coy look. "Jeff."

"Jeff who?" Tam wrinkled her forehead, running through all the Jeffs she knew in her mind. "Wait, Jeff Abrams? Steven's father?"

At Abby's nod, Tam said, "No wonder you keep offering to pick Angela up from their house. What's going on? How'd this happen?"

"The first time I picked up Angela, we started talking. I like him." Abby gave a casual shrug. "But you know what people say about him."

"I don't think he's really a player. He's gotten a bad rep. He's a nice guy." Tam sipped her chai latte. "And since when have you cared what other people think?"

"I don't usually."

Tam shook her head. "I've never been good at that. Even with Tony. That was part of our problem. I always did what he wanted." *Except for one thing.*

"Why, Tam?"

Tam shrugged. "It was just easier. I don't know." She'd always had a problem talking about her feelings. That's why she didn't make friends easily. Acquaintances yes, but close friends who shared secrets and talked about everything? No.

Abby waited for Tam to say more, but Tam didn't know what else to say. It wasn't that she didn't trust Abby. She did. She just hated putting her feelings on display. They were her private thoughts, not something to be aired out like laundry flapping in the breeze.

"Tell me more about Jeff."

"I was married before," Abby said.

"I know that." Tam gave her a look. What did that have to do with Jeff Abrams?

"I mean before. I was married when I was eighteen, to my high school boyfriend."

Tam looked at Abby in surprise. In all the years she'd known her, she'd never mentioned being married twice. "What happened?"

Abby looked away. "He died—in a car accident. It was sudden and horrible, like it was with Tony. We'd only been married for six months and had our whole life planned, and then just like that, a car ran a stop sign and he was gone."

"I'm so sorry."

Abby took a breath. "He was the love of my life. It's still hard to talk about even after all these years. When I got that call about Tony, it was like hearing about Ben dying all over again."

Tam reached out and touched Abby on the arm. "I never knew. You've always said you didn't believe in marriage."

"I did believe in marriage, and I tried to find that again, but my second husband turned out to be such a loser. I chose to ignore that Randy was just a sweet-talking asshole who was too lazy to lift a finger and treated me more like a servant than a wife. I should never have married him." Abby paused and sighed. "Anyways, that's why I felt so bad for you. I know what it's like to lose the love of your life."

Tam dropped her hand into her lap. Before she could stop herself, she blurted out, "I thought Tony was the love of my life, but then he—" She stopped herself and looked up into Abby's eyes.

"He what?"

Tam waved a hand. "He did something . . ."

Abby waited, but when Tam didn't continue, she said, "I would never say anything against Tony, especially now that he's gone, but I've always gotten the feeling there was something wrong in your marriage."

"You have no idea." Tam gave a short laugh.

Abby tilted her head. "You know you can tell me anything. I won't judge, Tam."

"I know." Tam looked down. "It's just hard for me to talk about."

"Yeah, I know. It hasn't been easy being your friend all these years." Abby nudged Tam's hand with her cup and laughed. "But it's okay. I'm here if you ever want to talk."

"Thanks. What about Jeff?"

Abby shrugged. "It's early days yet. I like him and he likes me. That's good for now." She suddenly slapped a hand on the table, startling Tam. "You know what you need?"

"What?"

"You need to get laid. I'm not talking about a relationship; I mean a one-night stand. If this doctor already has a girlfriend, then I'll find someone for you."

"You think sex will fix my problems?"

"No, but it'll make you feel better." Abby grinned.

And Tam grinned back, wondering if Abby was right. Sex wouldn't solve all her problems, but maybe it would stop her from fantasizing about naked male bodies.

23

TWO DAYS BEFORE Christmas, Tam got the I-800 approval letter from United States Citizenship and Immigration Services. She had refiled the I-800A after she got her amended home study. She'd pored over the form with the one Tony had filled out as her guide. Seeing Tony's neat handwriting in front of her reduced her to tears. How could his handwriting still be here on earth, when his body wasn't? Tony had taken care of the paperwork and now she realized how tedious it was. She was ready to tear her hair out as she plodded through one form after another.

Her parents and brother and his family arrived that afternoon, and they went out to dinner at the Chinese restaurant in town to celebrate.

"So now what, Tam?" Wei asked. "What's the next step?"

"I have to wait for an email from the National Visa Center, which I'll use to file for Charlie's immigrant visa." Tam played with her chopsticks, watching Angela laughing with Wei's kids. "Once I do that, I have to wait for the Article 5 letter to be issued."

"What that?" Zhong-Ying scrunched her nose up at the chicken in garlic sauce Tam had ordered. She claimed it wasn't "real" Chinese food.

"Basically it says I'm approved as a suitable adoptive parent and that Charlie would be able to enter and reside permanently in the United States. Then a couple of weeks after that, I should get my travel approval, and then I'll be able to book my plane tickets." Tam removed the offending dish from in front of her mother and put a giant portion on her plate, giving her mother a pointed look. Zhong-Ying sniffed and tossed her head.

"Ayi, can I have some?" Wei's daughter asked, and Tam scooped some onto her plate.

"Me too, Tam." Angela held out her plate to be served.

"Angela, you shouldn't call Tam by her first name. Either Ayi or Auntie Tam," Zhong-Ying scolded the little girl.

"But Tam said I could—" Angela started, and Tam jumped in.

"I'm not her ayi, I'm her—" Tam cut herself off. "I told her she could just call me Tam. Kids do that these days." Tam gave Angela a reassuring smile, because she looked upset by Zhong-Ying's scolding.

"So disrespectful." Zhong-Ying shook her head.

"So, wow," Wei said loudly as he speared a shrimp with his chopsticks. "Things are moving along with the adoption."

"Yes." Tam took a gulp of her glass of beer, thankful for Wei's interference. "It's really happening."

"Nervous?" Wei refilled her glass when she set it on the table.

"Yeah. Up 'til now, it's just been a lot of paper chasing. But I'm actually going to meet Charlie soon." She looked around the table at her family and realized she loved being surrounded by them, even with the way she and her mother bickered. Maybe she really should think about moving back to California. But she didn't voice the thought out loud. She didn't want her mother to crow like a rooster. She had vowed to enjoy her family's visit and not antagonize her mother.

"So exciting," Zhong-Ying said. Tam nodded in agreement.

But she was worried. Jenny still hadn't found Angela's birth certificate, so she hadn't been able to apply for a passport. With the arrival of the I-800 approval letter, Tam called Jenny again that night after dinner. Jenny still hadn't looked through the box from Mia's apartment thoroughly, and she promised to do it the next day.

Two days after Christmas, Tam dropped Angela off at Bee's so she could take a yoga class with Adam. It had become their thing, meeting once a week at the studio, sometimes moving their conversation to the coffee shop after class.

"The new foster is from a puppy mill," Bee said when she opened the door. "She's really scared, so I'm glad you're here."

"Stella and I will help her." Angela pushed past Bee and disappeared into the back room with Stella. Wei had taken his family and their parents into the city for the day. Angela had been invited too, but when Bee had told her about the new foster, she had decided to stay.

"Bee, thanks for everything." Tam hesitated, and then, filled with gratitude for all this woman had done for her and Angela, she reached out and hugged Bee. Tam usually hated the American way of kissing and hugging people on greeting. But ever since her talk with Abby, she'd been trying to be more open. And to her surprise, she found it wasn't uncomfortable, especially when Bee squeezed her back.

It had been drizzling all morning, but the drizzle was now turning into a steady rain. Bee looked up at the sky. "I made banana bread. Do you want some before class? You're early today."

Tam's stomach growled. She hadn't eaten much lunch. "That'd be great."

Tam sat at the kitchen table, and while Bee cut slices of the bread, Tam asked, "Why do you live alone? Is it by choice?"

Bee laughed long and hard. "No, not by choice. I was married for many years to a wonderful man named Kevin McKenna. We bought this house together, planned to raise our kids here. But we never had any, so I turned my attention to our dachshunds at the time. That's how I got involved with the rescue groups."

"What happened to Kevin?"

"He had a heart attack ten years ago. He was so young—only fifty-two. We were high school sweethearts." Bee sniffed as she placed a plate in front of Tam. "He loved me with all his heart. He didn't care that we couldn't have children. He said it wasn't meant to be and we had each other and our dogs and it was enough. And it was, until he was gone suddenly one day." Bee chuckled softly. "That man loved his steak. He was a true Irishman—loved his meat and potatoes and beer. And he hated to exercise. I guess it caught up with him."

"I'm sorry, Bee. I didn't mean to pry." But she was glad she'd asked. How had she not known that both Abby and Bee had lost their husbands? Maybe that's why they'd been so willing to help her.

"You're not prying. I would have told you before, but I didn't think you'd be interested in an old woman's stories."

Tam's face burned with shame. Was she really that self-absorbed? "I'm always interested in your stories. I'm sorry I've been so distracted."

"You've had good reason." Bee waved a hand at Tam.

"And you're not old. You're only in your early sixties, right?"

"Yes. Kevin and I were the same age." They sat in companionable silence eating their bread and listening to the rain patter on the sunroof.

"I should go." Tam was about to stand up and put her plate in the sink when her cell phone rang. She picked it up.

"Hi, Jenny," Tam said. "Did you find—"

Before she could finish her sentence, Jenny burst out, "Tam. I so sorry!" Then she babbled in Cantonese, none of which Tam understood.

"What's the matter? Can you speak in English? Or at least Mandarin? I don't understand anything you're saying."

"Sorry, sorry," Jenny shouted. "I come up and see you now, okay? Neil will run nail salon by himself. I come now." Then she switched back to Cantonese.

"Wait, what? You're coming here from Flushing? Why?" What could be wrong that Jenny was taking off in the middle of the day to come all the way out here to see her? And on a Friday, one of her busiest days?

"I tell you when I get there," Jenny said. "I call to make sure you home. I'm on the 7 subway on way to Grand Central to catch train. You pick me up at train station?" Jenny told her what time the train arrived.

"Um . . ." Could she go to yoga class and make it back in time to pick Jenny up? No. Damn. She had really been looking forward to seeing Adam again. But Jenny sounded frantic. Maybe she should offer to drive to Grand Central to get Jenny? But the thought of driving into midtown Manhattan almost gave her a panic attack. "Okay, I'll pick you up at the Dobbs Ferry train station. But tell me what's wrong right now. You're scaring me."

"Don't worry, no one dead," Jenny said and hung up before Tam could ask more.

Tam was waiting in her car when Jenny emerged from the train station. The minute she opened the car door, Tam asked, "What's wrong? Why are you here?"

Jenny slammed the door. "Let's get to house first. I don't want to say when you driving."

Tam stared at her in frustration, but Jenny was calm now, not frantic like she was on the phone. They drove home in silence. Tam couldn't fathom what could have made the woman come all the way up here. Then her heart skipped a beat. The last time Jenny insisted she had to see her in person, she ended up getting custody of a child.

As they pulled up to her town house, she saw Abby standing on her front stoop with a bottle of wine in hand. Tam suddenly remembered she had invited her over for dinner and Abby said she would come after yoga class to help. Tam's family wouldn't be back until after dinner, and Abby wanted to say hello to them.

Abby walked up to her. "I was starting to think I got the date wrong. I actually went to yoga and you didn't show up. Adam asked about you." Catching sight of Jenny, Abby leaned over and whispered, "What's Jenny doing here?"

Tam shrugged. As soon as they were inside, Jenny headed for the couch and patted the seat next to her. "Tam, sit. I glad you here, Abby. She going to need friend."

Abby frowned and looked at Tam.

Giving Abby another shrug, Tam sat down and Jenny grabbed both of her hands.

"I so sorry to be the one to tell you this. But I had to tell you in person."

"What? What's so important that you had to come all the way

up here?" Tam was annoyed now. "Not that you're not welcome anytime, but you're really stressing me out."

Jenny was quiet for a moment, and then she said, "I found Angela's birth certificate. It was in a photo album of pictures of Angela."

Tam let out a breath, not even realizing she'd been holding it. "But that's great news. Now I can finally get her a passport." She was relieved to hear this. She shifted in her seat, trying to get her hands back from Jenny, eager to get the document so she could start the passport application process. She'd get it expedited, just in case.

"Tam, I saw who listed as her father." Tam went still. She searched Jenny's face, trying to see if she could possibly know. But how could she? There was supposed to be no name listed. She was afraid to look in Abby's direction.

"I so sorry, Tam," Jenny said. "I not going to tell you, but Neil said you had right to know. And I didn't want to say on phone."

Tam grasped on to the first thought that popped into her head. "Neil knows too?"

Jenny nodded. "I told him." She took a deep breath and Tam knew she was about to say out loud the thing she'd been trying to hide from for the last five years. She cast about desperately for a way to distract Jenny, but before her brain could form a coherent thought, Jenny spoke.

"It was Tony. Tony was Angela's father."

24

*One Month
before the Accident*

MIA'S HANDS STILLED on the large envelope mixed in with the junk mail. It was from the Vital Records Office. She tore it open and stared at Angela's amended birth certificate.

Her face burned as she remembered how angry Tony had been when she called him and told him he was Angela's father. In this terrible, hoarse voice he'd said, "I threw my own little girl out of my home? I've missed out on almost five years of her life. How could you do that?"

Mia's heart had been pounding so hard, and tears were streaming down her face as she'd tried to explain to him that she thought she was protecting Angela and Tam. She'd lied to him and told him Angela was Kenny's and then broken up with Kenny because she didn't want him to claim the baby, telling him that she had cheated. She'd lied to everyone, and now this whole mess was her fault. She'd thought it was better that everyone thought Angela was Kenny's. But now that Angela kept asking where her father was, she started to have doubts.

"Why now?" Tony had asked. "Why are you finally telling me now?"

"Because Angela is asking about her father." She hadn't told Tony it was also because that feeling of doom, as if something bad was going to happen to her, was pressing down on her every day. And if something did happen, Angela would be left without any family unless she told Tony the truth.

He'd called her back after a few days, as she'd known he would. Family meant everything to him, and she knew there was no way he'd turn his back on his daughter now that he knew the truth. He wanted to visit her but asked that she not tell Angela he was her father until they'd figured things out. And he'd asked who was listed as Angela's father on her birth certificate.

"No one. I put down 'unknown.'"

Tony had let out a breath; of relief or frustration, Mia couldn't tell. "I want you to get it amended. Hire a lawyer if you need to. I'll pay the expenses. I want my name on her birth certificate."

Mia's heart had risen on hearing that. Maybe things would be okay. Tony was willing to claim Angela as his without asking for a paternity test. And with each visit with Angela, she could see him falling under their daughter's spell. How could anyone not? Angela was the sweetest, most loving little girl in the world. And now Mia held proof in her hand that Angela belonged to Tony and would be taken care of if anything happened to Mia.

If only Tam would forgive her too. Tony wanted to wait until they brought their little boy home before telling Tam that Tony was Angela's father and that he'd arranged to see Angela once a week on

Thursdays. He'd told Tam he was teaching an afternoon class on that day with office hours after, but in reality, he was coming to Flushing to spend time with Angela. Mia thought it was a big mistake for Tony to lie to Tam. If they were really repairing their relationship, how was it good to lie to her? But Tony wouldn't listen to her. He wanted to wait.

Mia took out a photo album of pictures of Angela from when she was a baby up until now and placed the birth certificate in it for safekeeping. She wished they could tell Tam now. She couldn't stop the feeling that time was running out. And besides, Tam already knew Tony was Angela's father.

25

TAM STARED AT Jenny, unable to utter a word. She heard Abby gasp, but she didn't turn to look at her. Jenny started apologizing and babbling in Mandarin. "I'm so sorry, Tam. If I knew, I never would have encouraged you to take Angela. Tony was Mia's cousin. I know only second cousin, but still . . ." She switched back to English. "That's so not . . . nice."

"It's awful. Even if they were distant cousins," Abby said. "Are you sure?"

Jenny nodded and pulled the birth certificate out of her bag and held it out to Tam. Tam didn't take it, knowing that if she moved, she would fall apart. Abby grabbed it from Jenny, and as Abby stared at the document, Jenny went off again on one of her Cantonese rants, speaking so fast that Tam couldn't catch her breath. She felt as if she was drowning under Jenny's words.

"No fucking way." Abby swore under her breath.

Tam sat frozen, struggling to get air into her lungs, her mouth open and a hand on her chest. This couldn't be happening.

"Tam. Tam! Are you okay?" Abby was staring at her in concern.

Tam tried to speak, but the only sound that came out was a tiny gasp of breath. Was it possible to die of shock? Was this what it felt like to die, her heart about to explode as her body was deprived of oxygen?

"Mia was my friend, but I know not how she do this," Jenny said.

Abby swore again. "How could she have done that to you? You told me you were friends with her. And she lived with you!" When Tam still didn't answer, Abby said, "Tam. Breathe. It's okay."

Jenny added, "You must hate her."

Tam shuddered at Jenny's words. She had hated Mia at one point, but Mia was dead. She knew it was irrational, but sometimes she wondered if it was her fault Mia had died. If she'd been nicer to Mia, would she have lived?

Abby lowered her voice and said gently, "What about Angela? Are you going to be able to keep her, knowing that she's your husband's daughter?"

Tam finally snapped out of her stupor. "Yes, of course I want Angela."

"But how you possibly keep her, knowing what you know now?" Jenny wrung her hands in distress, her eyes flashing sympathy at Tam.

Abby spoke softly. "Jenny's right. You're not going to be able to help how you act around her, now that you know the truth. It wouldn't be fair to Angela."

"I wouldn't do that to Angela."

Abby rubbed her back. "It might not be the best situation for you to raise her. Her mother slept with your husband."

"No." Tam scrambled to find any excuse to make that statement not true. "Maybe . . . maybe she didn't sleep with him! Maybe he only donated his sperm because she wanted a baby." She knew she was grasping at straws, and from the look the other two women exchanged, she knew they felt the same way.

"I so sorry, Tam," Jenny said. "I feel very bad. But I take Angela for now. Don't worry. We figure it out."

"No!" Tam raised her voice. "You're not taking Angela." Tam swallowed and her shoulders slumped forward. In a quieter voice, she said, "I knew Tony was Angela's father."

The other two women stared at her, Abby with her mouth open, and Jenny with a look of confusion on her face.

"What?" Jenny asked.

"I knew. It was a few months after Angela was born and they were still living with us. I looked at Angela one day and thought how she looked so much like Tony in his baby pictures. And then I remembered something Mia told me, and I did the math and realized she couldn't possibly be Kenny's like Mia said."

"Well, they're cousins, so isn't it normal that Angela would look like him?" Abby asked.

Tam got off the couch and started pacing. "Yes, but it was more than that. Little things that happened in the past, things that Mia had said, triggered something in my mind. And I put it all together."

"Wow," Abby said. "Did you confront Tony?"

"No. I never said anything to him." Tam sighed and paused to pick up Angela's birth certificate. With a heavy heart, she made herself look at it. She needed to see the proof that it was really true. And there it was, in black and white in front of her.

Father: Tony Li Qiang Kwan

And then she noticed Angela's name was written as Angela Meili Kwan. Tam had registered her at school as Angela Guo. Guo was Mia's last name and the name on all of Angela's records.

Focusing on the names, she said, "I never told him I knew. I told him I wanted Mia to leave, and to take Angela with her. I said either they left or I would." She swallowed and then continued. "And he agreed."

Abby stared at her in shock. "He kicked out his own daughter?"

Tam put the birth certificate down and looked at her hands. She could have kept this next part to herself, but she was tired of feeling guilty. She wanted, needed, to get it off her chest.

"No. He didn't know Angela was his daughter. I confronted Mia after I suspected it and she admitted the baby was Tony's. But she convinced him Angela was Kenny's baby."

"He had no idea he was kicking his own daughter out of his house?" The disbelief was apparent on Abby's face.

Tam hung her head. "No. And I didn't tell him," she whispered. "I just wanted them out of my house. I wanted my husband back. I didn't think about Angela then. I only thought about myself. I felt so betrayed, and in my own home!"

Jenny hadn't said anything through her confession, but now she came to Tam's side. "Mia shouldn't have slept with your husband, but I not believe you let him put out own daughter. Mia was devastated. Said she had argument with Tony. She stayed with me until I found her apartment in same building."

"Yeah, but what was she supposed to do?" Abby defended Tam. "Let her husband's mistress and child stay in her home?"

Tam shivered at Abby's reference to her husband's mistress. "Mia was really upset. She kept saying she was sorry, but all I could see was the two of them together. I couldn't take it anymore and told her I never wanted to see her again."

Neither Jenny nor Abby said anything, so Tam continued. "Tony told me Mia was going to live with us in our spare room, just for a month or two, when she first came here. He said he was going to help her get a visa. Then he told me she couldn't afford to get her own place, so she stayed. And the ironic thing was, when she got pregnant, he wanted her to move out, but I stuck up for her. Me!" Tam jabbed herself in the chest with a finger. "She was my friend. I told her everything and she stood by me through all the miscarriages. I told Tony we couldn't ask her to leave. She needed our help. I had no idea then that she was carrying my husband's baby. I stuck up for her!"

Abby shook her head. "That's awful. I'm so sorry. You never told me about the miscarriages."

Tam hung her head. "I know. It's hard for me to talk about. But Mia was there, in my house, always there when I needed someone. I trusted her and she betrayed me."

"I can't believe he brought his mistress to live in your house," Abby said.

"What he think, she his concubine?" Jenny paced in front of Tam. "This America, not old China. What he thinking?"

Tam covered her ears. "Don't say that! She was his cousin, first or second, but still, his *cousin*—not his mistress or concubine."

"I'm sorry, Tam."

Abby and Jenny continued talking, and Tam dropped her face into her hands, trying to block them out. She couldn't believe this was all coming to light.

Looking back, Tam's intuition had been screaming at her that something wasn't right about Mia's pregnancy. Mia had told Tam that she refused to tell Kenny about the baby. And Tony had been acting funny around that time. Maybe Tam already suspected, but she refused to believe Tony would betray their marriage, especially with his cousin. She'd pushed those thoughts aside, and the three lived together, if not happily, then peacefully.

That all changed when Angela was born. Tam had had to fight her feelings of jealousy and grief all through Mia's pregnancy. She didn't know how she'd feel when the baby actually came. But Tam fell in love with Angela. She doted on the baby, buying her presents, holding and cooing at her, and watching her so Mia could catch up on sleep. Tam used to stare at Angela, wishing she were hers. She didn't know she could love a child who wasn't hers so much. It wasn't until Angela was a few months old that something clicked in Tam's mind. She knew there was no doubt Tony was Angela's father. Her mind and heart filled with mounting rage; she waited for a day when she knew Tony would be home late, and she confronted Mia.

"Angela is Tony's, isn't she?" Tam asked in a low voice. She didn't trust herself to speak any louder because she was afraid she'd start screaming and never stop.

Mia turned away from her and gave a little laugh. "What are you talking about? She's Kenny's."

"Don't lie to me, Mia. I just remembered you told me you and Kenny weren't having sex at the end of your relationship. I did the math and there's no way she's Kenny's if what you told me was true." Tam grabbed Mia's arm and forced her to turn around. "Look at me. Look me in the eyes and tell me she's not Tony's. Tell me."

Mia raised her eyes and looked at Tam. She started to speak, but Tam tightened her grip on her arm and said again, "Tell me she's not Tony's."

They stared at each other for what felt like hours. Finally Mia said, "I can't," and dropped her eyes. "I'm sorry, Tam," she whispered.

Tam let her hand fall away from Mia's arm. She felt like she was losing her mind. "How could you? I thought we were friends. How could you?"

When Mia stayed silent and stared at the floor as if she wished it would open up and swallow her, Tam asked, "Does he know?"

Mia shook her head and spoke in both Mandarin and English. "He asked me when he found out I was pregnant but I told him I was due a month earlier than I really was. I told him there was no chance the baby was his. I told him Kenny's the father."

"Yet Kenny has never made a move to claim Angela. It's because he knew she couldn't possibly be his, right?" Mia's silence confirmed what Tam had suspected.

"You're disgusting. I want you out of our house. Both of you." Tam's voice was shaking and she was so angry she was afraid she'd strike Mia. "He's *my* husband and *your* cousin. Your cousin!"

"He's not my—" Mia started to say, but Tam cut her off.

"I don't want to hear it. I don't want to hear any more. I don't ever want to speak to you again. Leave Tony and me alone. Do you understand?"

Mia nodded and whispered, "I didn't put a father's name on the birth certificate."

Tam stared at her for another minute, then turned away without a word. Her heart was pounding with the strength of her emotions. She normally hated confrontations, but the thought of Tony being with Mia made her so angry she couldn't keep quiet. She sat in their bedroom and waited until Tony came home and then gave him an ultimatum. "Either Mia and the baby move out, or I will." For the first time, she stood up for herself and refused to back down. She didn't stop to ask herself if she still wanted Tony. She only knew in that moment that she needed Mia and Angela out of her life. She'd deal with Tony later. And Tony had taken one look at her face and agreed without asking questions.

From that moment, she hardened her heart against Mia and Angela and what she'd forced Tony to do. She never saw Mia again, and she thought Mia had kept her word not to contact them. And she'd refused to discuss it with Tony. He'd tried, but she shut him down, not wanting to hear the excuses because she was afraid he would say he loved Mia more than he loved her.

"It obvious to me you can't keep Angela," Jenny said, breaking into Tam's thoughts. "I no blame you. If that were me, I probably do same thing. But this not best place for Angela. She no stay here."

"Yes, she can," Tam said, enunciating every word. "I know I didn't think of her best interests five years ago, but that was then. We've become a family and she belongs with me."

"But she's your husband's daughter," Jenny said. "You even said you not want her when I first told you Mia put you as guardian. Now I know why. I take Angela."

"Jenny." Tam was frustrated. "You're not taking her. She's staying with me."

"It not healthy for her," Jenny insisted. "You only took her 'cause you had to."

"You're not listening," Tam said loudly. "Angela and I need each other. We're family."

"Don't be selfish!" Jenny yelled. "I sorry for you but we need think of Angela first. Neil and I take her. We won't let her go to foster home."

At that moment, Angela burst through the front door. "No! I

want to stay with Tam!" She was breathing hard and turning red. Bee came huffing up to the door as Angela asked, "Don't you want me? Why does Jenny Ayi want to take me away?"

Oh, no. They'd left the front door ajar. Tam's hands flew to her mouth and she struggled to remember what they'd just said, wondering how much Angela had heard.

"You promised I could stay with you!" Angela's wails pierced Tam like arrows through the heart. The little girl threw herself at Tam, and she recovered enough to open her arms and catch her. As the women watched helplessly, Angela clung to Tam, sobbing as if her heart would break.

26

*One Month
before the Accident*

"MAMA?"

Angela had just come home from an outing with Tony and now sat in Mia's lap on the couch. She'd been telling Mia about their day, snuggled up against her. Mia held her, feeling grateful that Angela still wanted to be close to her and wishing they could stay like this forever.

"Yes, my Angel?" Angela had fallen silent after telling Mia about the ice cream sundae they'd gotten that afternoon.

"Is Uncle Tony my daddy?"

"What?" Mia's jaw dropped in shock, and you could have knocked her over with a feather. She always knew Angela was an intuitive little girl, but how in the world had she figured this out by herself? Mia had thought she was too young to understand, but now she could see she had underestimated her.

"Is he the prince from the stories you always tell me?"

Mia had promised Tony she wouldn't tell Angela yet, but she

couldn't lie to her face. She'd lied to so many people already, and she wouldn't do it to her daughter.

"Yes, Uncle Tony is your father."

Angela tilted her face, her serious brown eyes trained on Mia's face. "Why is it a secret?"

What to tell her? Mia prayed for strength and fell back on the only thing she could think of: the fairy tales.

"One day, a long time ago, a poor girl fell in love with the prince. They grew up together and the girl always thought she would marry the prince when she grew up. But then he met a princess and married her instead, and the girl was sad. So the girl did something really bad and that's how the prince and princess both got captured by the evil witch."

Mia paused for breath and looked down to find Angela listening to the story intently. "The girl and the prince had a baby and the evil witch sent the prince and princess away. But the prince has been trying to find a way to tell the princess that he has a beautiful little daughter without the evil witch finding out. If the witch finds out, she might make the princess stay with her or take the little daughter. We have to wait for the right time."

Angela thought about it, and Mia was surprised she didn't question the story, because she herself was confused. "So it's not because he doesn't love the little daughter?"

"Oh, Angela. The prince and princess both love the little daughter very much. Everything's just all messed up and the little daughter's mama is trying to fix it."

"Okay." Angela thought another moment and then seemed to accept it. "I'll keep it a secret for now." She leaned in and whispered, "But I'm so happy Uncle Tony is my daddy."

Tears sprang to Mia's eyes. How did their lives get so twisted?

She hated how complicated Angela's story was. How was she ever going to tell her daughter that her mother had been in love with her father since she was little girl, but he married someone else, so she schemed to get him back? But then she became friends with Angela's father's wife and realized too late that she shouldn't have come between them and betrayed her friend? Angela wasn't old enough to understand. And even when she was old enough, would she ever forgive Mia for how she came into the world?

27

TAM AND ANGELA had a quiet dinner together after Angela had calmed down and everyone had left. Abby had driven Jenny to the train station and Jenny had left in a huff. Tam was angry too. Who was Jenny to tell her whether she should keep Angela? Mia had appointed her the guardian, knowing Tam knew the truth.

The only saving grace was that Tam's parents hadn't been there. Tam could only imagine the uproar that would have happened if her mother had witnessed the scene.

"Should we take Stella for a walk?" She wanted to talk to Angela but didn't want to do it in the house in case her parents and brother and family came back. And also, the walls were closing in on her and she needed air.

They walked in silence in the darkened night. "How much did you overhear?"

Angela looked up. "A lot."

"Oh." After a pause, Tam asked, "How much?"

Angela was quiet.

"Do you know what any of it means?" Tam chose her words carefully. She wasn't sure how Angela had interpreted what she'd overheard.

Angela nodded. "Yes."

When she didn't say any more, Tam prompted her with, "Yes?"

"Yes. Uncle Tony was my daddy."

Tam stopped walking and Angela and Stella halted next to her. Tam crouched down to Angela's level. "You knew?"

"Yes. Mama told me right before she died."

"She did?" In all the time since she'd come to live with Tam, Angela had never once hinted she knew Tony was her father.

"Mama said it was a secret, and I couldn't tell anyone." Angela looked at Tam with worry in her eyes. "I never told anyone, not even Lily." Then she looked down. "Well, I told Stella. But Stella promised she'd never tell anyone neither."

"Did Tony know Mia told you?" Tam asked.

Angela shook her head. "No. Mama said it was our little secret. Did Mama and Uncle Tony do a bad thing?"

Tam sighed. She didn't know how to explain the situation to Angela without casting blame on her parents. "It's complicated. Adults sometimes do things they shouldn't, but none of it has anything to do with you. Okay?"

Angela tugged on Tam's hand. "Are you mad at me?" she asked in a small voice.

Tam hugged Angela hard. "No, I'm not mad at you. None of this is your fault. And guess what. Technically, it makes me your stepmother." Which was why it had made her feel funny to have Angela call her Auntie Tam.

"Like in the fairy tales?" Angela asked, her eyes wide.

Tam laughed. "Well, I hope I'm not wicked like the stepmothers all seem to be. But yes. Like that."

They started walking again. "Why was Jenny Ayi mad at you?"

Tam considered her words. "I guess she thought I might not want you to live with me. But she's wrong. I love you very much. You and Stella are my family now, and you're not going anywhere. And, hey, I saw from your birth certificate that your last name is Kwan. So that makes us even more family. Okay?"

Angela searched Tam's face, and whatever she saw there must have reassured her, because she nodded. "Okay."

They kept walking, the silence between them comfortable now. But Tam couldn't keep her thoughts at bay. Tony had fathered his cousin's child. She had hidden the truth from everyone; she hadn't even told him the truth. She thought she was a good person, but was she really? Had she kept her little secret because a part of her was punishing Tony for his affair with Mia? He cheated on her, so she wouldn't tell him Angela was his daughter. Ha! Gotcha back!

She knew in days past, in China and even in the States, it wasn't unusual for parents to marry their children to their second or third cousins, sometimes even first cousins, but it seemed so wrong to her. She was embarrassed and repulsed that she was married to a man who would do something like that. It was bad enough that her husband had a child with someone else when she couldn't even bring her babies to term; it had to be his cousin. She wished now that she'd had the guts to confront Tony and to tell him Mia had lied. But it was too late; he was gone. And as it turned out, Mia had already told him the truth.

"YOU DID WHAT?" Tam shouted into the phone on New Year's Day. Her parents and brother and his family had just left for the airport. "You got a lawyer?" Tam was incredulous. "Why are you doing this, Jenny? Do you really think I'm such a monster?"

Jenny was hell-bent on taking Angela away, calling and texting Tam several times a day. Tam never knew the woman could be so stubborn, and no matter what she said, Jenny refused to believe the best place for Angela was with Tam.

"You no monster. I feel bad for you," Jenny said. "But I don't think it right that you raise Angela. You always will think, she the product of Tony's cheating. How that be healthy for her? One of my clients from nail salon is lawyer. She help us petition for guardianship of Angela."

"Why can't you understand I don't feel that way anymore?" Tam cried. "What do I have to do to convince you I love Angela and don't hold her accountable for anything her mother or father did? Why are you doing this?"

Jenny was quiet for a moment. "Because if that me, I be so . . . You must be so . . . so . . ." Jenny trailed off, searching for the word.

"Disgusted?" Tam supplied. "Repulsed? Yes, okay. I do feel disgusted. But it has nothing to do with how I feel about Angela."

"I not involved, so I can do better for her."

"From the moment she was born, Angela has held a special place in my heart. I wished she were my child. I loved her, and it hurt to send her away with Mia. When I found out Mia had appointed me as guardian, it felt like a second chance to make it up to Angela. I knew I had to do it. And having her in my life has been the best thing to ever happen to me. She has nothing to do with what her parents did."

Jenny remained stubborn. "You can't know for sure you always feel this way."

"Damn it, Jenny! I'm sick of arguing with you. If you think you can take her away from me, you've got another think coming. I can't talk to you anymore. I'm calling my lawyer." And with that, Tam hung up, wishing she could slam the phone down, but it was hard to slam down a cell phone.

She sat still until her heart had calmed to a normal rate, thankful she was in the town house alone.

She picked up her phone and called Mia's lawyer, who had helped her get guardianship of Angela.

"This is Tamlei Kwan," she said when he picked up. "I have a problem."

After speaking to the lawyer, Tam felt a bit better. He told her it was unlikely that Jenny and Neil could make a case strong enough for Angela to be taken out of Tam's custody. There was nothing about Tam's life that made her unsuitable as a guardian. But depending on how determined Jenny was, she could make it uncomfortable and time-consuming for Tam if she persisted in trying to get guardianship. He suggested Tam might want to officially adopt Angela if she was sure she wanted to keep her.

She didn't need this. She had enough thoughts running through her head, wondering if Tony and Mia had resumed their affair after Mia told him the truth. Or was Tony only visiting his daughter? And why hadn't he told her Mia had contacted him?

She needed to do something. Checking the app for the yoga studio on her phone, she saw there was a class starting in forty-five minutes. She stood to go change. Yoga was exactly what she needed now.

When she walked into the studio thirty minutes before the class with the intention of stretching before it started, she was surprised to see Adam on his mat. They were on the only ones in the studio. She unrolled her mat next to Adam and sat down, sending him a shy smile.

"Are you okay?" Adam's forehead scrunched in concern. "You look tired."

Tam ran a hand through her hair. "It's . . . There's a lot going on right now."

"You want to talk about it?" He gestured around the studio. "We have some time before people show up."

Tam hesitated. She couldn't explain why Adam's presence always made her feel as if she was lit up like a Christmas tree. She knew he had a girlfriend. He'd always kept their interactions on a friendly level, never overstepping into anything resembling flirtation. It was all very innocent, wasn't it? Maybe that's what made their friendship possible, because she knew she couldn't have him.

She was usually reticent to talk about her personal problems, but thoughts of Tony, Mia, and Angela swirled around in her mind until she felt as if she would burst. Before she stopped to think, she blurted out, "Angela is my husband's child."

Oops. Did she really just say that out loud? Tam turned her head away, embarrassed. Yet there was a part of her that was relieved at finally being able to say what was really on her mind.

Adam touched her on the arm. "Did you just find out?"

Tam shook her head. "It's a long story, but I knew. And I didn't tell Tony. It's all very complicated." She fell silent, not sure how or even if she wanted to tell him their whole sordid tale.

"I'm so sorry you had to go through that." He squeezed her arm before withdrawing it, and Tam immediately missed the warmth of his hand.

Tam nodded, fighting tears. She extended her legs out in front of her, folding over in a stretch so that he couldn't see her face. "And now Jenny's trying to take Angela away. She thinks I won't be able to raise her, but I knew she was my husband's child when I took guardianship of her. Jenny contacted a lawyer."

"Oh, Tam. I'm sure she doesn't have much ground to stand on."

Tam nodded. "That's what my lawyer said."

"Let me know if there's anything I can do to help."

Tam smiled at him, and then they fell silent. After a moment she decided to be bold and ask about his girlfriend.

"How long have you and your girlfriend been together?"

"Almost five years. She moved in with me last year. I think she's expecting a ring soon." Adam had a sheepish look on his face.

"Oh." Did he seem unhappy about that thought? Or was it just her wishful thinking?

"Funny, I was just thinking about her. She's a good woman, but she doesn't have a lot of compassion for others. If something or someone doesn't work in the grand scheme of her life, she wants no part of it."

"Hmm." Tam tilted her head. What did he mean by that?

"Don't get me wrong, Jessie has a lot of great qualities, but she's not as open to things as you are. She wouldn't have taken Angela in your situation."

Tam flinched on hearing Jessie's name. Somehow, when she was just a nameless woman, it seemed okay to be having this personal talk with Adam. But hearing her name reminded Tam that she was a real person, someone who wouldn't be happy if she knew what Tam was thinking about her almost fiancé. And having been the one who was cheated on, she would never do that to another woman. In a desperate attempt to change the subject, Tam said, "Did you know when I first saw you, I thought you looked like the Marlboro Man?"

"Ree Drummond's husband?" Adam's eyebrows rose.

"You watch *The Pioneer Woman* on the Food Network?" Tam was surprised when Adam nodded. "No, not her husband. The real Marlboro Man from the ads."

Adam laughed.

"So you cook, then?" He was not only cute but he could cook too?

Adam nodded. "When I have time, I like to try new recipes."

"Me too." Tam was relieved they were back on safer ground, and they talked about their favorite recipes while people started trickling into the studio and setting up their mats.

When the teacher walked into the room and welcomed everyone, Adam leaned over and whispered, "If you ever need a friend, I'm here. I can help with Jenny if you need it."

"Thank you." She smiled even as she wondered if he too was trying to establish that they were just friends.

She lay down on her mat, her thoughts back on Jenny. She thought the woman had become a friend and never dreamed she would be the one to threaten the bond between Tam and Angela. If Jenny was going to fight her, then Tam was prepared to fight back. The one thing she knew in all this confusion was that she couldn't love Angela more, and she would do anything to keep her. She was going to legally adopt her so nothing could come between them again.

28

*Three Weeks
before the Accident*

JENNY HUNG UP the phone and wrote something in the appointment book she kept behind the counter. "Huang Tai Tai will
be here at noon for a bikini wax, but I'm already booked for a man-
icure and pedicure. Can you take her? You're the only one who can
tolerate her when she starts cursing and screaming."

Mia rose on her toes to peer out the front windows and didn't
answer. Jenny looked up and asked, "Are you listening to me?"
When Mia still didn't answer, Jenny turned to look behind her.
"What are you looking at?"

"I'll be right back." Mia put down the cloth she was drying her
hands with and slipped out the front door before Jenny could ask
any more questions.

She crossed the street and stalked behind the truck parked at the
curb. "What do you want, Kenny?"

He didn't answer, just leaned against his truck and watched her.

His co-worker, a young blond man with a sunny face, raised a hand in greeting. "Hey, Mia. Good to see you."

"Hi, Joe." Mia's face broke into a smile. She'd always had a soft spot for Joe, who looked up to Kenny like an eager puppy and was always so friendly. "What are you two doing here?"

"We had a stop in this neighborhood and Kenny wanted to see if you were working." Joe gave her a grin. "He's still infatuated with you."

"Unfortunately." Mia rolled her eyes as Kenny shot death looks in Joe's direction. She turned her back on Kenny and addressed Joe. "So what's new with you?"

"Teresa and I just had a baby. A beautiful little girl named Hope." Joe's face shone with pride as he pulled up a picture on his phone to show Mia.

Mia admired the tiny baby before handing the phone back to Joe. "She's so beautiful. Congratulations." She turned to Kenny and placed her hands on her hips. "Why are you lurking in front of the nail salon?" she asked when he still didn't speak.

He pushed himself off the truck and took a step toward her, causing a tingle of unease to run down her back. "Guess who I saw on the streets yesterday."

Mia dropped her hands and rolled her eyes. Really? He was going to play guessing games with her? "Who?" She sighed in exasperation.

"Your cousin Tony. He was holding Angela's hand." Kenny's voice lowered so that Joe couldn't hear, and his eyes squinted into small slits. "Imagine my shock when I saw them together. They look so much alike. I don't know why I never saw it before." He took another step toward her, and Mia stepped backward, the tingle of unease turning into apprehension. "He's her father, isn't he?"

Oh, shit. Kenny had figured it out. Mia scrambled frantically to say something as her heart beat so loudly she could barely hear the traffic sounds on the street or the bad names Kenny was now calling her in English and Mandarin. She brought a hand up to her head, shaking it in the hopes of clearing the roaring that was filling her ears and making her feel faint. She swallowed hard and breathed a sigh of relief when the noises around her came back into sharp focus.

"You're a fucking whore, Mia," Kenny shouted. "A whore who had a bastard with your cousin." He placed his hands on her upper arms and shook her, causing Joe to jump forward in alarm.

"Hey, now, Kenny," Joe said. "What are you doing? That's no way to talk to Mia."

Mia didn't notice the people giving them a wide berth as they passed on the sidewalk. She didn't see the stares from the kids across the street or the concerned looks from an older man who was trying to decide whether to intervene. All she saw was the crazed expression on Kenny's face as he continued to curse her out even as tears formed in his eyes.

"Kenny, stop." She could barely be heard above his hollering. "Tony's not—"

"Fuck you, Mia." Joe finally got Kenny to let go of her, but the look in Kenny's eyes nearly broke her. He looked like he'd lost his best friend, and her heart went out to him even as she feared what he'd do now that he knew the truth. "I love you so much. I wanted to marry you. And all this time, you were carrying on with your cousin? You let everyone think Angela was my baby and told me you had a one-night stand."

"I . . . He's not—" Mia could hear her voice rising and fought for control of her breathing, which was coming in short gasps. "It was a one-night—"

"Stop lying to me!" Kenny roared, lunging for her and causing Joe to place both hands on his chest. The older man who'd been debating whether to help also moved forward.

"Calm down, man." Together with Joe, the older gentleman forced Kenny to back away from Mia.

"Get out of my way. This is none of your business." But Kenny halted in front of the stranger. He'd always had respect for elders. Mia could see the battle on his face as his wish to bat the man aside to get to her warred with his reluctance to harm an older man.

"I'm fine," Mia said to the man. He stared hard at her and Joe and then nodded.

"Call the police if he lays a hand on you," the man said as he walked away.

Mia looked toward the nail salon, wondering if Jenny could see what was going on, but realized they were standing behind Kenny's truck. Jenny couldn't see them from inside. Kenny was silent now, his eyes as red as his face, as Joe shot him puzzled looks.

"Kenny, I'm sorry I lied. I never meant to hurt you. I just—" She broke off, not sure what to say to him. She'd made such a mess of things for everyone. How was she going to fix it so that Angela wouldn't ever have to be ashamed of her family and where she came from?

"I have to go." She turned to cross the street and Kenny grabbed her arm.

"You're mine, Mia. No one could ever love you like I do."

"Kenny, let her go." Joe jumped forward, but the look Kenny shot him had him backing up a step.

"Stay out of this, Joe," Kenny said.

"We . . . I . . ." Mia tried to speak, but there was too much to explain to him now on the sidewalk. "I've got to go back to work."

She tried to pull away, but he had a firm grasp on her arm. "Let me go."

"Never."

She looked up and met his gaze, shivering at the intensity in his eyes. He finally let go and she ran across the street, not bothering to say good-bye to Joe or to look both ways. As she let the front door close behind her, she stopped to catch her breath. For the first time since she met him, Mia was scared of Kenny.

29

THE DAY BEFORE Chinese New Year, Tam woke to an email from her caseworker, Sandra, saying she got her travel approval. Tam called Sandra as soon as she saw the email and gave her three dates to apply for the consulate appointment. "I'll put the request in today, but you might not get an answer right away," Sandra warned. "It can take up to seventy-two hours for the US Consulate in Guangzhou to confirm, and Chinese New Year is tomorrow. All of China shuts down for a week to celebrate, so you probably won't get an answer until after the holiday."

Tam was frustrated that they'd have to wait another week to make their travel plans. They were so close! They'd gotten Angela's expedited passport already, and she knew the little girl was excited to go on her first plane ride.

"Why aren't we going to Lily's house for Chinese New Year?" Angela asked. "Is Jenny Ayi still mad at us?"

Tam was worried that she hadn't heard from Jenny for a couple of weeks now. At least when Jenny had been calling constantly, Tam knew what the other woman was thinking. With this radio silence, it made Tam jittery, not sure what was coming.

"She's not mad at you, Angela."

Angela looked sad. "I miss Lily. I want to spend Chinese New Year with them."

"I know." It was really too bad Jenny was letting their disagreement get in the middle of the girls' friendship. Then again, Tam hadn't reached out to her either. She was still so mad from their last conversation. But Tam decided to swallow her pride for Angela.

"Do you want me to call them?" she asked. Angela nodded, and Tam dialed Jenny's number. Bracing herself to be nice, she was disappointed when the call went to voicemail. She hung up without leaving a message.

"No answer." Angela's smile fell when she realized she wasn't going to get to talk to Lily. Trying to cheer her up, Tam hugged her. "Never mind. We're going to have a great celebration ourselves tonight. Abby and Bee will be here soon, so we'd better get ready."

Her parents called it Lunar New Year because they, like many Taiwanese, believed it wasn't just a Chinese holiday. It was a tradition in Tam's family that on Lunar New Year's Eve, they gathered around a pot of stock placed at the center of the dining table. While the hot pot was kept simmering, each family member added ingredients, such as a variety of vegetables, fish and squid balls, thin slices of beef, seafood, tofu, bean threads, and whatever else they happened to have on hand, to the pot. They dipped the cooked food into a sauce made of raw egg, soy sauce, *sha cha* (a savory and slightly spicy sauce), hot sauce, and sliced scallions.

Angela looked sad as they prepared the ingredients. "Mama and I used to go to this hot-pot restaurant for special occasions." Her voice was so forlorn that Tam stopped what she was doing and put her arms around the little girl. "I miss my mama."

"I know. I miss Tony too. Did you know I was the one who introduced your mama to hot pot?" Angela listened intently as Tam told her about how fascinated Mia had been, since she'd never had a hot pot, and how much the two of them loved it and would huddle over a pot of boiling stock, talking, laughing, and eating for hours, until they thought they'd burst.

The doorbell rang and Angela went to answer it.

"*Xin nian kuai le!*" Abby said. Angela had taught her how to say Happy New Year in Mandarin. They each brought a *hongbao* for Angela. It was a tradition to give children these lucky red envelopes to bring happiness and good luck, regardless of how much money was inside.

Tam turned on the pot at the center of the table and poured in the hot chicken stock she had prepared earlier with her mom's help on the phone. Tam watched from the kitchen as Angela kneeled on her seat in order to reach into the pot. The little girl's face was flushed from the heat and she laughed at something Abby said. You'd never know from looking at her that her mother and father had died five months ago. She'd been through more turmoil than most kids her age. Tam vowed to make things better for Angela. She deserved it and Tam would do everything she could to protect her.

30

*Two Weeks
before the Accident*

MIA SCREAMED AND threw her cell phone across the apartment. It landed on the couch with a soft plop.

"Why won't he stop calling?" she shouted to the empty studio. Angela was downstairs with Lily. Kenny had started calling her the night he'd confronted her on the street and he wouldn't stop. And no, she wasn't talking about a call here and there. Kenny was literally calling her over and over again. The ringing had driven her up the wall, and even after she turned off the ringer, it still rang in her ear until she thought she'd lose her mind.

Mia walked to the couch to pick up her phone and saw it was still vibrating. She huddled on the couch, shaking. She kept her finger on the soft reset button until the phone went dead and it no longer vibrated. Drawing a big breath, she waited for the shaking to stop.

Kenny had been mad at her before, but this was a whole new level of crazy. She knew he'd been following her ever since she broke up with him, but that was harmless. And if she had to be honest, she'd liked it, that he still wanted her after everything. But this—this obsessive calling and showing up everywhere was starting to get to her. When she left the apartment in the morning, he was parked across the street. When she left the nail salon to get lunch, she'd see him on the next block, his eyes trained on her. And when she was hiding inside her apartment, he'd call her repeatedly like this.

She couldn't take it anymore. He had to stop. She would call the police.

But in the next breath, she knew she'd do no such thing. Because she was here in the States illegally. The police couldn't help her, unless she wanted to risk getting deported.

31

*Three Days
before the Accident*

"I NEED A favor."

Well, that was a first, Tony wanting a favor from her. Mia's eyebrows rose and she placed him on speaker so she could put the phone down and finish getting ready to go out with Chris. Chris was taking her for a special dinner, and she had on a light blue sundress with thin straps and a full skirt that made her feel pretty and feminine.

"What do you need?" Her spirits lifted despite Kenny's harassment. He was still following her and calling her, but he'd eased off slightly.

"I want to get Angela something special for her fifth birthday."

"There's a doll she really wants, but it's kind of expensive." Angela had wanted it so bad, but Mia just didn't have the extra money. It had broken her heart to see the stoic way Angela had put the doll back on the shelf after giving it a final hug.

"Can you take me to the store when I come get her on Thursday? I can come early."

"Um . . ." She'd have to leave the salon for a bit, but she was sure she could make an excuse to Jenny. "Sure. It's on Main Street." It was only down the street and around the corner from the nail salon, so she wouldn't be gone long.

"Thanks, Mia." Tony paused and then said, "Tam and I should be getting our letter of acceptance for our little boy soon."

"That's great, Tony." Mia was genuinely happy for them. And maybe a part of her hoped Tam would forgive her once she had a child of her own and understood what a mother would do for her child.

"I'm going to tell Tam soon about Angela." Tony stopped and Mia held her breath. "I'm just waiting for the right moment."

"You're not going to wait until after you get back from China?"

"I think I should tell her before we go. I just have to do it right. Tam loved Angela. I think she'll be okay." His voice was filled with doubt.

"It'll be okay." She felt the first spark of hope. She walked to the window to see if Chris's car was out front. "Oh, shit."

"What's the matter?" Tony asked.

"Shit, shit, shit." Kenny was out there. She hadn't seen him in the last two days and thought he'd finally given up. But now he was back, right as Chris was due to pick her up. She didn't need this today.

"Mia, what's wrong?" Did she imagine it, or was that concern in Tony's voice? Could he be softening toward her?

"It's nothing. Kenny's been following me and harassing me." She told Tony everything Kenny had been doing.

"Mia." She was surprised by the alarm in his voice. "That's not good. You need to call the police."

Mia peered out the window again. Maybe she should text Chris to meet her around the corner and she could sneak out the back way.

"I can't call the police. Don't worry, he's all bark and no bite."

"I don't know, Mia . . ." Tony sounded doubtful. He hung up after she reassured him she was fine and that she'd see him in three days. But the feeling in the pit of her stomach that something bad was going to happen wouldn't go away. It'd been growing stronger despite her hopes for the future. Exasperated that the dread was overcoming her optimism, she pushed it to the back of her mind and reached for her phone to text Chris. Her life was getting better. Nothing bad was going to happen.

32

The Day
of the Accident

THE TRAFFIC NOISES were deafening as Mia and Tony hurried down Roosevelt Avenue toward the toy shop on Main Street. Tony had just gotten a call and Mia knew it was Tam. How she longed to grab the phone from Tony and speak to Tam. Tell her she missed her and she was so sorry and explain everything to her. But she fisted her hands at her sides and controlled herself.

"I shouldn't be home late. Thanks, Tam." Mia's heart lurched to hear the way Tony's voice softened when he said Tam's name. They stopped at the corner of Roosevelt and Main to wait for the light to change, and she berated herself. She was such a fool to try to get between a husband and wife. Tony loved Tam, not Mia, and he'd proven that when he told Mia she and Angela had to move out of their apartment. Why couldn't Tam see that? Why didn't Tam realize Mia meant nothing to Tony, and Tam was the one he loved?

There was a screech of brakes, and what sounded like a hundred car horns suddenly filled the air. Mia looked up and saw a beverage-distribution truck that had just gone through a red light and was now blocking traffic on all sides in the middle of the intersection.

". . . just a lot of traffic," Tony was saying into the phone.

Mia's heart rate picked up when she realized it was Kenny's truck. Joe was driving, but it was Kenny Mia was focused on. They locked eyes, and for a second, time stopped. There was no mistaking the ferocious look on Kenny's face when he finally broke their gaze and looked back and forth between Mia and Tony. He threw his hands up, and the contents of the coffee cup he was holding sprayed all over the interior of the cab. Even from across the street, Mia could see the arc of the liquid as it splashed over Joe. Mia gasped when Joe's hands left the steering wheel and clawed at his face.

She tugged on Tony's arm. "Tony!"

He put the phone aside and asked, "What's the matter?"

"It . . . he . . ." She couldn't get the words out, because the truck suddenly lurched erratically and Kenny reached over to grab the steering wheel.

Tony turned back to his conversation with Tam.

Mia tried to shout a warning because the truck was now barreling toward them, but nothing came out. Surely Joe would slam on the brakes any minute now, right?

She screamed and backed up, trying to drag Tony with her. Kenny was yelling something at her, waving one hand frantically as he fought Joe for control of the steering wheel. What was Joe doing? His hands were now covering his eyes, and he was rocking back and forth. Why wasn't he slowing down?

She heard people yelling and more car horns blaring, but her entire focus was on Kenny as the truck cut a clear path directly to her and Tony. People sprang out of the way, but Mia's feet had turned to lead, and she couldn't get out of the way fast enough. Tony finally looked up, saw the truck descending on them, and yelled out, "HOLY SHIT!" right as the truck overtook them and a roaring sound filled Mia's head. And then there was nothing.

33

THE THURSDAY AFTER Chinese New Year week, Tam
headed out on the trail after school for a run. She didn't go far, just
enough to release some tension and work off the impatience of waiting for the US Consulate in Guangzhou to open again. As she unlocked her front door on the way back in, she heard her cell phone
ringing on the kitchen counter. Rushing inside, she glanced at the
caller ID and saw it was the detective who was investigating Tony
and Mia's accident.

"We finally got a confession from Kenny Wong and Joe Walsh.
Joe was the one driving, like all the eyewitnesses said." Tam listened
in silence as the detective told her the rest, and then she thanked him
and hung up, stunned. After a moment, she dialed Abby's number.

"Abby."

"Tam? What's the matter?"

"Where are you?"

"I'm at Jeff's."

"I . . . He . . ." Tam couldn't get her voice to work.

"Are you okay?"

"The detective called. He wasn't driving."

"Who? What? Wait. I'll be right over." Abby was there in fifteen minutes. "What happened?"

Tam had calmed enough to speak. "Kenny and Joe finally told the truth. Joe was driving the truck, not Kenny."

"What? What happened?"

"Apparently Kenny saw Mia and Tony on the street together and he spilled his hot coffee all over Joe. It got in Joe's eyes and he couldn't see. Kenny tried to take control of the wheel, but in the chaos, Joe stomped on the accelerator instead of the brakes and the truck plowed into Tony and Mia. It was an accident." Tam was still processing what the detective had told her.

"Oh my God. So Kenny really didn't run them over on purpose? Why did he lie and say he was driving?"

"Joe just had a baby and Kenny was afraid he was going to get in trouble. He told the police he was driving and told Joe to stay quiet. Joe was in shock, so he didn't speak up. He let Kenny cover for him. But then he couldn't take the guilt anymore. He'd always liked Mia and his running her over was giving him nightmares. He finally came clean to the police."

Abby nodded in silence, waiting for Tam to continue.

Tam twisted her fingers together, taking a breath before going on. "Kenny also felt so guilty. He didn't mean to cause their deaths. He was angry when he found out Angela was Tony's, but he never meant to hurt Mia. He loved her, was obsessed with her, but said he would never have hurt her. He thought he deserved to be punished. That's why he told everyone he was driving. He wanted to take the blame if someone was charged for the accident."

Abby shook her head in disbelief. "I can't believe this. As awful as it is, I can't imagine what the two of them have been going through if this was all just a horrible accident."

"I can't get the image of Tony and Mia standing on that corner and that truck just plowing over them out of my head. And I was talking to Tony when it happened!"

"Oh, Tam. I'm so sorry." Abby put an arm around Tam. "You don't deserve all this."

Tam played with the end of her shirt as tears dripped down her face. "I'm just so sad that this is how Tony's life ended." There was so much inside her that wanted to get out, and she couldn't hold it in anymore. She needed to talk about Tony.

"I thought when I married Tony, it was forever," Tam said in a soft voice. "A friend dragged me to the lecture he was giving at Columbia on Eastern influences on Western pop culture. I thought I'd be bored out of my mind, but he was so engaging. I went up to him afterward and said, 'I love the way you talk.' I meant to say I loved his talk, but I was tongue-tied."

Abby laughed. "I can totally see you doing that."

"He invited us out for a drink, but my friend made an excuse. Tony and I had such a good time. He was so smart and we just talked and talked. Drinks turned to dinner. And he asked me out again at the end of the night. I'd never met anyone like him."

"He was smart," Abby said. "And he did love you. I saw it."

Tam sighed. "I always thought I loved him more than he did me. By the time Mia moved in, things had cooled between us and I wondered sometimes if he had a girlfriend on the side. I just never thought it was Mia."

"We may not have gotten along well, but he didn't seem like the cheating kind to me," Abby said.

"I thought maybe he thought the old Chinese way of having multiple wives or concubines was okay. He was so traditionally Chinese in the way he thinks."

"I never got that feeling from him," Abby argued. "I think there's more to the story with Mia than what you know."

"What else is there? They had an affair and had a child together." Tam smiled through her tears as memories assaulted her. "Did you know he was really superstitious? When we were buying this town house, he drove our poor real estate agent crazy."

"How?"

"He refused to see a house because it faced north. He said the north and northwest represent evil and bad luck. And the next house didn't work because the front door opened right onto the stairway. He said all our luck would fly out the door."

"Is that feng shui?" Abby asked.

Tam nodded. "Another house was bad because we could see from the front door right through the back door to the yard. He said all our wealth would go right out the back door. And another had too much energy coming at the house because it faced a perpendicular street." Tam laughed, remembering the look of despair on their agent's face with each rejection. "The last house we saw before this one was across from a cemetery, and Tony refused to get out of the car. He claimed he could feel the ghosts. Our agent actually cried tears of happiness when Tony approved of this town house."

Abby laughed too, and she was about to speak when Tam's phone rang. Tam looked at it with a mixture of fear and hope. Was it the police again? Or maybe Sandra calling with a consulate appointment confirmation?

But it was Jenny. "Tam?"

Tam braced herself for another difficult and frustrating discussion. "I was starting to get worried that I hadn't heard from you. Are you still working with a lawyer to take Angela?"

"No." Jenny's voice was quiet, and Tam realized Jenny sounded like she had a cold.

"Are you okay?" Tam asked.

"Yes, but I have something to tell you. You come see me in Flushing?"

"Oh, no. Not this again. Every time you insist on talking to me in person, you drop a bomb on me. Just spit it out, Jenny."

Jenny was quiet for so long that Tam thought she had hung up. Then Jenny said in Mandarin, "I found Mia's journal. I saw it before but I thought it was for her English class."

"Okay," Tam said with caution. "I'm sure Angela would love to have it. I'll get it from you next time I see you."

"I read it." There was a pause, as if Jenny expected Tam to reprimand her. When Tam didn't say anything, Jenny continued. "I read the whole thing. Now I understand everything, why Mia did what she did."

"What?"

"Tam, Mia was an orphan."

"I know that," Tam said. "Her parents died when she was fourteen; that's why she lived with Tony's family."

"No," Jenny said. "She wasn't Tony's cousin. She had no family. She was abandoned as a baby and grew up in an orphanage. She's not related to Tony at all. She's a real orphan!"

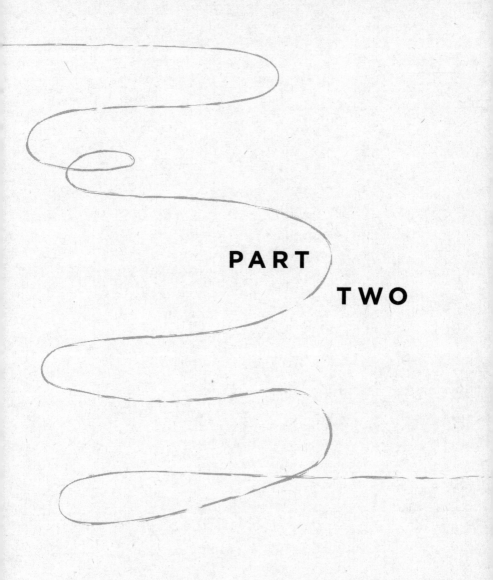

PART

TWO

34

MIA'S JOURNAL

My dear Angela,

I hope I will be with you when you are finally old enough to read what I have written in this notebook. I hope it is not your father or Tam who gives this to you because I am gone. Even though I fear in my heart that the ayis in the orphanage are right, that I am a yao zhe baby who will die young, I hold on to the small hope I will live to see you grow up.

But in case I don't, this journal is for you. If I'm not around to tell you myself, I want you to understand and not grow up hating me. Everything I did was out of a desire to be loved, to have a family of my own. You have no idea what it's like to grow up knowing no one wants you. Maybe that's why I've held on to the love I have for your father so tightly, even when I knew he wasn't mine to love. Somehow, I justified it because I've loved him since I was only six years old. I can't say I am proud of the things I've done or the people I've hurt. You may be shocked and appalled when you finally hear how you came into this world. I've written it all down, all the awful things I did, because you deserve to know the truth.

I love you so much, Angela. You are the light of my life and the child of my heart. This is my story, the story I based all those fairy tales I made up for you on. I hope as you read this, you will find it in your heart to forgive and understand why I did the things I did. I will love you forever, connected by the red thread of fate, even if I am no longer with you.

Love always,
Your Mama

ON A COLD and blustery day in the middle of February, Tam and Angela boarded a plane bound for California. They were on their way to visit Tam's parents for two days before flying on to Beijing to see Tony's mother and Fei-Yin, and then finally to Guangzhou to meet Charlie.

Angela quivered with excitement as they buckled their seat belts. "My first plane ride," she whispered to Tam, all traces of her sadness at having to leave Stella for two weeks forgotten in the buzz of this new experience. "I can't wait to see China, where my mama was born."

"Me too." Tam smiled at her. "I've never been to China either. Only Taiwan."

They held hands as the plane took off, and Angela squeezed Tam's hand hard when the plane began to climb. Once it had leveled and Angela was happily watching a movie on the personal screen in front of her, Tam settled back in her own seat with a sigh. The last week and a half had been frantic.

The same day Jenny had dropped that bomb and told her Mia wasn't related to Tony and had grown up in an orphanage, Tam had also gotten her consulate appointment and made her travel arrangements. Nine days after booking the flights, they were on their way to California.

Even in the midst of packing and getting ready for their trip, Tam had found time to travel to Flushing to get Mia's journal from Jenny. Jenny had handed her the black-and-white composition book filled with Mia's neat handwriting in Mandarin.

"I know this for Angela," Jenny had said. "But I think you need read it." Jenny held on to the notebook until Tam looked up and met her eyes. "She wrote about what happen with Tony. She in love with Tony since she was little girl."

Tam studied Jenny's face. She was still angry with Jenny for trying to take Angela away. "Just tell me."

"I think it better you read for yourself."

Tam narrowed her eyes, but Jenny's gaze didn't waver. "Fine. I'll read it. After I get someone to translate it."

Jenny finally let go of the notebook, and Tam tucked it into her tote bag. She turned to go, but Jenny stopped her with a hand on Tam's arm. "I'm sorry, about everything. When you get back from China, we get Lily and Angela together, okay?"

She looked so contrite that Tam relented. "Okay. Angela would love that."

Jenny smiled. "See you soon."

Tam had flipped through the pages on the train ride back to Dobbs Ferry. Who could translate it for her? The most obvious person was her mother, but Tam didn't want to tell her that Angela was Tony's daughter. Just thinking about doing that gave Tam a headache. She was too ashamed to tell her mother that she'd been right about Mia.

Zhong-Ying had never been happy about Tam's friendship with Mia. "I don't understand why she must live with you. A young marriage like yours doesn't need an outsider. She seems so needy, wants too much from Tony. She needs to move out."

Tam could already hear her mom's voice in her head: *See, I knew something was wrong. Not natural.*

She'd thought about asking one of Tony's colleagues, but the contents of the journal were so personal, and she knew Tony wouldn't have wanted his colleagues to know about their family secrets. Maybe she could find someone in China to translate it for her. The notebook sat now in her carry-on at her feet.

Angela leaned over and pulled her headphones off. "Are we almost there?"

Tam laughed. "Not even close, Angela. We just left. It'll be a few hours yet." She looked up and saw the flight attendants coming down the aisle with their carts. "Do you want a drink?"

Angela reached to release the tray in front of her. "Apple juice, please." Once she had a cup of apple juice and a tiny bag of pretzels in front of her, Angela turned to Tam. "Can we FaceTime with Dr. Adam when we get to California?"

Tam had taken Angela to see Adam for her shots. He'd given Tam his cell phone number and said to call him from China with any questions. Did her heart start pounding with excitement that he'd given her his phone number? Hell, yes. But they were just friends. Really. An involuntary sigh escaped her lips.

"Are you okay?" Angela gave Tam a curious look.

"I'm fine." Tam patted her cheeks. "And no, we're not Face-Timing Adam. He only gave me his number for emergencies."

Angela pouted, but then she brightened. "Well, we'll definitely see Dr. Adam again when we get home. He has to see Charlie." She put her headphones back on and was soon engrossed in the Disney movie again, taking sips of her apple juice and happily swinging her legs.

Tam couldn't help but smile at Angela's obvious infatuation with Adam. It seemed Tam wasn't the only one with a little crush on the doctor. Tam shifted in her airplane seat, thinking about their friendship. And that's all it was, because there was no way she'd ever become the other woman. Not after finding out she'd let Mia (who she now knew had been in love with Tony for years) live with them and they'd continued their affair right under her nose.

The smile fell from her face as she imagined Tony and Mia together. She squeezed her eyes shut to block the image from her mind. Her hands clenched and it took several minutes before the haze of anger cleared from her brain. Because the truth was, if Tony and Mia were still alive, she'd want to kill them for how they'd deceived her. Not literally, of course. Kenny's hot cup of coffee had taken care of that. And now he and Joe were under investigation to see if either would be charged in Tony's and Mia's deaths.

Even though she grieved for Tony and Mia, Tam hoped Kenny and Joe weren't charged. They'd both suffered enough, unable to get past the accident and the knowledge that they'd ended two lives. The police told her Kenny had asked to speak to her, but Tam just couldn't. Not yet. She leaned her head against the headrest and closed her eyes. While she didn't think Kenny should go to jail for the accident, she couldn't imagine facing the man who had inadvertently killed her husband and Mia.

35

"LOOK AT HER," Tam's mom said as they watched Angela running around her parents' backyard with Wei's kids and their cousins' kids. "She loves being here. You should move back."

Tam opened her mouth, but then closed it without saying anything. Because for once, she actually thought her mom might be right. She'd left California because the closeness of her extended family had suffocated her when she was in her twenties. But now Tam longed for the comfort of family, of being with people who had to love her. Plus, Zhong-Ying had been cooking all of Tam's favorite Taiwanese dishes, making Tam realize how much she missed all this. Maybe she should move back.

Tam took Angela to the office of the family software business the afternoon before they flew to China. While Tam's father showed Angela some of the programs on a computer, Tam stopped by her brother's office. He was on the phone, but when he saw Tam in the doorway, he gestured for her to come in and ended his call.

Wei studied her face. "How are you? You okay?"

Tam gave her brother a small smile. "You really want to know?"

He nodded. Tam hadn't planned on telling her family anything on this trip, but she'd always been able to talk to Wei. She closed his door behind her, and the whole story about Tony and Mia poured out, like a gush of water from a hose.

When she finally ran out of words, he said, "Never doubt that Tony loved you. I saw the way he treated you. But what happened with Mia is messed up, and the way they died." Wei reached out and briefly laid his hand on top of hers. "You'll be fine. You're strong."

She felt anything but strong. But she suddenly realized who could translate Mia's journal for her. Wei. He'd kept up with Chinese school long after Tam had quit to try out for the cheerleading squad (which she didn't make, but she'd refused to go back to Chinese school). He'd also studied Chinese all through college and beyond. He was fluent and could read and write, which came in handy in the family business.

"I need your help." Tam reached into her bag for the black-and-white composition book. She'd been carrying it with her everywhere and placed it on Wei's desk now.

"What's this?"

"Mia's journal to Angela. Jenny thought I should read it. She said Mia wrote about what happened with Tony."

Wei flipped through it and looked up at Tam. "And you want me to translate it for you since you can't read it?"

Tam nodded.

Wei smirked. "I told you Mandarin would come in handy at some point in your life. You shouldn't have quit Chinese school."

Tam didn't say anything, just gave Wei the stink eye. "Sorry," he said. "I won't tease you. I see this is important. I can start working on it tonight."

"Thanks, Wei," Tam said softly. "It means a lot. It's the only thing I have to help me understand what happened, since I can't ask them."

"Do you want me to email them to you as I translate, or all together once I'm done?"

"Send them as you go along. I really want to start reading as soon as possible." She went around the desk and hugged him.

"You should talk to Ma, tell her the truth," Wei urged. "She worries about you, so far away."

"I will, but not this trip. I'm already nervous about everything. I don't have anything left to deal with her."

Wei looked at her. "Why do you need to deal with her? Just tell her the truth. She understands more than you think." He stared at her intently, and Tam felt as if he were trying to tell her something. It'd been like this since they were young. Wei was the one who understood their mother, while Tam always seemed to get in a fight with her.

When Tam didn't say anything, Wei shook his head. "Listen to your older brother. Talk to Ma. Soon."

Tam sighed. "I will." She turned to go and muttered under her breath, "One of these days."

THREE DAYS LATER, Tam stood in their Beijing hotel room after a morning of sightseeing and opened the safe. She was relieved to see their passports, the orphanage donation in new bills, and their extra money still inside. She had been nervous to leave so much cash in the room, more than six thousand dollars, but it was better than carrying it with her.

"Angela, are you almost done?" she called toward the bathroom door. "We need to hurry."

She slammed the safe shut and stared down at her bare left ring finger. She'd finally taken her wedding ring off when they arrived in China, and it was now sitting in the safe along with the money. She was starting a new stage of life without Tony. It still pained her to think of him and how he died, especially when she started to read the first few pages of Mia's journal, which Wei had sent to her. But she knew she had to move on, and taking off the ring he gave her seemed like the right first step.

Tam gathered her purse and the bag of presents for Tony's mother. Their guide in Beijing was about to take them to the *hutong* where she lived with Fei-Yin.

"Angela, are you ready? Mr. Yang is waiting."

Angela finally emerged from the bathroom, her face pale.

"Are you okay?"

Angela held a hand over her stomach and said, "My belly hurts."

Tam crouched down in front of her and said, "I know. My belly hurts too. I haven't seen Tony's mom in so long. And remember, she probably won't know who we are."

Angela nodded. "I know. But I'm still a little scared to meet her."

Tam hugged her. She knew how the girl felt. She was nervous for Angela to meet her grandmother too.

36

MIA'S JOURNAL

Once upon a time, there was a little girl who lived in an orphanage in Guangdong Province for all of her childhood until she aged out at fourteen. That little girl was me.

I didn't have a very good start to life. When I was only a few weeks old, my birth parents put me in a cardboard box with a thin blanket and placed the box outside a Social Welfare Institute. There was a note pinned to the blanket that said they were sorry they couldn't afford my medical care and listed my birth date but no name. Do you have any idea what's it's like to wonder if my parents ever gave me a name? Or was I a nameless baby, a nobody because of my congenital heart defect?

This was why I wanted to give you the perfect name, Angela. I wanted you to have a name that meant something, to know you were wanted. I took one look at your little scrunched-up face when you were born and I knew you were my angel.

The ayis, nannies who took care of us at the orphanage, named me Mei. Mei wasn't even a real name. It's short for mei mei, or little sister. When I was old enough, I asked my favorite ayi, Xing Xing Ayi, if they didn't give me a real name because they thought I was going to die. She smoothed back the flyaway hairs from around my face and told me that the other ayis were afraid to pick me up because I was so tiny and so sick. They thought I wouldn't survive. But Xing Xing Ayi believed in me.

She had taken a special interest in me because she said I reminded her of the infant daughter she'd lost. Her daughter was born prematurely and her lungs and other organs hadn't developed properly. Despite the doctor's best efforts, the baby passed away before she was even a month old.

If it weren't for Xing Xing Ayi, I would have died as an infant too. I needed surgery for my heart defect, but the orphanage didn't have the funds. Xing Xing Ayi turned to an American volunteer called Xiao Cici. The director had grudgingly allowed her to come once a week because her husband made a big donation to the orphanage. Xing Xing was one of the few ayis who would even talk to her. Most of the ayis eyed the white woman with distrust, muttering under their breath that the wai guo ren was butting her nose in where it didn't belong. When Xing Xing Ayi told her about me, Xiao Cici started a fundraiser among her group of expats to raise money for my surgery.

The other ayis thought Xing Xing was crazy to get attached to me. They truly believed I was going to die soon and scolded Xing Xing for wasting her energy on me, telling her to focus on the stronger, cuter kids who might have a chance at a life. But Xing Xing Ayi stood her ground. She's the one who taught me to go after what I believe in.

She fed me more, held and rocked me, and whispered to me to hang in there until Xiao Cici was able to raise the funds for my surgery and get it approved through the higher-ups in the orphanage. It took months

*for the request to move through the multiple levels of directors, and by
the time my surgery was approved, even Xing Xing wondered if I was
going to make it.*

*But I did. She said I was a fighter. Against all odds, and against all
the pessimistic predictions of the other ayis, I survived my surgery and
recovered. Xiao Cici took me home with her for a few weeks after I was
discharged from the hospital. The director and Xiao Cici actually had a
tug-of-war with me at the hospital. The director tried to pull me out of
Xiao Cici's arms because she didn't want her taking me home, but Xiao
Cici wouldn't let go. I still remember the thrill that would run down
my spine at the image. I loved to hear how Xiao Cici fought for me, and
I made Xing Xing Ayi tell me the story a million times, clapping my
hands when she got to the part about the fight.*

*My heart was the reason I never went running with Tam. She used
to tease me and call me lazy, but I never told her the real reason why. I
didn't want her feeling sorry for me. And I didn't want to prove those
ayis right by dropping dead from running.*

*Because those other ayis considered me a yao zhe baby, one who
would never live to adulthood. And even when I recovered, they still
avoided me. They believed I was bad luck; they shook their heads with
pity whenever they saw me and generally ignored me.*

*But I proved those ayis wrong; I have lived to adulthood and I have
you. I will always provide for you, even if I have to beg or steal to keep
you fed and happy. You will never live in an orphanage the way I did.
That's why I changed my mind and realized I had to tell Tony the truth.
When that feeling came back a few months ago, the feeling that the ayis
were right and I will die soon, I knew I needed to make sure you are
taken care of in case something happens to me. And who better to take
care of you than your father and Tam, who was there when you were
born and who loved you as if you were her own?*

37

TAM AND ANGELA piled into the van in front of their Beijing hotel along with the Donovans, the family from Long Island who were adopting a boy from the same orphanage as Charlie.

Paige, the Donovans' ten-year-old daughter, grabbed Angela's hand. "Let's sit in the wayback together." The girls had bonded on a tour of the Forbidden City and Tiananmen Square that morning, and now they scampered to the back together. They'd all been astounded that car seats weren't required for Angela in this country.

The Donovans had adopted Paige over nine years ago from China. Paige's long black hair hung down to her waist, and she was long-legged like both her parents. Tam couldn't get over how much she physically resembled her parents, even though she was Chinese and they were Caucasian.

"Why can't you speak Mandarin?" Tam heard Angela ask Paige.

Tam turned to see Paige duck her head in embarrassment. "My parents made me go to Chinese school, but I dropped out. I wanted to play lacrosse and soccer and hang out with my friends on the weekend."

Kelly Donovan smiled at her daughter. "I think she's completely Americanized. We try to keep the Chinese culture and traditions in our house, but she can't speak Mandarin, I'm afraid."

Tam smiled at Paige. "I dropped out of Chinese school too."

Paige's eyes grew wide. "You did? But you can speak Mandarin."

"Not very well. I have a five-year-old's understanding of it. Now I wish I had stayed in school."

Sean Donovan laughed. "Hear that, Paige? Maybe you'll consider going back to Chinese school."

Paige gave them a doubtful look. "Maybe."

Mr. Yang, their guide, had the driver drop Tam and Angela off at the entrance to the *hutong* where Fei-Yin lived, about a mile north of their hotel. "I'll be back in three hours, okay?"

They waved as the van drove off, taking the Donovans to the Hongqiao Pearl Market to do some shopping and buy a pearl necklace for Paige while Tam and Angela visited with Tony's mother. Tam was glad the adoption agency had provided a guide to help them navigate around Beijing. She was disoriented from being in a new country, and it was nice to not have to rely on her iffy Mandarin to get around.

Tam pulled her down jacket tighter around her as she and Angela walked along the narrow streets of the traditional residential area. The travel agent had warned her that Beijing would still be cold like New York, while Guangzhou, where they'd meet Charlie and finalize the adoption, would be more like Florida.

Tam glanced at the paper with the directions she'd jotted down to Fei-Yin's gray-brick home. She slowed her pace and looked around. They had just come from a bustling, modern part of Beijing, with tall buildings, big hotels, and shopping malls, and entering this alleyway was like stepping back in time. The homes were all inter-connected, one old walled courtyard home right next to another. Tam looked down the street, and here and there she saw old men and women sitting on wooden chairs, chatting to one another with mugs of tea in hand, or playing what looked like chess.

Angela was walking slowly in front of Tam, looking right and left. It was like being in a maze, and Fei-Yin had warned them about getting lost. They could hear shouting in the distance, and as they turned a corner, they saw a woman pedaling a three-wheeled cart. Tam listened closely and realized she was saying over and over again, "*Mai pijiu! Mai pijiu!*" Tam laughed; she'd never seen a street vendor selling beer right at people's doorsteps, much like the ice cream man did at home in his truck.

Looking down again at Fei-Yin's directions, Tam counted the number of homes they passed and peeked into one open door. She saw a small courtyard with a tree growing in the middle of it and a bicycle leaning against a wall. Small pots of plants lined the court-yard, and all sorts of tools were strewn about. A honey-colored dog sat in front of the door to the inside. Angela darted toward it, but Tam pulled her back.

She finally found the right home, with the red door and two lions flanking it, and just as Fei-Yin had said, the outer door was open. They walked into the small but neat courtyard. It was much tidier than the one they'd just seen.

Tam called out, "Hello?"

A woman emerged from the inner door, wiping her hands on a small towel. She looked to be in her early thirties and had shoulder-length hair.

"Angela! You look just like your mama." Fei-Yin spoke in flaw-

less English. She held Angela in her arms and greeted Tam, beckon-
ing them inside. "Xing Xing is in here."

She led them into the sparsely furnished central room, where an
old woman was seated in a large sofa-like chair with a blue blanket
wrapped around her. A space heater next to her warmed the room,
which was a welcome relief from the biting cold outside. The smell
of ginger and garlic lingered in the air, mixing with the sweet and
pungent odor of the incense sticks burning at the altar at one end of
the room. Tam glanced around at the modern furniture, all steel and
glass, which was a stark contrast to the neighborhood outside.

Tam went to Tony's mother's side, and her heart dropped to see
how frail she was. She knelt next to the chair.

"*Ni hao.* It's me, Tamlei, Li Qiang's wife. It's so good to see you
again," Tam said in Mandarin.

Xing Xing didn't respond, only stared straight ahead. Angela
spoke up from Tam's side. "*Wo shi* Angela." I'm Angela.

Xing Xing turned to study the little girl, her forehead crinkled
as if puzzling out who this was. Suddenly, she broke into a big smile.
"Mei! You've finally come back to see me."

Angela turned to Tam, worry clouding her eyes. "That's Mama's
Chinese name."

Tam reached out to touch Angela's cheek. "It's okay. You look
like your mama. She probably thinks you're her." She was going to
introduce Angela as Mei's daughter, but now she thought better of
it. The old woman seemed so overjoyed that Mei had come to see
her, and she didn't want to confuse her further.

Xing Xing didn't say anything else, but her eyes roamed over the
little girl's face. Fei-Yin had told her that Xing Xing very rarely recognized her anymore, and on the few occasions when she did speak,
she spoke of the past, about her mother and being a young wife.

They spent the next few hours in that room, visiting with Fei-Yin and Xing Xing. Tam was glad the old woman didn't know her son and Mia were gone. She watched Angela come alive as she talked to her mother's friend and hovered by her grandmother's side.

When Angela ran into the bathroom to wash her hands before eating the lychee nuts that Fei-Yin was peeling, Tam asked, "Did you know Angela is Tony's child?"

"Yes." Fei-Yin's hands stilled and she looked straight into Tam's eyes. "I know what Mei did was wrong. She shouldn't have slept with your husband. I'm not condoning what she did. But she's been in love with Li Qiang since she was six. I tried to tell her to let him go, especially when he married you, but she just couldn't. She loved him so much." Fei-Yin wiped her hands on a napkin. "I hope one day you can forgive her. I know she loved you like a sister."

Tam didn't respond. Her heart was in turmoil. She'd loved Mia too. But Mia had betrayed her.

Fei-Yin turned to Angela when she came back into the room. "Would you like to hear stories from when your mama and I were growing up? And when she first met your father? Even though the orphanage wasn't a nice place, we did have some good times together. And Xing Xing watched out for us as best as she could. Your grandmother was so good to us."

Angela nodded eagerly. "Yes. I want to hear about my mama and my baba." She pulled her chair next to Xing Xing, and Fei-Yin passed her the plate of peeled lychees. Angela ate the sweet, juicy fruit with one hand and held her grandmother's hand with the other. She listened with wide eyes as Fei-Yin told them many stories, holding tightly to Xing Xing's hand the whole time.

38

MIA'S JOURNAL

I told you about the orphanage, remember? Everything I said about it was true. It was located in southern China, with its humid subtropical climate. The summers were unbelievably hot and stifling, and the orphanage always had a certain smell: sour milk, soiled diapers, and sweat from so many bodies. There were bugs everywhere: mosquitoes that buzzed around our ears and left red welts all over our bodies, flying cockroaches as big as a baby's hand, cicadas that roared outside, louder than the cries inside, and bedbugs that infested the entire building. One foreign volunteer once ran out of there, screaming about the fucking bugs. She never came back, but for weeks, the older kids imitated her and shouted, "Fook n buh!" whenever they saw a bug. I told Tam that story once, but I didn't tell her it was when I was living in the orphanage. She thought it was so funny, and we ran around yelling "Fook n buh!" and then laughing hysterically until Tony thought there was something wrong with us.

We didn't have much in the orphanage. We were starved for attention, the babies stuck in a crib all day long and the older kids confined within the walls that imprisoned us, except for a few lucky ones who got to go to school. We were always hungry. Most days, the only thing we were given was milk powder, and hot water for the babies and rice or congee for the older children. If we were lucky, sometimes we got bits of vegetables or meat with the rice. I remember one time I was so hungry I picked up a bug and tried to eat it. An older girl named Fei-Yin (Yes! your auntie Fei-Yin—we've known each other since we were little girls) grabbed the bug out of my hand and threw it away. She shoved her rice bowl at me and told me to eat the rest of hers because her teacher had given her leftover dumplings at school. And wanting so much to believe her, I picked up her bowl and devoured the rest of her rice. I became her loyal friend after that.

The one bright spot in my dull life was Xing Xing Ayi. Her real name is Xin Yuan, but when I was four, I gave her that nickname. She was singing a song about stars, xing xing, and she said I suddenly laughed and pointed to her. To me, she was a star, and the nickname stuck.

Sometimes, she'd bring in little gifts for some of the kids, a piece of candy or a sticker, but to us, they were treasures. When I told her Fei-Yin had shared her rice with me, she brought Fei-Yin a whole bag of chips, all to herself. You should have seen the other kids' eyes growing bigger as they stared at the bag. Of course Fei-Yin shared, because that's the kind of person she is. I wouldn't have. I would have shared with only Fei-Yin, but not the other kids, who were mean to us. Some of the bigger kids used to hit or pinch us, leaving bruises on our arms and legs. But when *Fei-Yin* shared with them, they stopped hitting us, so maybe she was smart to share.

As I got older, *Xing Xing Ayi* would take me and *Fei-Yin* home for a couple of days every once in a while when we were sick. She called us her fragile flowers. Like me, *Fei-Yin* needed heart surgery, and *Xiao Cici* had raised the funds for her too. The director refused at first to let *Xing Xing Ayi* foster us because she didn't believe in giving special attention to anyone. But *Xing Xing Ayi* was so persistent, and the director eventually relented.

The times I spent in her home were some of the best times of my childhood. It was there that I met and fell in love with her son, *Li Qiang*.

39

ANGELA WAS SILENT as they made their way back to the street where Mr. Yang would pick them up. They passed more vendors on their bicycles hawking their wares. Tam recognized the Chinese words for "chicken eggs," and knew what the man shouting out *"Jidan!"* was selling. And when they heard another vendor yelling he had toilet paper for sale, they looked at each other and burst into giggles.

Angela didn't speak until they walked into their hotel room. "We're going back tomorrow, right?"

"Yes," Tam said. "Mr. Yang is taking us to the Great Wall in the morning, but we'll visit again in the afternoon. Were you glad to see them?"

Angela nodded. "I wish we could see them more."

"I know." Tam drew Angela to her, and the little girl leaned against her, silent once again.

They were back in the *hutong* by midafternoon the next day. This time, Xing Xing did not recognize Angela at first. She stared blankly into space as Angela told her about their visit to the Great Wall and showed her the jumping pictures she and Paige had taken on the wall.

"You look like little ninjas, flying high above the wall," Fei-Yin said. Angela held the phone up for Xing Xing to see and then glanced at Tam when the old woman didn't react. Tam could see the disappointment in Angela's eyes.

"The best part was the toboggans we took to get down. We whizzed down the mountainside really fast," Angela said. "It felt like we were flying and everything was okay."

She fell silent and stared at her grandmother. Tam wanted to comfort her, but before she could say anything, Xing Xing suddenly spoke.

"You're a good girl, Mei." Xing Xing reached out to touch Angela. "You remind me of myself. When I was a child, my mother always said to me, *xiao tian xin*—she called me little sweetheart—you can be anything you want to be. You don't have to be a concubine like me." She settled back in her chair and smoothed a hand over the blanket. "You see, my mother was my father's second wife. Did I ever tell you that? His first wife only had daughters, so he married my mother hoping to get a son. But she only had one child, me. And so he took a third wife and she gave him the son he wished for."

Fei-Yin translated softly for Tam, and they exchanged a look. Tam remembered how Fei-Yin had said Xing Xing mostly talked about the past now.

"My mother was treated the worst in that household, neither the first wife nor the wife who gave him a son. My father didn't have time for me. I was just another useless daughter. But my mother would whisper to me that I was just as important as my little half brother. The family wanted to marry me off when I was sixteen to a rich man who was looking for a fourth wife. But my mother refused to let them. She threatened to kill herself and come back to haunt the family if they did. My father must have believed her, because he set us up in our own little place and left us alone after that. My mother never told me what she did to make him believe her, but I think she attempted suicide and had him thinking she really would take her own life in order to save me." Xing Xing had a sad smile on her face. "I never saw my half brother and half sisters again."

Tam turned to Angela, thinking the little girl would be afraid or confused by what the old woman was saying. But Angela was completely engrossed in her grandmother's story, her eyes wide and her lips slightly parted.

"That was right around the time of the New Marriage Law, which outlawed the practice of concubines. Women and men were equal in marriage and should have the right to choose their own partners. I remember how my mother rejoiced. She wanted me to find my own husband. Unlike the women of her time, she didn't believe in arranged marriages or a man having several wives." She closed her eyes. "But in a way, she did arrange my marriage to Yaping, your *shushu*. He was our postman's son and he used to help his father deliver the mail. One hot day, she invited him into our home for a drink. She pinched my cheeks to make them rosy and put the cold tea in my hand. She thought he would make a fine husband for me. And she was right."

When Xing Xing opened her eyes, they were so clear Tam could have sworn there was nothing wrong with her mind. She looked like the feisty woman she'd met all those years ago.

"We wanted many children, but it wasn't to be. We only had one child, our son, Li Qiang. It means "strong," did you know that? We knew he was strong, because I was way past the childbearing age when he was born. I'd prayed to Guan Yin for years, ever since we lost our daughter when she was only a few weeks old. I told you about her, remember, Mei? At first I prayed to the Goddess of Mercy to protect my little daughter's soul from torment. I got pregnant three more times after that, but none of them took. Their spirits weren't strong enough for this world. I continued to pray to Guan Yin to protect us in our sorrow and to bring us more children. I had all but given up when we had our baby boy. He was born healthy and strong, a miracle baby, and we named him Li Qiang."

Tam swallowed over the lump in her throat. She never knew she and Tony's mother had shared the same heartache of multiple miscarriages. She had no idea Tony's Chinese name meant "strong." She didn't know his mother had had a daughter before him who didn't live past a few weeks. There was so much she hadn't known about Tony and his family.

"He was such a good strong boy." Xing Xing's face shone with pride. "We raised him to be a good man. When he met you and the other children from the orphanage, he told me he was going to go to America, become successful, and come back and adopt a child or two. He dreamed of marrying a kind woman, someone with a big heart who would want to help those kids as much as he did. And they'd have children of their own."

Tam's mouth opened and tears clogged her throat. Had she lived up to what Tony wanted in a wife? Was she kind with a big heart? Or had he regretted marrying her, wishing instead he'd married Mia, who knew what it was like to grow up in an orphanage and had carried his child?

"But he didn't have any children. Our family seems to have bad luck when it comes to children." Xing Xing tilted her head and her brow furrowed. "Does he have children? Why can't I remember?" She looked at Fei-Yin in confusion. "Where's Li Qiang? Why hasn't he come to see me?" And just like that, the spark of clarity in her eyes died, replaced by the blank look she'd had when they first arrived.

When it was time to go, Angela held tight to Xing Xing. "Bye, Nai Nai," she said, calling her by the Chinese term for paternal grandmother. The old woman didn't say anything, but she placed a hand on her granddaughter's cheek, and there were tears shining in her eyes. The two clung to each other. Tam knew it was likely that they'd not see each other again. Tam's chest hurt, as if her heart was literally breaking for the little girl, who'd lost her mother and father so recently and was now saying good-bye to the only living blood relative she had left in the world.

40

I was six the first time Xing Xing Ayi took me home. I had a bad cold and a cough that shook my whole body, and Xing Xing Ayi was afraid it would turn into bronchitis or worse. She lived about twenty minutes from the orphanage on a block crowded with apartment buildings. Laundry hung from most windows, some strung between the buildings and waving in the breeze like colorful banners advertising the lives of the people within.

She had a sixteen-year-old son, born ten years after her little girl died, and she and her husband considered him their miracle child. She was so proud of him, of how smart he was, at the top of his class. When she brought me home that day, he was sitting at the kitchen table studying. The sun streamed through the open window, and even at six years old, I knew there was something special about him. He looked so studious and handsome, his face scrunched up as he concentrated on the book in front of him, and the sun picked up highlights in his black hair so that it looked like it was on fire.

I fell in love with him at first sight, as I was trying to hide the cough that was threatening to erupt out of my mouth. I didn't want to cough in this handsome boy's face and make him move away from me. I wanted to stare at him for the rest of the night. Even at that young age, I knew he was the one I was tied to by fate. He was my destiny, the one I was connected to by the red thread.

He was kind to me. He treated me like his little sister whenever his mother brought me home. He always had a little treat waiting for me—moon cakes during the Mid-Autumn Festival, lotus-seed buns, and egg tarts, which were my favorite. He knew how much I loved those egg custard tarts and always tried to buy them for me when I was visiting. I knew their family didn't have a lot of money. Their home was really only one big room consisting of the kitchen, living area, and a small alcove where Li Qiang slept, a tiny bedroom for his parents, and a small bathroom. They didn't have a refrigerator or hot water. But to me, their place was the home I'd always dreamed of, and I treasured the days I was allowed to visit.

I would get upset whenever Xing Xing Ayi had to take me back to the orphanage, and I would sulk and refuse to speak to her for days. I was mad when she took Fei-Yin home. Even though Fei-Yin was my closest friend, I thought Xing Xing Ayi was mine and I didn't want to share. I couldn't understand why she didn't adopt me and bring me home for good. But as I got older, I realized she couldn't adopt me because they didn't have the money to do so, or to get around the one-child policy. I learned to stop sulking. If she couldn't adopt me, then I wanted to be allowed to visit her home as much as possible.

Sometimes, Li Qiang would come to the orphanage with his mother. I remember how proud I was to stand by his side and show off to the mean kids that this big handsome boy was my special friend. After helping his mother in the main room, he'd come to me and we'd go visit the kids hidden away.

He'd take my hand and we'd sneak off to visit the kids kept in the secret room. I told you about these kids in the fairy tales, remember? They all had a special need or deformity. There was Yuyuan, an eight-year-old boy with Down syndrome. And little Ming, who had a type of dwarfism and was so tiny, even at fifteen. And a girl about my age named Fan Fan who had spina bifida and was paralyzed from the waist down. I remember how much you loved to hear about Fan Fan, Angela. She was real. She was my friend. In the fairy tale, I told you she was a mermaid who couldn't walk on land. But the Fan Fan in real life was just like the mermaid Fan Fan. She was always smiling and helping others.

These kids were hidden away, but I knew they were there and had told Li Qiang about them. Whenever he came to the orphanage, we found time to sneak into their room and pass out the chips and cookies Li Qiang brought, or stickers and crayons to keep them occupied. They were delighted to see him and crowded around him, vying for his attention. He was so gentle and kind to them all, helping with simple projects or opening bags of chips and feeding those who couldn't do it themselves.

Fan Fan loved Li Qiang too. She told me how she wished she could grow up to marry someone like him. I thought my life was bad, but I guess hers was worse than mine. Because I really thought I was going to grow up and marry Li Qiang, while she would be stuck in institutional life forever.

One day, when Li Qiang was visiting the orphanage, Fei-Yin was sick in bed and couldn't participate in the games he was playing with the other kids. Afterward, Li Qiang went and sat at Fei-Yin's side for an hour, holding her hand and telling her stories that made her laugh. I was so mad. I didn't like seeing him hold her hand like that. And I resented the attention and time he was spending with her. In that moment, I hated her. I even imagined she was faking being sick in order to gain his sympathy.

I wanted Li Qiang to leave her side and come with me to visit our kids, but he just ruffled my hair and said after he read a book to Fei-Yin.

I pushed his hand away and ran from them. I sat sulking in a corner with a book and refused to talk to him when he came to find me later. I wouldn't look at him and stared at the book as if it was the most fascinating thing in the world. And I responded with my snottiest voice that I was busy. See, Angela, I could be just as snotty as you are to me when you don't get your way.

He stared at me for a moment and then shrugged and left. I had wanted him to persuade me to go with him, and I sat seething in the corner. A girl named Yan walked by and smirked at me, telling me the book I was reading was upside down. I wanted to throw the book at her and slap the smile off her face.

I was so mad that when Fei-Yin got better, I did something bad to her.

I was hungry and knew that Gong, an older girl Fei-Yin's age, had hidden a bag of cookies she'd stolen from someone at school that day under her pillow. I waited until I knew Gong was busy somewhere else, and I took her cookies and hid in a closet and ate every single one. Later, when we were going to bed and Gong discovered her cookies missing, she threw a fit.

She threatened to beat up whoever had stolen her cookies, and I told Yan, who was a friend of Gong's, that Fei-Yin took them. Yan gave me a funny look because she knew I was friends with Fei-Yin, but later I

saw her whispering to Gong and pointing to Fei-Yin. I smiled in satisfaction that I had gotten back at Fei-Yin for holding Li Qiang's hand.
See how you like it, I was thinking. But that night, after the ayis
were all sleeping, Gong dragged Fei-Yin out of her bed. She took her
outside and beat her up, bad. When I saw Fei-Yin's black eye and swol-
len face the next day, I was filled with so much remorse I couldn't look
at her. I didn't mean for her to get so hurt. Fei-Yin told the ayis she had
fallen out of bed and hit her face on a corner of the bed. I should have
taken care of her, but instead, I avoided her until her face was almost
back to normal.

When Li Qiang was eighteen, he left for America to study. I was
heartbroken. Xiao Cici had pulled some strings and gotten him a full
scholarship and visa to study at a great university in New York. This
was the same university that her husband had graduated from. Xiao
Cici told me how brilliant Tony was and how he would have gotten a
scholarship without their help. It made my heart proud, as if I had
something to do with his success.

I was sad when he left for America. Xing Xing Ayi brought me
home to say good-bye. When I told him I didn't want him to go, he
reached out and ruffled my hair, telling me he would be back for visits.
Even though he came home every year for a month at the winter holidays,
it wasn't the same, and I missed him something awful.

The years passed and Fei-Yin and I grew up with the other orphans. I never told her I was the one who had gotten her beaten up by
Gong. I tried to make it up to her in other ways. When she was sick,
I'd make sure to grab enough food for Fei-Yin and bring it to her in
bed. When she got her period and thought she was dying since no one
had told us what to expect, I was the one who told Xing Xing Ayi and
brought her to Fei-Yin in the bathroom. She picked Fei-Yin off the floor
and sat us both down and explained the facts of life to us. Fei-Yin and

I stared at each other in horror. We would bleed from down there every month?

Fei-Yin and I grew closer as we got older. She'd often tell me stories at night about the families we'd both have soon. Sometimes, the stories were about the rich American family who would take me out of China and give me everything I wanted in life. Sometimes she would tell about the Chinese family whose baby was confiscated by birth-planning officials in an effort to improve the birth-planning record of a township. That baby was Fei-Yin, and the family would somehow manage to pay off the officials and get Fei-Yin a hukou, a household registration, and they would be reunited and live happily ever after. Her stories filled me with hope; we were able to forget for a while that we were the forgotten ones, abandoned because we were girls or had a birth defect that our families couldn't or wouldn't take care of. We learned at an early age that life was cruel and grew up yearning for something we couldn't have, but Fei-Yin's stories made me feel better.

I often thought about my birth parents, wondering if they missed me and if they'd want me back now that my heart was fixed. I liked to think they had a hard time giving me up, since they kept me for almost a month before abandoning me. I tried to imagine what happened. Did my father and his family make my mother give me up because I was a girl and they were hoping for a boy? Did my mother fight for me as hard as she could before yielding to the family's wishes? Maybe my mother and father had both wanted me, but they were so poor they couldn't get my heart fixed. That was my favorite version of what happened. They desperately wanted to keep me, but they couldn't afford the medical attention I needed and they loved me so much that they gave me up so that I'd have a chance at a life.

Whatever the actual case, I spent many years hopefully waiting for them to come back. I imagined they'd kept track of me, and now that my *heart was fine, they'd show up one day to claim me. But my hopes faded with each year that went by, until I knew that the only chance I'd have at a family was if I was adopted. I didn't care if they were rich or as poor as dirt. I just wanted a family who desperately wanted me, as much as I desperately wanted a family.*

41

THEY FLEW TO Guangzhou the next day. Mr. Yang dropped them off at a small airport with instructions to "stay in this spot. In forty-five minutes, go to that line and check in." No one spoke English and all the signs were in Chinese. Kelly Donovan chewed on her lips, her eyes darting around as she stayed close to Tam. "I'm so glad you're traveling with us. I hate not being able to understand the language and read the signs."

Tam made a face. "I can't read the signs either, and my Mandarin is only just passable."

She proved this when the airport staff thought Sean Donovan had a bomb in his suitcase. They jabbered at her in rapid-fire Mandarin as she desperately tried to figure out what they were saying. With much gesturing and charades, the offending items, Sean's portable speakers, were identified, and they were allowed to board their plane. And in no time at all, they were landing in Guangzhou. Tam squeezed Angela's hand as they walked off the plane. The real reason for their trip to China was about to begin.

"Hello, hello!" An energetic woman in her thirties with long black hair and dressed in a pink twinset waved a sign bearing their names. "My name is Tiffany. I will be your guide while you are in Guangzhou. Welcome, welcome, Donovans and Kwans!" With great cheer, she herded them out to a waiting van. On the ride to the hotel, she handed out paperwork to the two families, which included an update on each child and his most recent measurements and daily routine. Tiffany helped them check in and then accompanied them to their rooms on the Executive Floor.

"We always recommend our families stay on this floor because you'll have access to a lounge that serves breakfast and dinner, as well as drinks and snacks. Many families have found it helpful to have these amenities available in the early days when they are getting acquainted with their new children." There was a lilt to Tiffany's accented English that made Tam think of a lullaby.

Tam's eyes were beginning to droop, and she'd have given anything to lie down for a bit, but Tiffany startled her by clapping her hands loudly.

"I will take you to the Executive Lounge now for dinner. You must eat, get energy for tomorrow to meet your little boys!"

Tam caught Kelly's eye as she unlocked the door to their room, which was down the hall from the Donovans'. Tam's mouth quirked at the corners and she lifted a brow at Kelly. Apparently, Tiffany took her guide duties seriously. After dropping off their bags in their rooms, they followed Tiffany to the lounge.

"Eat, eat!" Tiffany waved her arms with enthusiasm toward the buffet of Chinese and Western foods. Cowed by Tiffany's exuberance, they meekly obeyed, filling their plates and sitting at the table Tiffany had commandeered for them.

"I will meet you in the lobby at eleven o'clock tomorrow and take you to the bank where we will wire transfer your donation to the orphanage. This process has been known to take several hours. We're scheduled to meet your children at two." Tiffany clapped her hands so loudly that Tam dropped the dumpling she was about to place in her mouth as she wondered why they couldn't just give the cash (that they were told to bring) to the orphanage, instead of giving it to the bank and having them wire it. Maybe because they had to change the currency? Tam poked at her dumpling. She was finding it difficult to eat while Tiffany talked. She couldn't get the chopsticks to work, and the food was sliding around on her plate. She didn't know if she was tired or nervous about tomorrow, or if the chopsticks in China were extra slippery. All she knew was that she couldn't seem to get a morsel of food into her mouth while Tiffany was talking.

"I will bring baby bottles and formula for each family, since the paperwork says your children are still drinking from a bottle," Tiffany said. Tam and Kelly exchanged a glance. Charlie was three and a half and the little boy the Donovans were adopting was three. They were still using bottles?

"Okay!" With another vivacious clap, Tiffany stood up. "I will leave you to enjoy your food and I will see you tomorrow. I'm only a WeChat away if you need me!" She waved and was gone before anyone could react.

"Is it just me or do you feel like we were just bombarded by a tornado?" Sean asked.

Paige and Angela giggled while Kelly hit her husband on the arm. "Stop it. She's nice."

Sean turned up his hands. "I didn't say she wasn't nice. She's just so . . . enthusiastic. I need a nap."

Tam laughed and stood. "Me too. I'm going to go unpack and rest. Maybe we'll meet you back here for cocktail hour later?" Tiffany had informed them they served free cocktails and dessert at night.

When Tam and Angela got back to their room, they saw that what looked like a Pack 'n Play with a thin mattress on the bottom had been delivered while they were at dinner. Tam stared at it. In less than twenty-four hours, the crib would hold a little boy, her new son. In that moment, Tam wished more than anything that Tony were there. This was his dream, to adopt a child from the orphanage where his mother had worked. Xing Xing's words echoed in her mind, and she blinked, almost sure that if she turned her head, Tony would be standing next to her. All the paperwork and scrutiny by the American and Chinese governments were about to end. He should have been by her side, anticipating meeting the son they'd waited for.

A hand slipped into hers, and Tam jumped.

"Are you okay?"

Tam cleared her throat. For a moment, she'd thought it was Tony who took her hand. "Yes. I'm just sad that Tony isn't here."

Tam hugged Angela close and they stood for a moment, both staring at the crib.

Tam finally pulled away. "Why don't you take a bath while I unpack?" Angela had wanted to jump in the giant jetted tub as soon as she saw it. She gave a scream of delight and ran into the bathroom. The wall separating the tub from the bedroom was all glass, and Tam raised the blind so she was able to see into the bathroom from the bedroom area.

As she unpacked, the sounds of Angela splashing happily in the tub faded into the background, because all she could think about was the little boy she was about to meet. Would he be scared and unresponsive? Or would he act out like the adoption agency said the children sometimes did? By the time Angela got out of the tub, Tam had finished unpacking and had worked herself up into a nervous mess.

"Can we go get dessert?" Angela bounced on her heels.

"Aren't you tired?" Tam was ready to collapse onto the giant king-size bed. She wished she had half of Angela's energy.

"No. Let's go!" Angela grabbed her hand and pulled her out of their room.

They found Kelly in one of the oversize chairs in the lounge, a glass of red wine in hand. Angela ran off to find Paige, who was filling a plate to take back to her dad in their room. Tam poured herself a glass of pinot grigio and joined Kelly at the table. "I'm so nervous about tomorrow. I think I'm going to throw up."

"Drink up," Kelly said. "Alcohol will help." She took a healthy swallow of her wine and sighed. "I can't stop imagining the worst. It was different last time. Paige was a healthy baby." The Donovans' little boy had a congenital heart defect. His file said he'd already had surgery.

Tam tapped her glass lightly against Kelly's. "Here's to our boys."

"And probably our last quiet night," Kelly said.

They fell into a comfortable silence, each lost in thought about the day to come. This wasn't how Tam had pictured she'd become a mother all those years ago when she first married Tony. And yet, fate had thrown her and Angela together and it was now about to add a little boy to their patchwork family.

Her phone dinged with a WeChat message just as they were

heading back to their rooms. Looking down, she saw it was from
Wei.

WEI: Just emailed you more of Mia's journal.

Tam's heart pounded. She'd become so engrossed in Mia's story
and couldn't wait to read more. She quickened her pace, and once in
the room, she helped Angela get ready for bed. When the little girl
was snuggled in the king-size bed they would share, Tam turned a
small light on at the desk and reached for her laptop. Her fingers
trembled as she opened the document Wei had sent her and began
to read.

42

Do you know how heart-wrenching it was for me to realize my family was never coming back for me? It broke my heart, Angela. I waited and waited for them, but they never came. And as each year passed and no one applied to adopt me, my yearning for a family only grew.

Xiao Cici, whose real name I learned is Cecilia Armstrong, had worked hard over the years to help the orphanage navigate the paperwork for adoptions. She had partnered with an adoption agency in California, and they worked on getting more of our dossiers ready. But only the healthiest, youngest babies were adopted at first. By the time it became popular for Americans to adopt the abandoned girls of China, I was already ten years old and my chances diminished every year. They wanted a cute little baby, not an older child with a birth defect.

Fei-Yin is four years older than me, and she aged out of the system the day she turned fourteen. I was terrified as I listened to her sobs, and they tore at my heart. I was sorry she'd never have her own family, but at the same time, I was glad she wasn't leaving me. I couldn't imagine life at the orphanage without her.

As my own fourteenth birthday drew near, I'd often catch Xing Xing Ayi and Xiao Cici talking quietly together, sending me worried looks. Xiao Cici had gone back to America for several years, where she continued to work with the adoption agency to advocate and raise money for the orphanage. She'd only returned a few months ago when her husband's work brought them back to China, and I knew Xing Xing Ayi had asked her to double her efforts in finding me a family. I had watched as many of the younger, healthier children were adopted, and I wanted it to be my turn, for me to be the chosen one. What was wrong with me? Why was I not wanted? I desperately wanted a mama and a baba of my own. I knew Xiao Cici pushed hard to find me a family, and it almost happened. But something fell through, and the couple pulled out, and no one would ever tell me why. On the eve of my fourteenth birthday, Xing Xing Ayi and Xiao Cici were both there. I had resolved that I wouldn't cry, but the minute they pulled me into their arms, I dissolved in tears. I was about to age out of the adoption system without being chosen. My dream of a better life was shattered.

A dark cloud descended over me, and I was shrouded in despair. What would become of me? Fei-Yin had stayed on at the orphanage because she excelled at school and they hoped she'd receive a scholarship to university. Some of the older children who had aged out still lived there and worked to earn their keep. Some of them disappeared, but I never asked where they went.

One day, I was summoned to the laundry room and told I would be working there. First they gave me the job of hanging up the wet clothes. But the basket weighed so much I couldn't pick it up, no matter how hard I tried. I wasn't very big and those baskets weighed more than I did.

Gong, the older girl who had beaten Fei-Yin up all those years ago, yelled at me to move my lazy butt. I held back my tears and tried to drag the basket. But the clothes spilled out, all over the dirty floor, and Gong clocked me over the head, and I went down. The next thing I knew, I was lying in Xing Xing Ayi's arms and she was yelling at Gong.

Xing Xing Ayi wasn't a big woman, but the girls and other ayis respected her because she'd been there for so long and had the support of Xiao Cici, who proved over the years that she could use her clout to get things done at the orphanage.

After the laundry basket incident, I was put in the washroom, and I immediately wished I was back lugging the heavy baskets. The smells in the washroom of the urine- and poop-soaked diapers and the sweaty clothes were enough to make anyone gag. The heat from the room and the pervasive odor soon made me light-headed and short of breath. Without warning, I felt myself blacking out, and before I could catch myself, I slumped to the floor.

Once again, I awakened in Xing Xing Ayi's arms, but this time she wasn't yelling. She smoothed the hair from my head and told me she was worried. The orphanage was getting too crowded, more babies coming in every day, so they had to put two, three, sometimes four in a crib. She didn't know how long I could stay at the orphanage, since there was no way I'd get a scholarship to school like Fei-Yin had.

I remember being so scared that I gritted my teeth to keep from crying out in fear. Xing Xing Ayi told me the director was going to pull me out of school soon, and she didn't know what was going to happen to me.

Gong told me that night that if I couldn't help around the orphanage, they would put me out on the streets to become a beggar or sell my body for food. I didn't know if she was saying this just to be mean, but I couldn't sleep. I tossed and turned all night, images of living on the streets *and begging filling my dreams. As much as I hated life in the orphanage, the alternative made me want to pee in my pants. I cursed my fate, and as I often did when things were bleak, I thought of Li Qiang. I dreamed he would come back to China and rescue me.*

As the weeks passed, I tried as hard as I could in school, but the numbers made no sense and I couldn't write a suitable essay. I wasn't smart like Fei-Yin. At the orphanage, they moved me to the baby room to help with the feedings and changings. I thought I had finally found a job I could do, but the ayis there soon complained to the director that I took too much time with each baby, holding them and talking to them. They said I disrupted their routine and was more of a hindrance than a help. The nightmares escalated at night so that I became afraid to sleep. I would lie on my scratchy pallet in the dark, my eyes wide as I listened to the sounds of so many children in the same room, snoring, coughing, or tossing in their sleep. Was this better than finding my own way in the outside world?

Then Xing Xing Ayi pulled me aside one day and told me about these special schools, kind of like a medical school where they teach you skills like physical therapy and massage therapy. But all the programs were full. And that's when she asked if I wanted to become an assistant to a woman who practiced traditional Chinese medicine. She was a neighbor of Xing Xing Ayi's and was looking for help. She said I'd assist in acupuncture treatments, help with the massages, and learn about Chinese medicine and qigong. It'd be kind of like the programs, only I wouldn't live with her.

I couldn't believe it. I was so happy to be given this opportunity. But where would I live? I asked Xing Xing Ayi if I would stay at the orphanage and she said no. And that's when she asked if I wanted to live with her and her husband. Since Li Qiang was in America, they had room and I'd be earning my own keep. They would expect me to help out around the house. I remember the stern look she gave me when she said this, but she couldn't fool me. I'd met her husband, Kwan Xiansheng, many times when I stayed with them, and he was just as kindhearted as she was.

Can you imagine how I felt at that moment, Angela? I was finally getting the most unbelievable gift. I didn't get my own family, but I would finally escape the orphanage and no longer fear living on the streets. I vowed then and there I'd be the best assistant this doctor ever had, and I would work so hard she'd wonder what she ever did without me.

And best of all, I was going to live in Li Qiang's home. Even though he wouldn't be there most of the year, I'd be in his home and see him every day when he came back from New York. My heart almost burst with happiness. My new life was about to begin.

43

TAM WOKE EARLY the next morning, the anticipation of meeting Charlie setting off butterflies in her stomach. At the same time, she couldn't get the image of Mia as a little girl living in the orphanage out of her mind. How scared and lonely she must have been, desperate for the love and affection of a family, which Tam had taken for granted all her life. How terrified Mia must have felt, knowing she was about to age out at only fourteen, ill-equipped to live on her own, her chance at having a real life gone. If it hadn't been for the kindness of Tony's mother, Mia might have ended up on the streets or, at best, stuck in a menial job.

Tam had read everything Wei emailed long into the night, until the words blurred before her eyes and she couldn't hold her head up any longer. She knew she should have gone to bed early in anticipation of today, but she couldn't stop reading. It was like staring at the scene of an accident; she was horrified but unable to tear her eyes away.

After breakfast and two coffees at the Executive Lounge with the Donovans, they went back to their respective rooms to prepare for Tiffany's arrival. Tam had brought cheese puffs, Goldfish crackers, and small bags of M&M'S. She put them into the monkey backpack she and Angela had chosen for Charlie, along with a ball and a teddy bear.

Her phone dinged with a WeChat message. It was from Adam, wishing them luck. Tam smiled and thanked him, and her WeChat dinged again. This time it was her mother, requesting a video chat.

She picked up and her mom asked, "Did you meet him yet?"

Tam laughed. "Hello, Mom. No, not yet. We're about to leave."

"Okay, I just wanted to say good luck." Zhong-Ying paused. "And to tell you Wei told me everything."

Tam sucked in a breath. "What? What did Wei tell you?"

"He told me about Tony and Mia, and that Tony is Angela's father."

"What!" Tam dropped the backpack on the bed and her mouth opened in shock. "I'm going to kill him. I told him not to tell you."

"Why shouldn't he tell me? I'm your mother. And why didn't you tell me yourself?"

"I didn't want to get into it before we left for China." Tam sat down on the bed and closed her eyes, wishing Wei was in front of her right now so she could wring his neck.

"But you told Wei."

"Yeah, but he's, I don't know, calmer than you. I knew he wouldn't make a big deal out of it." Tam opened her eyes and looked at the clock. It was almost time to meet Tiffany. Could her mom have called at a worse moment? The woman really knew how to time things.

"Big deal!" her mom shouted. "Of course it's a big deal. I'm your mother. I can help."

"Mom, it was a lot for me to take in, and I didn't know how to tell you. You wouldn't understand."

That was the wrong thing to say. Her mom sputtered and started speaking a combination of English and Taiwanese. "Not understand. You know not what I've been through in my life. Let me tell you about the time before—"

Tam rolled her eyes and cut her mom off. "Since when did you think your husband had a mistress who you thought was his cousin? You and Dad have been married forever."

"I have stories I can tell you, but you never want to listen. You too busy for your mother. Think you know it all and your mother too old to understand. Well, I understand because when I was living in Taiwan—"

Tam cut her off again. "Mom. Stop it. This is why I didn't tell you. I'm about to meet my new son and I can't deal with this right now. I've got to go. Bye." And she hung up, knowing how much her mom hated to be hung up on.

Her WeChat immediately dinged again, twice, and she sighed, thinking it was her mom. But the first message was a text from Wei.

> **WEI:** Hey, wanted to give you the heads-up that Ma saw notebook as I was translating and I ended up telling her the whole story. Sorry! She'll probably call you soon.

It was followed by the embarrassed-face emoji.

> **TAM:** She already called!!!

WEI: Oops!

TAM: I'm going to kill you, but I need you to translate so I guess you get to live for now.

The other text was from Tiffany, saying she was in the lobby.

"Angela, we've got to go." Tam gathered the bags, and together they went out the door to meet Tiffany and the Donovans.

"The bank is a few blocks away, so we'll walk," Tiffany said, leading them out of the hotel. "The driver will pick us up when we're done and take us to the Civil Affairs Office to meet your new children." She clapped her hands, and Tam saw Kelly, who was standing next to Tiffany, jump at the sound.

They followed Tiffany to the bank and handed over their documents for the money transfer. Tam couldn't imagine it would take as long as Tiffany said, but as the first hour went by and they continued to sign this and hand over that document, she started to think maybe Tiffany was right. By noon, they didn't appear any closer to getting the money wired. Angela and Paige were practicing dance steps from Paige's ballet class. When Angela crashed into a man, Tiffany herded everyone into a back room.

Two and a half hours later, both families' wire transfers finally went through. "Quickly, quickly," Tiffany said as she made shooing motions with her arms and herded them into the van. Tam and Kelly shared a look. Did Tiffany think she was tending a flock of sheep?

"Okay, everyone." Tiffany turned to address them from the front seat. "Take a deep breath. You're about to meet your new sons. We'll be there in twenty minutes."

Tam did as Tiffany suggested, but that only made the butterflies in her stomach worse, and the driving didn't help. The driver, Mr. Thomas, dodged between cars and buses and honked his horn when a truck weaved and cut in front of them. On a long freeway overpass suspended high above the city, they had a near miss with a bus that came so close she could see the contents of the steamed bun a little girl was eating.

They passed old quarters of Guangzhou; gray cement blocks piled on top of one another with bars on the balconies like zoo cages. Laundry waved without shame, and here and there a green plant reached its leaves out of the bars as if yearning for freedom. The old buildings were squeezed in the shadows of high-rise offices and construction sites for luxurious skyscrapers.

Mr. Thomas finally pulled up at their destination. Everyone piled out of the van on shaky legs, and Tam looked at their little group. Everyone was silent, and Kelly looked as stricken and sick as Tam felt. Tiffany led them down an alleyway toward the building. She rushed them through the doors and into a small elevator. Tam was just starting to feel claustrophobic when the doors opened again and they stepped into a dim hallway before walking into a large room.

On the wall to their right, she saw in red letters ADOPTION REGISTRY CENTER OF GUANGDONG PROVINCE. Ahead of them was a long cushioned seating area. She peered around Tiffany and saw an empty room. Where were the kids?

"I just called the directors. They'll be bringing the children out in a few minutes. Does anyone have to use the bathroom?" Tiffany asked.

Sean raised his hand. "I do." Tiffany pointed to the men's room, and just as he went in the door, Tam saw two men and a woman coming toward them. She didn't see where they came from, but suddenly they were there and getting closer. And the woman and one of the men each held a child in their arms.

"Oh, no. They're here. Sean! Get out of the bathroom now. The kids are here," Tiffany yelled through the door of the bathroom.

Sean burst into the room. "I thought I had time to pee," he said, but then his attention was drawn to the kids. Tiffany went to meet them, and a moment later, she called out: "Jia Ping's family." She beckoned to the Donovans and they approached the little boy the woman was holding. Tam could see tears in Kelly's eyes as she reached out and took Jia Ping, or Aidan, as they named him, in her arms. He immediately started crying, and Sean and Paige crowded around as Tiffany translated for them.

Rocking back and forth on her toes and heels, Tam tried to stay in the moment to remember everything. She was aware of Angela next to her, but everything else faded away. Her attention was on the gray-clad little boy in the man's arms. Was that him? Was that Charlie? *Oh, Tony, how I wish you were standing here with me.*

Just as she thought she couldn't wait anymore, Tiffany called out, "Jia Li's mommy," and Tam and Angela stepped forward. Before she could really look at the little boy, he was in her arms. Tiffany grabbed Tam's cell phone and took a video of their first moments with Charlie. Tam gingerly held the little boy and he stared back at her with wide, terrified eyes but didn't make a sound. Unlike Aidan, who was wailing loudly, Charlie only stared, and then shifted his eyes to Angela. Tam couldn't feel anything. She stood there gently rocking the little boy until Tiffany told her to sit down. Angela handed the teddy bear to Charlie and he clutched it like a lifeline.

"This is one of the ayis who took care of the children." Tiffany gestured to the woman. "Feel free to ask her any questions. And these"—she motioned to the two men—"are directors from the orphanage."

The directors presented them with a plaque thanking them for their donations and for adopting the children. The ayi gave them each a small photo album of pictures of the boys and a backpack. Tam knew she signed some paperwork Tiffany thrust in front of her, but for all the attention she paid it, she could have just signed away a kidney.

Tam had pictured this moment so many times, first with Tony by her side, then later by herself. It was both what she expected and not. She felt detached, as though she were floating above the scene watching the drama unfold. Thoughts flitted in and out of her mind, and she couldn't seem to grasp that she was actually holding Charlie in her arms. She didn't cry like Kelly or jump up and down like Paige and Angela, or bow her head as if giving a prayer of thanks like Sean. Her mind was a void and her feelings were numb, as if coated with a layer of Novocain.

"Come, let's take a group photo." Tiffany lined them up in front of the ADOPTION REGISTRY CENTER OF GUANGDONG PROVINCE sign. Tam thought she smiled, but later when she saw the picture, she looked like a deer caught in headlights.

"Okay! Time to go back to the hotel!" Tiffany shouted, and Tam jolted. Before she could move and say good-bye, the two men and the ayi disappeared.

Tiffany cheerfully guided them back out and into the waiting van. The entire group was silent, obeying her commands without question.

"Parents, congratulations!" Tiffany gave one of her signature claps inside the van. "These two lucky boys are now part of your wonderful families and will bring you much joy. And they may not poop for a few days as they get accustomed to the food outside of the orphanage, or they might have diarrhea."

Despite her state of disbelief at finally having Charlie in her arms, Tam's mouth twitched at Tiffany's remarks.

Tiffany beamed back at Tam. "If that happens, no problem. I will take you to the pharmacy and find medicinal herbs to fix that up!" She brushed off her hands as if washing away a pesky bug. "I will leave you at the hotel to get acquainted with your new children, but if you need me, I'm just a WeChat away. Tomorrow, we will return here to the Civil Affairs Office and complete the paperwork. They will interview you, and then the boys will officially be your sons. Any questions?"

Tiffany dropped them off at the hotel, and Tam was surprised to see it was already five o'clock. After making a plan to meet the Donovans in an hour for dinner, Tam and Angela brought Charlie to their room. She wanted to change him. He was bundled in so many layers of clothing, he could barely move. He'd still yet to say anything, but he held tight to the teddy bear.

When Tam took off the big puffy sweat suit he wore, she was shocked to see how thin he was. Removing the shirt he wore underneath, she could feel every rib under her fingertips.

"He's so skinny," Angela said. "He looks like one of those starving children on TV."

"I can't believe how tiny he is," Tam said.

Charlie looked more like a nine-month-old baby than a boy of three and a half. He stared at them with a blank expression and didn't make a sound. She'd noticed his breath didn't smell good and she pulled out the puffs and Goldfish she'd forgotten about. Putting some in a snack cup with a lid made of soft flaps that allowed him to reach in but prevented the snacks from spilling out if tipped over, she gave the cup to Charlie. He took it and immediately started eating. He ate like he was starving, and Tam couldn't take her eyes off the little hand pinching a snack between two fingers before bringing it to his mouth.

Angela sat on the floor next to Charlie, fascinated by their new family member. Tam collapsed into the chair at the desk, so emotionally drained she felt as if someone had sucked out all her insides, leaving just a hollow shell. She was still having trouble believing that Charlie was actually here in this room with them.

Tony, can you see him? We finally got him.

She slumped against the desk, and her elbow jostled the mouse of her laptop, making the screen come to life. Tam glanced at it, and there, waiting in her inbox, was an email from Wei. Instantly she was alert and sat up straight, her hand reaching for the mouse to click open the document. Her curiosity to read Mia's journal outweighed her fatigue and emotional turmoil. She glanced at the kids, and seeing they were fine, she turned her attention to Wei's email.

44

MIA'S JOURNAL

I can still remember those first few weeks out of the orphanage as if it were yesterday. The bag I packed was pitifully small. When I said good-bye to Fan Fan and the other kids in the special room, Fan Fan gave me a hug. She asked if I would be back to visit them and to let her know when I married Li Qiang.

I promised I would and left before they could see me cry.

But Fei-Yin and I cried together. This would be the first time we'd live apart in our lives. She'd gotten a scholarship to university and would soon be living there. She had needed surgery right after she aged out, and when the orphanage refused to use the funds that were raised for her, Xiao Cici had gotten angry. She and her husband had fostered Fei-Yin and paid for her surgery themselves.

I asked Fei-Yin if she was upset that Xing Xing Ayi had asked me to live with her. Fei-Yin gave me a hug and said no. She was about to go to university and she thought it was my chance to make something of my life, that I deserved this. She told me to forget what the ayis always said about me, that I was a yao zhe baby destined to die young. She said it was just a stupid superstition.

I hung my head, suddenly filled with shame for what I had done to her all those years ago when she'd always stood by me. I knew I had to tell her the truth. And I finally did. I told her I was the one who ate Gong's cookies and then told Yan that Fei-Yin did it. I was so ashamed I couldn't look in her eyes. I waited for Fei-Yin to yell at me, to tell me I was a despicable person and that she hated me, but instead, she told me she'd always known. Yan had told her that day.

I couldn't believe she'd known all these years! And that she was still my friend after I'd betrayed her like that.

But she just smiled at me and said she understood. I was hurt that Li Qiang spent so much time with her when she was sick. And she told me I'd made it up to her in many ways since. You see, Angela, even then she had a more generous heart than me. If the roles were reversed, I would have been angry that she threw me under the bus. And I would have been jealous that Xing Xing Ayi hadn't asked me to live with her before I left for university. I gave her a hug and vowed to be a better friend from that day forward.

Even though I had been to Xing Xing Ayi's house plenty of times, this time was different. I was here to stay and didn't have to return to the orphanage in a couple of days. When I stepped inside, I was filled with so much joy I wanted to twirl and dance. This would be my home now. I would sit on the faded blue couch with the worn spots on the cushions, underneath the framed paintings of birds and peonies, Xing Xing Ayi's favorite flowers. There was the tiny kitchen where I'd help cook our food and the altar with a statue of Guan Yin, the Goddess of Mercy, on one side, and a shrine to Kwan Xiansheng's and Xing Xing's ancestors on the other. And most precious of all, I had my own little sleeping alcove where once Li Qiang had slept and dreamed. The happy Buddha statue he'd kept on the shelf above his bed was still there, and I rubbed my hand across it, unable to believe my luck.

Kwan Xiansheng was wonderful to me. He told me he was happy to have me live with them because Xing Xing Ayi had been sad, not having anyone to boss around at home since Li Qiang went to America. I loved how he bantered with Xing Xing and the way she swatted his arm when he teased her. I wanted a relationship like that.

He told me to stop calling him Kwan Xiansheng, Mr. Kwan, and to call him Shushu, Uncle. When I heard, my patched-up heart nearly burst out of my chest. I knew they both worked hard, he as a postman but also taking other jobs to supplement his income, and I vowed to do whatever I could to make their lives easier.

I worked hard for the next few years. I learned so much from the doctor, Madame Zheng. She taught me about qi, the body's vital energy, or life force, and about the meridians, or channels they circulate through. She knew so much about herbal medicines, and her office was stocked with jars of various roots, twigs, and bark, as well as other more mysterious and strange substances that I knew were from animal sources. The room always smelled musty, with an earthy scent rising from the medicinal plants and animal parts, such as the dried seahorses (to aid in asthma, heart disease, and impotence) and fetuses of anteaters and tiger penis (to increase a man's virility). I knew to most people it wasn't a pleasant odor, but to me, it was the smell of freedom. I was no longer trapped behind the walls of the orphanage. I'd much rather be breathing in the smell of snake oil, maple bark, and ginseng root.

Madame Zheng taught me how to assist when she performed acupuncture, and later, she even allowed me to assist when she performed moxibustion, the burning of an herb above the skin to apply heat to *acupuncture points. But best of all, she taught me about tui na. To my surprise, I had a natural gift for it. Madame Zheng said when it comes to massage, people either had the touch or they didn't. And I did. She showed me the acupressure points and how to open the body's qi to get the energy moving in the meridians and the muscles. She told me that tui na wasn't about how strong the masseuse was; rather, it works deeply with the positive energy of the body. I learned how to use rhythmic compressions along different energy channels of the body to establish harmonious flow of qi throughout the body to bring it back into balance. I paid attention to her teachings, and soon she was letting me work on most of her patients. I knew Madame Zheng was happy with my work because she often praised me and told me she didn't know what she'd done before I became her assistant.*

I had moved in with the Kwans in the summer, so I had to wait many months before Li Qiang came home that first year. When he did, I couldn't wait to show him how grown-up I'd become. I was still six months shy of my fifteenth birthday, but I felt as if I'd aged years since I'd last seen him. I felt for sure he'd see me as a woman this time, and not the little girl he last saw.

But to my dismay, he treated me just the way he always had. He ruffled my hair and called me Mei Mei. He'd brought a doll for me; it was called Barbie, and he said all the girls in America were playing with them. I might not have known much about America back then, but I would bet no fourteen-, almost fifteen-year-old was playing with Barbie. I swallowed my disappointment and thanked him, happy to see him again, even if he still considered me a child.

I insisted he have his sleeping alcove back. I'd happily sleep on the couch for the month he was home. I was content on the lumpy couch and glad to have him across the room in the dark, where I could hear his deep breathing when he slept. It was still more comfortable than the itchy straw mats I'd slept on in the orphanage.

Li Qiang was working part-time in New York while he went to school, and he'd bought some much-needed items, like a fridge for his parents. It was a luxury to be able to buy fresh food and not worry it would spoil. He told me all about his studies in New York. He was almost done with his master's program and hoped the university would eventually hire him as an assistant professor. That was the year he gave me my English name, Mia, and told me not to be in a hurry to grow up. He told me to call him Tony, since he was now calling me Mia, but the unfamiliar name tasted strange on my tongue. When he left to go back to New York, he promised to write often.

Madame Zheng started giving me more responsibilities that year. Xing Xing Ayi and Shushu were very kind to me, and in return, I tried to take over as many of the chores at home as possible. I cleaned the house on my days off so that Xing Xing Ayi didn't have to do it after working at the orphanage all day. I learned to cook and was soon in charge of most of our meals. I also did all the laundry, which was much easier to do for three people than it was for hundreds of kids. It was all worth it when Xing Xing Ayi came home one day and said that I was such a good girl. She told me how nice it was to come home to a clean house and a meal she didn't have to prepare.

I beamed with pride. It wasn't often someone said I was useful. It made me want to work harder to make sure they never regretted their decision to bring me into their home.

Life was good for a few years. I continued to learn from Madame Zheng, and I no longer looked so skinny and malnourished. Fei-Yin was doing well in her studies. We'd get together every once in a while and catch up over chang fen *or* yuntun mian, *wonton noodles. We* talked about the kids still left in the orphanage, and she asked if I'd gone back to visit Fan Fan and the other kids in the secret room.

I was ashamed to admit that I hadn't. I couldn't meet her gaze. Since I left the orphanage, I'd gone back with Xing Xing a few times to visit the special-needs kids and bring them treats like Tony used to do. But every time I stepped foot back in the orphanage, my heart would race and I would feel the walls closing in on me, and it became harder and harder to visit. I hadn't been there in months.

Fei-Yin told me Fan Fan wasn't doing well. She said all the years of living in that room had caught up to her, and she'd lost the spark she used to have in her eyes.

I didn't say anything, my body infusing with heat at the guilt of not visiting Fan Fan like I'd promised. I got to escape the orphanage while she was stuck there, probably for the rest of her life.

Fei-Yin told me she was trying to find Fan Fan's family. Maybe someone would want to help her. She also told me about her new boyfriend, a kind boy named Wang Bolin from Beijing who didn't care that she was an orphan. And in turn, I talked about my love for Tony, which hadn't faded in all these years.

But Fei-Yin scoffed, saying Tony was too old for me, more than ten years older. She told me not to waste my time on him and that she would introduce me to one of Bolin's friends.

But I didn't want to meet Bolin's friends. Even though Tony was thousands of miles away and it sounded like he was never moving back, I couldn't forget about him. I didn't want a smart or cute university boy like Fei-Yin was encouraging me to meet. I wanted Tony.

Tony had bought a computer for his parents the second year I lived with them, and he taught me how to use it. I couldn't believe the things you could look up on the Internet, even with the Chinese government censoring certain websites. It opened up a whole new world for me. We used the computer to email Tony when he went back to New York, and it kept me from missing him so much. Being able to send him a message whenever I wanted made the many months he was away bearable. He never once mentioned having a girlfriend, so I naively continued to believe I would marry him once I was old enough.

But then, the December I was seventeen, he came home and told us about Tam.

45

·

CHARLIE ATE EVERY bite Tam gave him at dinner. Tam had to feed him, as he wasn't strong enough to grasp a spoon and bring the food to his mouth, and she saw Kelly doing the same with Aidan. Sean voiced out loud what they were all thinking. "I can't believe these boys are three. They look and act like babies."

"Can Aidan walk?" Tam asked. They'd put Charlie down when it was time for dinner, and while he could walk, he waddled from side to side with his arms outstretched. He'd also yet to say anything, despite prompting from Tam, and she was starting to doubt that he really was walking and talking like the adoption officials had told her. She knew he was definitely not toilet trained, as he was wearing a diaper.

"Not very well," Kelly said. "Why would they lie to us on the reports?"

Tam shrugged. "I don't know. But I can't believe how tiny they are. And look at the way they're eating. It's as if they've never seen food before."

It physically pained Tam to see how eager the boys were to get food into their mouths, and they ate as if they couldn't get enough. In the end, she had to stop feeding Charlie because she was afraid he would explode from the sudden intake of so much food.

"Can you show me how to change a diaper?" Tam asked Kelly as they were walking back to their rooms. She ducked her head in embarrassment. "I never learned because they told me he's toilet trained."

"Sure." Kelly laughed. "Bet you didn't think we would be taking care of babies, right?"

Charlie was content after dinner, and even though he didn't know what to do with the toys they gave him, he didn't fuss or seem distressed. He was more interested in playing with the bags that held the toys, and Angela spent time with him on the floor. He still didn't speak or make any noise, but his quiet demeanor made Tam think everything would be okay.

But that all changed the minute the lights went out. It was as if the flip of the switch also turned something on inside him, and the little boy let out all his fear and bewilderment at finding himself in this strange room with these strange people. Tam thought he'd eventually tire himself out and stop crying, but she was wrong.

"What's wrong with him? Why won't he stop crying?" Angela whispered. The little girl looked as distraught as Tam felt. They'd turned on the lights and tried to distract him. They gave him the teddy bear, toys, and the snack cup he'd latched on to from the moment they gave it to him that afternoon. But nothing worked. No amount of soothing and rocking would quiet him.

"I don't know," Tam said. "I don't know what to do." She stared at Charlie's distressed face, cheeks wet with tears and eyes screwed shut, as he let out his anguish in cries that were tearing at her heart. It had been a long and emotional day, and she was reaching her breaking point, even as it seemed Charlie reached his.

He cried and cried, for an hour, then two, then three. Tam and Angela were close to tears themselves as his screams escalated, and nothing they did made it better. She brought him into the bed with them, but he refused to lie down, even when Tam put him on his back. He immediately sat up, his eyes darting around the room. At three in the morning, Angela finally fell into an exhausted sleep, but Tam stayed awake. She was the adult here, but oh, how she wished she wasn't right now. She wanted nothing more than to crawl under the covers and not be responsible for the distraught boy. She alternated walking him in her arms with lying down in the bed and holding him close, but nothing consoled him. She thought she would tear her hair out at the screams and finally understood why some women had been driven to the point of dangerous actions they would never have taken if only their babies would be quiet.

In desperation, she reached for her phone and texted Abby on WeChat. When she didn't get an answer, she fisted her hands to her mouth and screamed silently. She needed to talk to someone; she'd made a big mistake with this adoption and she now knew she was crazy to think she could raise two children by herself. She couldn't do it. She needed to stop this adoption right now. She called her mom on video chat before remembering she was mad at her, and she was about to hang up when her mom answered. She took one look at Tam's face and said, "Tam-ah. It's okay, I'm here." All traces of her anger from earlier were gone.

"Mom." That was all Tam could say. The relief she felt just having her mom on the phone spread like a tidal wave through her body.

"Hi, Charlie," her mom said. His sobs quieted for a moment as he stared at Tam's mom. "He looks so tiny. Is everything okay?"

"I don't know," Tam said. "He's so much smaller than they said, and he won't stop crying. I think I made a mistake."

"I can get on the next flight to China," her mom said. "I'll hang up now and tell your baba to look up flights for me."

And with those words, the tears she'd been trying to hold back burst out of Tam. She cried for Tony, and for Mia, and for herself. Her tears mixed with Charlie's and flowed down her cheeks, intermingling in a way their blood did not.

Her mom made soothing noises while Tam and Charlie wept together. But when her mom shouted to her father to look for flights, Tam finally spoke.

"It's okay." She sniffed, trying to stop her sobs. "We'll be fine. Just tell me what to do to get him to stop crying." She was so tempted to take her mom up on her offer, but she couldn't ask her to drop everything and fly to China. Her mom gave her some tips, but nothing worked.

"Mom, I can't do this. I can't raise two children by myself. This is a big mistake."

"No, it isn't," her mom said firmly. "It's the first day and he's scared. You're going to be fine. Just say the word and I'll get on a flight."

Her phone dinged and she looked at it.

ADAM: How'd it go?

"Mom, it's the kids' doctor. Maybe he has some advice."

Her mom's forehead scrunched up. "The doctor calls you in China?"

"Well, he's a friend. I know him from yoga class."

"Hmm . . . sounds fishy to me," her mom sniffed. And just like that, Tam's feelings of gratitude toward her mother disappeared. Why was her mom so judgmental when she knew nothing about Adam? They talked for a few more minutes and then Tam hung up, irritated.

TAM: Not good. Can you talk?

Her resolve not to bother him had crumbled after hours of Charlie's screaming.

The next minute, her phone dinged with a video chat request from Adam.

"What's going on?" Adam asked.

She told him as she walked around the room with Charlie. She was afraid to stop moving, even though it was hard to hold the phone and the little boy at the same time.

"You're doing fine, Tam," Adam said. "He's not crying right now."

"That's because I'm walking. The minute I stop, he'll start again." She shifted him in her arms. Despite his small size, he was getting heavy and her arms ached. She walked into the bathroom and sat on the toilet. Charlie whimpered.

"Hi, Charlie," Adam said. "It's nice to meet you." Charlie stared at Adam and was quiet.

"Does he seem okay to you?" Tam asked.

"He looks fine. He's alert and he's following my image with his eyes." Adam had Tam run through some simple tests. "He looks good. He's responding appropriately. I'll know more once I examine him in person, but I don't think you need to worry."

"Thank goodness."

"Will you be all right until morning?" he asked. "I can stay on the phone with you."

Tam took a breath and said, "No, it's okay. I feel better now." She tried to laugh, but it came out more like a strangled choke.

"Call me anytime, okay?"

She thanked him and hung up. The minute Adam's face disappeared, Charlie whimpered again. She walked with him for another hour before she collapsed on the bed in exhaustion. She couldn't hold him anymore. She closed her eyes, listening to his cries, and thought she'd just rest for a minute. But the next time she opened her eyes, she could tell it was morning by the sun peeking around the curtains. Charlie was sitting beside her on the bed, wide-awake.

The rest of the day didn't get any better. She was so nauseated from lack of sleep that she could barely eat breakfast. Angela was quiet, having slept fitfully, but Charlie was alert for someone who hadn't slept at all. He ate hungrily and hadn't cried once since the sun came up. By the time they made their way back to the Civil Affairs Office to complete the adoption, Tam was so queasy she threw up in the bathroom before they were called in. She was sick with worry. She knew she was making a big mistake. She was going to stop the adoption before it became official.

She was even surer of it when she sat before the interviewer and her mind went blank when asked why she wanted to adopt Charlie. She couldn't think of a single reason, and her mouth opened and closed with no sound coming out. She was about to succumb to tears again when Angela spoke up next to her.

"Because he was meant to be a part of our family." Angela took Tam's hand as she continued. "Charlie and I both don't have a mama or baba anymore, but Tam is our new mommy and we're going to be a family together."

Tam stared at Angela in awe. In her stress and exhaustion, she'd given in to fear. But Angela's words made her remember why she'd gone through with this. Charlie needed a family as much as Angela. She had no idea how she was going to get through these next few days. But the thought of Mia growing up in an orphanage and Tony and his mother's dedication to helping the orphans of China cut through her panic. She could do this. She felt a breeze pass by her left ear and could almost feel Tony's presence at her side. *You got this, Tam. I believe in you.*

Once the adoption was official, a strange calm came over Tam. She'd done it; she was officially Charlie's mother, and she couldn't stop the tears that fell from her eyes. *Tony, he's ours. No matter what happened between us, this was the one thing we wanted together. And it's finally happened. I miss you.*

Tiffany took them to a superstore on the way back to the hotel.

"I guess we need diapers and clothes, since nothing we brought fits him," Tam said.

"And a stroller too," Kelly called from in front of a display of strollers.

"Good idea." Tam inspected them, and in the end, she bought the same one as Kelly, a lightweight model that folded easily.

But when she placed Charlie in it, he screamed to be let out, waving his arms. He calmed when she picked him up and went back to looking around the store with curious eyes. Nothing like retail therapy to sooth a child scared out of his mind.

"Kind of defeats the whole purpose of a stroller, don't you think?" Sean asked, as he gestured to Tam pushing the empty stroller while juggling Charlie and her purse in her arms.

By eight o'clock that night, Tam's arms ached and she was ready to pass out.

"What if Charlie still won't sleep?" Angela asked. "Is it possible for a little boy to just never sleep again?"

Tam shuddered. "I hope not." She brought her hands together in prayer. "Please, let him sleep tonight." She reached out to touch Angela's hair. "And to think, I thought *our* first night together was horrible. That was nothing compared to last night." They shared a small smile as each thought about that night, only six months ago. They'd come a long way since then.

Tam kept a small light on, and even though she talked to him the whole time she got into bed, he refused to lie down. She told him about their home and the people who were waiting to meet him. He fell over on his side, but the minute Tam stopped talking, he sat back up again.

"I think he's scared to fall asleep," Angela whispered. She slipped out of bed and went to the crib. She said to him in Mandarin, "It's okay, little brother. Your new mommy and I are here. Don't be scared." Charlie blinked a few times, and then his eyes closed, lulled by Angela's rhythmic Mandarin. Tam watched as Charlie lay back down again and stayed down.

Angela tiptoed back to her side of the bed and fell asleep almost immediately. Tam kept vigil, but after ten minutes, when it didn't look like Charlie was going to wake up, Tam relaxed. She was exhausted, physically and mentally. She closed her eyes, grateful to be lying down, and gave in to the sleep that overtook her almost immediately.

46

The March after Tony told us about Tam, he called to tell us he'd asked her to marry him and she'd said yes. While his parents exclaimed over the news (Xing Xing with happiness and Shushu muttering how he hoped she wasn't anti-China) and Tony put her on the phone to talk with his parents, I ran out of the house. I knew I was being rude, but I couldn't stay there and fake joy for the happy couple. I needed to be alone to nurse the enormous hole in my heart that Tony had just carved. But as I ran down the street with tears coursing down my face, I heard someone calling my name.

It was Yao, a neighborhood boy about my age. He'd come to my defense once when some of the kids were making fun of me for being an orphan. They'd asked what was wrong with me that even my parents didn't want me and wanted to know what living in an orphanage was like. I tried not to let it show that their words hurt me, but Yao told them to shut up. He was the leader of that group, and they left me alone after that. We'd become friendly, and Xing Xing had even teased me about my new boyfriend. I liked Yao well enough, but I only wanted one boyfriend.

He asked me what was wrong, but I shook my head and turned away to wipe the tears off my face. He wanted me to go to the park with him. I didn't want to go, but I also didn't want to be back at the house, hearing about the American girl who had stolen my husband from me. So I spent the afternoon with Yao.

The next time Tony called, I knew I couldn't avoid him. I congratulated him, but the words almost choked me as they came out of my mouth. I had to swallow hard to keep from screaming.

I wanted to know who he told her I was. How I hated the thought that she'd pity me when she found out I was an orphan his mother took in. But he surprised me. He said he'd told her that I was his cousin who came to live with his family after my parents died. He knew I didn't like to be reminded of my time in the orphanage.

My heart literally melted to hear how considerate he was of my feelings, and my love for him only grew. Until he said he'd always look out for me because I was like a cousin or younger sister to him.

I grimaced when I heard that. A sister? I didn't want him to think of me as his sister.

Tony and Tam were having an American wedding in California later that year, and Xiao Cici would be at the wedding, since she was back in California. And then Tony was bringing her to meet us in December. Xing Xing and Shushu were hosting a dinner at a fancy restaurant to celebrate a few days after they got here. I was dreading the time when they arrived. I didn't want to see my Tony with another girl. He was mine. I saw him first.

And then they arrived. I hid in a doorway across the street and spied on them as Tony helped his new wife through the front door. He had an arm around her waist, and the way he was looking at her! It's how I'd always imagined he'd look at me one day. A tender smile on his face, his eyes glowing and shining with a love so strong I couldn't bear it. I ran away down the street, looking for Yao. He always made me feel better.

By the time I came back to the apartment, they were seated for dinner. I came breezing in the door, calling out a casual greeting to the American girl, and threw myself into Tony's arms. I wanted her to see I was special to Tony and that she might be his wife now, but I'd always be his Mei. I was polite to her, but I studied her carefully when she wasn't looking. She seemed like a nice girl, shy and soft-spoken. She wore dark-framed glasses that I thought were too heavy for her face, and she didn't dress the way I pictured American girls did. She wore a plain shirt too big for her and a skirt that made her look shapeless. I think I would have liked her if she hadn't stolen my Tony from me. I wanted to see what he saw in her, what she had that I didn't. When I thought of him kissing her and making love to her, I could feel the steam rising off my body. I couldn't stand to be around her, watching him hold her hand and beam proudly whenever she spoke. I tried not to be around as much as possible the entire two weeks she was visiting.

And to make things worse, Shushu was really taken with her. I guessed he'd gotten over his grudge against her for being Taiwanese. He was solicitous of her, offering her the best seat and always making sure she had the best piece of fruit, or was comfortable. He laughed at her stories and listened raptly when she talked about her family's business.

Tony was quieter than usual, and I could see Tam watching him with worried eyes. I knew she thought he was ashamed of her. I've always been good at reading people. Maybe that came from silently observing everyone at the orphanage. If I had been feeling friendly toward her, I would have told her not to worry, that Tony wasn't quiet because he was ashamed of her; rather, he was afraid of what she would think of the humble life his parents led. He'd told me about Tam's family's wealth, and the grand house she grew up in, and I knew he was embarrassed by our poor neighborhood with all the laundry hung out for the world to see and bikes and random pieces of furniture littering the streets. You see, I knew him so much better than she did.

I was relieved when Tam went back to New York. Tony stayed another two weeks, and with her gone, I spent more time with him. This was the way things should have turned out, Tony and me with his parents. He told me he was afraid she was disappointed that he didn't come from more money. He was worried she wouldn't think he was good enough for her. How could he possibly think that? She was not good enough for him. I didn't care that she came from a wealthy family, that her parents ran a successful software business. I knew looking at her that she wasn't a materialistic person, but I didn't want to reassure him. I wanted him to have doubts. And I hoped that one day soon, he'd realize he'd made a big mistake.

47

THE DAYS IN China flew by. On the third day after getting Charlie, Tiffany took them to the local police station to apply for the children's passports. And on the fourth day, they went to the medical clinic for the children's checkup, where they learned that Charlie was only seventeen pounds. Seventeen pounds? At three and a half years old? Tam was flabbergasted.

Charlie, meanwhile, seemed to have accepted in his quiet, stoic way that he was stuck with these strange people for the time being. He started taking an hour-long nap in the afternoons and didn't cry at night after that first one.

"I can't believe he's sleeping through the night," Tam told her mom on one of their frequent phone calls. "I thought we were in for a battle every day, but he's sleeping about ten hours."

"See, everything will be all right. You only needed to get used to each other." For once, her mom's words were soothing, like a balm on a sunburn. Tam was grateful she'd been calling twice a day to check on them. "Has Charlie said anything yet?"

"No," Tam said. "I'm getting worried. But he did smile for the first time when we took him to get his passport." Tam looked over at Charlie, who was watching an episode of *Sesame Street* on her iPad with a bewildered look on his face. "He's got a deep dimple in his right cheek."

"He's a good-looking boy."

"Yes, he is." Tam's chest puffed with pride, as if she'd had anything to do with it.

"Has he pooped yet?" Trust her mom to get to the heart of the matter.

"No." Tam wrinkled her nose. "It's been four days. We gave him this herbal tea Tiffany recommended, and that didn't help. Kelly helped me give him an enema about an hour ago. Hopefully that'll do it. His belly is getting so big."

"I have a feeling there's going to be an explosion soon. I'd better go and let you take care of it." Tam could still hear her mom laughing as she hung up.

There was a knock on the hotel door and Tam opened it to find Angela, back from visiting Paige down the hall. Angela waved a hand in front of her nose. "What's that smell?"

"Uh-oh." Tam went to Charlie. She took off his diaper and found the biggest, messiest pile of poop she'd ever seen.

Angela's eyes grew big. "Lord have mercy!"

Tam turned to her, momentarily distracted. "Where on earth did you learn that phrase?"

"I heard some woman say it in the nail salon." Angela's eyes were glued to Charlie's diaper. In the next second, she ran into the bathroom yelling, "I'm not helping you with that. You said I didn't have to change poopy diapers," leaving Tam alone to face the mountain of excrement.

Charlie let out a tiny giggle. Tam turned to him, and when he saw he had her attention, he waved an arm and burst into a belly laugh.

"Oh, you think this is funny, huh?"

Angela poked her head out of the bathroom. "Did he just laugh?"

"Yes." Tam smiled at Angela and quickly got rid of the soiled diaper and wiped him off. "You think it's funny, don't you, leaving me this stinky pile of sh . . . I mean poop?" And Charlie giggled again, making both Angela and Tam laugh with him.

Tam's WeChat dinged and she looked at the message after washing her hands.

"Tiffany is in the lobby. We have to go down." Tam picked up Charlie, and Angela trailed after her, meeting the Donovans at the elevator.

"Ready for our 'meeting'?" Kelly made air quotes with her fingers. Tiffany had called this meeting to discuss their plans for the weekend, since they didn't have anything official to do until Monday, when they had their appointment at the American consulate to apply for the children's visas.

"As long as she doesn't clap her hands and scare the crap out of me." Tam smirked.

The elevator opened and they found Tiffany waiting outside the door. "There you are!" She clapped her hands together twice and Tam jumped in spite of herself. "Come, come, we have much to discuss."

She ushered them to a grouping of couches off to the side of the lobby, and as soon as they were seated, she asked, "So have we made a decision about visiting the orphanage?"

Kelly and Tam exchanged a look, but it was Sean who spoke up. "We're not going. Kelly will want to adopt every child if we go." Kelly shrugged but stayed quiet.

Tiffany turned to Tam. "What about you? I know Tony had wanted to go."

They had told the adoption agency they wanted to visit the orphanage. Tony had wanted to go back and see the orphanage his mother used to work in. And the same one, Tam now knew, that Mia had grown up in.

"I don't know. Part of me wants to because it was important to Tony. How long did you say the ride is again?" Tam asked.

"With traffic, it will take almost four hours each way."

Tam grimaced. She didn't think it was a good idea for Angela to see the orphanage where her mother grew up, at least not until she was older. And the thought of eight hours in a car tomorrow made her want to throw up.

As if sensing her indecision, Tiffany said, "You can always come back when Charlie and Aidan are older and visit the orphanage then."

Tam nodded. That sounded like a better plan. And maybe by then, Angela would want to visit the place where her mother had grown up and her grandmother had worked.

"Okay, now that that's out of the way, let's plan your sightseeing for the weekend, before our very important consulate appointment on Monday!" Tiffany clapped and proceeded to relay an itinerary that made Tam's head spin.

They played tourist all weekend. Tiffany arranged for the driver to take them to the Safari Park to see the wild animals, which Charlie and Aidan stared at with blank expressions, while Angela and Paige had a blast feeding the giraffes and cooing over how cute the pandas were. They went to Shamian Island, which was where the American consulate was located when Sean and Kelly had adopted Paige. Charlie sat quietly in his stroller looking around, but when several cars suddenly honked their horns loudly and scared him, Tam was gratified that he immediately turned to look for her and reached his arms to her to be picked up. And when they went to the park across the street from their hotel, Charlie beamed at her from his stroller and gave her a smile of pure joy that made her feel as if everything was going to be okay.

On Monday, Tam's birthday, they appeared at the American consulate at the appointed time to apply for the last important document they'd need before being able to return to the States. She didn't tell the Donovans or Angela that it was her thirty-eighth birthday. It didn't seem important in the face of what they were doing, and she celebrated quietly by herself that night with a glass of wine.

Four days after the consulate appointment, Tiffany presented them with the children's new visas.

"It has been my pleasure to guide you here in Guangzhou. Please, have a safe flight home and let me know how the children are doing in America." Tiffany hugged each of them, since her guide duties were now at an end. Tam held on to Tiffany a beat longer than necessary, suddenly not willing to let her go. As much as she and Kelly had laughed at Tiffany's enthusiastic ways, Tiffany had been their rock through this journey. She'd told them where to go and what to do, and Tam's heart fluttered for a moment in panic, wondering how she'd cope without Tiffany telling her what to do back home.

"I can't believe we're leaving tomorrow," Kelly said later that night, as they gathered for their last dinner in the Executive Lounge.

"He's doing so much better, even in just this last week." Sean pointed to Charlie, who was trying to feed himself with a spoon.

"I know." Tam cut up a dumpling and put it in Charlie's bowl. "He still hasn't said a word, but he's walking better."

Charlie smiled, the dimple in his cheek deepening as he reached with his fingers to pick up the dumpling.

"Are you still worried?" Kelly shot her a questioning look.

Tam nodded. "I don't think he has cerebral dysplasia, but he definitely has delays. The not-talking thing is really worrying me. But I guess I'll have to wait and see. Our doctor will examine him." Thinking of seeing Adam soon made her smile. It was comforting to know she had his support and he would take care of Charlie.

Kelly nudged Tam. "Look." She pointed at Charlie, who had just reached into his snack cup and put the puff he picked up into Aidan's mouth. They all watched as Charlie continued to put puff after puff into Aidan's waiting mouth.

"That is so sweet." Tam placed a hand on her heart. "I wonder if Charlie took care of Aidan in the orphanage."

"We need to stay in touch," Kelly said.

"We will," Tam promised. Sean was a fireman with the FDNY in Manhattan, and they lived on Long Island, so it would be easy to visit once they were all back in New York.

When it was time to say good-bye, Tam watched as Angela threw her arms around Paige. The moment was bittersweet. She couldn't wait to go home, but at the same time, their cozy hotel room had started to feel like home. This was where she, Angela, and Charlie had first formed their little family, and she didn't want to leave their safe haven to face the reality of life back in New York. Here, she didn't have to think about Tony and Mia and how she was going to get Charlie caught up and how much help he was going to need. Here, she could forget about everyone who had betrayed her and then had the audacity to die, leaving her all alone to deal with the mess they'd made.

Tam wasn't ready to face real life again. She wanted to stay in this safe cocoon forever.

48

WHEN THE PLANE touched down at JFK Airport, Tam was more than ready to get off. The long flight home was hell. The travel agent hadn't been able to upgrade them to business class, so the three of them were sitting in one row in economy. The flight was bumpy, and the plane dropped so many times, Tam was convinced they were going to die. She got no sleep, trying to keep Charlie entertained and letting Angela fall asleep against her shoulder, which made her entire left side go numb.

She was glad she had accepted Abby's offer to pick them up in Tam's car. When Tam saw her friend's pouf of curly blond hair waiting for them at baggage claim, she rushed to her like a starving woman toward the last morsel of food on earth.

"Welcome home!" A small Asian woman stepped around Abby and held her arms out. Tam stopped in her tracks, momentarily confused.

"Mom? What are you doing here?"

"You looked so overwhelmed and worried. I knew if I asked, you'd say you don't need help. I just decided to come. I called Abby." Zhong-Ying hugged Angela. Then she reached over and took Charlie out of Tam's arms, immediately lightening her load.

Tam gave her mom's arm a squeeze. "I'm glad you're here." Her mom smiled.

Charlie regarded his new grandmother with a puzzled look until she bounced him in her arms. He giggled and reached a hand to grab her glasses. Tam breathed a sigh of relief. Everything was going to be fine. Her mom was here to take over, much like Tiffany had in China.

But the minute they buckled Charlie into the five-point-harness car seat, basically rendering him immobile, his face screwed up and he let out a wail. He screamed most of the way home, fighting to be let out of the car seat. Tam could only imagine what he was thinking. She'd taken him not just out of the only place he'd ever lived, but also out of his birth country and into this foreign land. And now she'd strapped him tightly into this five-point harness, nothing like the strap across his lap on the plane or the stroller in China, which didn't have a seat belt. She wondered if he'd been restrained like that in the orphanage.

"I'm sorry, Charlie," she cooed, trying to distract him with the bear he was never without.

"I think he wants to go back to our hotel room," Angela said.

Tam sighed. "I know. I do too. It was kind of like home, right?"

Angela nodded. "We were a family there."

Charlie's cries had quieted to whimpers by the time they reached the town house. When Bee flung open the door and Angela saw

Stella standing there barking and wiggling her whole body in welcome, she gave a shriek and ran toward her dachshund.

"I've missed you so much!" She threw her arms around the little dog. Stella licked her face as if she'd never stop.

Tam smiled as she unbuckled Charlie and finally freed him. She gave Bee a hug and introduced Charlie, and then put him down. He toddled toward Angela and the dog, his face curious. He'd taken to following Angela everywhere in China. But then Stella tried to lick his hand and he recoiled in fear and ran behind Tam, screaming his head off.

"What all the noise?" Zhong-Ying walked in with Abby, dragging her suitcase behind her while Abby wrestled with Tam's and Angela's luggage.

"Oh, no!" Angela's face crumpled with disappointment. "Charlie's scared of dogs." She picked Stella up in her arms and sat down in front of Charlie. She tried to coax Charlie out from behind Tam, but Charlie only screamed louder, until Zhong-Ying plucked him up and into her arms. From the safety of his new grandmother's arms, he stared down at Stella in fear.

"What do we do?" Angela asked, hugging Stella tight against her body.

Bee walked forward. "Hold on to Stella, and let's try introducing them again."

Zhong-Ying gently placed Charlie on the floor, but the minute Angela approached him with Stella in her arms, he screamed and practically climbed up Zhong-Ying's legs.

After several attempts, Bee shook her head. "I hate to say it, but I think I should take Stella back for now and bring her over for a bit at a time until Charlie gets used to her."

"No!" Angela wailed in anguish. "I missed Stella so much!"

"I'm sorry, Angela." Tam tried to hug the little girl, but Angela ran to Tam's mother and buried her face against Zhong-Ying's side and wouldn't look at Tam.

Things continued to go downhill from there. Charlie cried and screamed the whole first night in their town house, as if trying to reprise his performance from the first night they met. Tam was deflated. She'd been lulled into a false sense of security that everything would be fine by how well Charlie had been behaving in China.

Her mom was sleeping in the basement, and Angela had gone to bed in her room, but now the little girl appeared at Tam's door. "I think he's sad he's not in China anymore." Her hair was a tangled mess and her eyes were droopy with exhaustion.

Tam shook her head and then, in desperation, she grabbed her iPhone, thinking music might help. She played the first song she saw, Adele's "Hello." The moment Charlie heard Adele's voice, he quieted. Encouraged, Tam turned the volume up and Charlie fell silent. She sang along softly for the entire song. The minute the song ended, he whimpered and would have started crying if she hadn't played the song again. She didn't sing this time, and he continued to whimper until she joined her voice with Adele's. She caught Angela's eye, and the little girl rolled her eyes. After Tam started the song again for the third time, Angela asked, "Are we going to have to listen to this all night? I like Adele, but you can't sing."

Tam swatted Angela on her behind. "Watch it, little lady."

Angela giggled and ran back to her room.

It only took ten replays of the song for Charlie to fall asleep. By then, Tam's voice was hoarse and she wondered if her life would ever be okay again.

IT WAS ADAM who suggested the next day that she get a white-noise machine and a night-light. "He's probably not used to all that quiet if he lived in an orphanage. Maybe the silence and dark are what's scaring him."

It worked. Sitting beside his crib the second night with the white-noise machine on, she watched him fall asleep and thought about Tony. She'd thought he was crazy when he said they should buy a crib. She'd wanted to get a toddler bed since Charlie would be three and a half by the time they got him, but he'd said, "Trust me. He's coming from an orphanage that doesn't have a lot of re-sources, and he's spent his whole life in a room filled with cribs. He'll be more comfortable in one, at least for the first few months he's home."

Now she realized Tony had been right. She leaned her arms against the railing. Tony was the one who wanted to name the little boy Charlie. "It sounds really American, doesn't it? And he can go by Charles once he gets older."

He spoke often about giving the little boy a chance at a life he wouldn't have had if he'd stayed in China. "I want him to have the best education, like I was given, and I want him to grow up knowing he can be whatever he wants. There's no censorship in America, and it amazes me every day what I can learn. I want to give our little boy that same freedom."

Tony believed in family above all else and in honoring elders, and he couldn't understand some of his students' disregard and disdain for older generations. He'd often commented to Tam that the kids today had no respect; they didn't realize how lucky they were to have the things that mattered most—a family and a future. This was what he wanted to give to Charlie.

She gazed down at the son that Tony had waited for, looking so small in his crib. Giving a big sigh, she leaned over to make sure Charlie was sleeping before slipping quietly out of the room.

THE NEXT DAY, Tam sat in the exam room in Adam's office with Charlie on her lap and her mom next to her. She hadn't wanted her mom to come, but she'd insisted.

"It'll help Charlie to have both of us there," her mom said. "Besides, I want to get a look at this doctor who calls you in China."

Tam rolled her eyes and had to bite her tongue to keep a sarcastic zinger from flying out of her mouth. She'd vowed to be nicer to her mom on this trip, since she was doing so much for her. But it was hard when her mom made comments like that.

When Adam walked into the room, Tam's face immediately heated, and she saw her mom glance at her sharply.

"Hi, Charlie. Remember me?" Adam voice was gentle, but his presence filled the small room. Tam shifted uncomfortably when he leaned down to kiss her on the cheek, with her mom radiating disapproval at her side.

"I am Zhong-Ying, Tam's mother." And she thrust a hand out, which Adam shook warmly. He said all the appropriate things, which seemed to placate her mom for the time being.

Adam gave Charlie a thorough exam. "He's severely undersize for his age. He's smaller than they wrote on his file. And developmentally, he's more like a one-year-old than a three-and-a-half-year-old." Tam had known this already, but having Adam confirm it made her realize how far behind Charlie was.

"I don't see any evidence of cerebral dysplasia though," Adam said, and Tam and her mom both breathed a sigh of relief.

After the exam, they spoke briefly before he went on to his next appointment. Tam looked after him, conflicted. He felt at once like an old friend and a new crush. In their texts while Tam was in China, he'd mentioned one day that he was going with Jessie to look at rings. Apparently, Jessie didn't trust him to buy the right one. Tam hadn't asked him since if he'd purchased the ring. She didn't really want to know. She resolved to think of Adam as a friend and nothing more. Her life was confusing enough as it was, and she didn't need any extra complications.

Tam could feel her mom's disapproval loud and clear as they walked out of the building.

"What?" she finally asked. Her mom shook her head but didn't answer. Tam could feel her frustration build. "If you've got something to say, say it. I hate it when you act all superior."

Her mom tapped her mouth. "Silence condemns more effectively than loud accusations."

Tam threw up her hands. "There's nothing to condemn. Nothing's going on with Adam."

Her mom tapped her mouth again and Tam said, "I give up."

Tam's mom ended up staying for three weeks. At first, Tam protested. "Mom, you don't have to stay. The adoption agency said we should limit the amount of people Charlie comes in contact with for at least the first month. They call it cocooning. That's why they advised coming directly here after we got him, instead of stopping in California on the way home. It keeps the children from being confused about who they belong to."

Her mom's nostrils flared. "Excuse me? I'm now considered 'people'? He belongs to you, which means he belongs to me. I'm family, not some random stranger off the street."

"I know, but what about the business? Doesn't Dad need your help?"

"I told your father and Wei they would just have to do without me for a while. You need help, whether or not you think you do." And her mom picked Charlie up and took him upstairs for a bath, giving Tam time to finish eating in peace.

Charlie had still yet to say a single word, in either Mandarin or English, and Tam was getting more worried each day. She had an appointment to get him evaluated, but what if he couldn't speak for some reason?

"Stop worrying," her mom scolded. "No point getting all worked up now. That doctor friend said there's nothing physically wrong with him. He'll catch up."

"What if he doesn't?" Tam was trying not to let the despair take over. Charlie had so much to catch up on developmentally, not to mention physically. She'd been expecting a walking, talking, toilet-trained toddler, but instead, she'd gotten a nine-month-old infant. She wasn't prepared for a baby. How was she going to take care of him by herself?

"He'll be fine," Zhong-Ying said firmly. "He just needs love and good food."

The day before Tam's mom flew home to California, Tam walked into her town house after a yoga class. She'd taken the maternity leave the school offered and wouldn't go back to teach until September. She'd also received the settlement checks from the beverage company. Even with putting Angela's portion aside in an account for her future, she wouldn't have to worry about their financial situation for the time being.

She paused and realized the place was absolutely quiet, which it hadn't been in a long time. She found her mother sitting in the living room with a cup of tea.

"Where is everyone?"

"Angela is walking the dogs with Bee, and Abby took Charlie for ice cream." Her mom pointed to the couch. "Sit."

Tam eyed her mom and walked to the couch as if approaching a tiger. "You sound so serious."

"I know how overwhelmed you are, so I haven't brought up Tony and Mia. But I'm leaving tomorrow, and I think we need to talk."

Tam turned her face away. Damn. She *really* didn't want to talk about it with her mom.

"Tam, I know you feel bad—"

She cut her mom off. "I really don't want to talk about this."

Her mom pursed her lips and narrowed her eyes. "Okay, but we need to talk about Angela. Wei told me you feel so guilty for making her leave your house. But it wasn't your fault. Tony started the lies. You shouldn't blame yourself."

Tam looked at her mother, determined to keep her mouth shut. But the feelings and emotions were bursting out of her, threatening to erupt, and she couldn't stay quiet any longer.

"I threw Angela out of our home," Tam cried. "When she finds out, she's never going to forgive me. I kept her from her father all those years, and then she only had a few months with him before he was killed. How could I have done that? Do you know how bad I feel, hearing Angela say how happy she was to find out Tony was her father? How much she enjoyed their time together when he visited her?"

She looked down, unable to meet her mom's eyes.

"Tam, look at me," her mom said. "No one would blame you for wanting Mia and Angela out of your house. You were trying to protect your marriage. And you didn't keep them apart. Mia could have told Tony at any time in those years. You'll tell Angela when she's old enough to understand. She does need to know about the past, but only so she can realize how much you love her. If you didn't, you would never have taken her in when her mother died."

Tam looked at her mom and couldn't keep the anguish out of her voice. "I made my husband throw his own daughter out of his home when I knew the truth. I loved Angela too, but I couldn't live in the same house with them. I let my hurt overpower the needs of a helpless little girl. How is that forgivable?"

Her mom got a fierce look on her face. "Tony was the one who set this whole chain of events into action. He lied to you, Tam. He told you Mia was his cousin and brought her into your home. Would you have agreed to let her live with you if you'd known she had no relation to Tony?"

"Stop it," Tam said. "I don't want to talk about it." She walked into the kitchen and poured a glass of water. She faced the refrigerator, taking big gulps of the cold liquid, and felt her mom come up behind her.

"You need to let it out. Get it off your chest. Let go of the guilt," her mom said.

"Oh, Mom. You just don't understand." But when her mom put her arms around her from behind, she leaned into her. She let herself be held for a moment, wishing she could be a kid again and have her mom take away all the hurt.

49

MIA'S JOURNAL

I was so depressed over the loss of Tony. I'll admit, I turned to Yao to comfort me. I wanted, no, needed to feel wanted, like I mattered to someone. So I let him kiss and touch me. He wanted to be my boyfriend, and I realized if I ever wanted to win Tony over, I needed more experience.

So one night, when I was closing Madame Zheng's shop, I told Yao to meet me there. Madame Zheng had a small back room that she used for storage. And it was there, on top of an old blanket I brought, that I lost my virginity to Yao. It hurt like hell and there was so much blood, but Yao held me afterward. He stroked my hair and told me how beautiful I was. I knew I wasn't beautiful, but I let his sweet words soothe my broken heart and I was content.

I confessed to Madame Zheng my wish to go to America. I thought she would be upset since she'd be losing an assistant, but she told me she might be able to help me find a job. I couldn't believe it. I thought she'd be angry that she'd spent all this time training me and then I'd leave her.

But Madame Zheng only chuckled and told me that she'd taken me on as a favor to Xing Xing Ayi. She didn't really need an assistant, but Xing Xing and Shushu had been so good to her ever since her husband died. So when Xing Xing told her she was trying to find a job for me, she told her she could use the help.

I was upset to hear that. All this time, I thought I'd been needed by Madame Zheng, when all along, she'd taken me on as a charity case. She must have read the look on my face, because she chucked me under the chin and told me not to read too much into this. She said she might not have thought she needed an assistant, but I'd turned out to be good for her and her business. She said I'd been indispensable to her all these years.

I felt slightly better at her words, and my mood improved even more when she told me she might know someone who could find me a job in New York.

When Tam and Tony came to visit that year, I spent as much time with them as possible, now that there was a possibility I'd really get to America. Despite my resolve not to like her, I found myself drawn to Tam and her quiet ways. I couldn't help but like her, and she shared her American magazines with me and tried to teach me some English. I asked a lot of questions about New York, and the more the two of them talked about their apartment in Astoria, Queens, and the life they led, the more I was determined to move to New York. It sounded like a dream.

As much as I was enjoying Tam's company, there were still times when jealousy would cloud my vision. When Tony pulled out a chair for her but left me to pull out my own, or when I'd imagine him going down on her the way Yao did with me, I could feel the resentment bordering on hatred shoot off me like sparks. Once, I caught her eye during one of those moments, and I could see by the little jolt of surprise on her face that she sensed what I was thinking. But I smiled, and she tentatively smiled back. I didn't want to make an enemy of her. I needed her on my side when I asked Tony for help in getting to America.

I introduced them to Yao at a noodle shop. I watched Tony out of the corner of my eye to see if he was jealous. But Tony only shook Yao's hand and smiled at him.

I sat so close to Yao I was practically in his lap. I let him put his hand possessively on my leg, because I had told Yao long ago that I was in love with Tony. I nuzzled Yao's neck, let him play with my hair, and snuggled with my head on his shoulder, all the while watching Tony for his reaction. Yao was surprised because I usually didn't let him touch me in public, but then he took full advantage and held me tight.

Tam and Tony left before we did because he wanted to take her to visit some old friends. The minute they were out the door, I slid off Yao's lap and pushed his hands off me. I knew Yao was aroused and thought we would sneak off somewhere to have sex. But I was miffed that Tony wasn't jealous and I told Yao I had a headache and had to go home. I saw the hurt on his face, but I didn't care. I was hurt too.

When Tam went back to New York that year, I finally told Tony I'd been dreaming of moving to America and asked if he would help me find a way. I'd emailed Xiao Cici, who was in California, and asked if she could help me get a visa. Her husband had many contacts in the American government. She told me she'd try to help me at the American embassy in Guangzhou when she and her husband returned to China in a few months. If she could somehow get me a visa, and if Tam and Tony would let me stay with them until I found a place of my own, I thought my American dream would finally come true.

50

THE DAYS FOLLOWING her mom's departure were hard.
Tam was overwhelmed, running on not enough sleep and just scrap-
ing by, grateful at the end of each day that all three of them had
survived. Her mind never shut down, worrying about Charlie's
speech delay and his poor performance on all his evaluations, even
though that meant he'd be getting help from the school. She worried
about Angela and not being able to give her enough attention and
about her separation from Stella. Tam's mind was in overdrive every
moment she was awake, and with each sleepless night, her worries
multiplied until she felt as if she would smother under all the pressure.

But almost exactly a month after they came home, Charlie finally
spoke his first word. He yelled out "Bye!" and waved as Angela was
leaving for the school bus. Angela and Tam looked at each other in
amazement, and then at the same time, both reached out to hug him.

"Oh, my goodness." Tam picked Charlie up and danced around

the room with him, causing him to giggle. "You can talk!" Relief flooded her body, making her feel weak, like a wet noodle. She sank onto the sofa and held him close while he continued to say, "Bye, bye, bye," like a broken record, as her mind said, *Thank you, thank you, thank you.*

That same day, when Bee brought Stella over after school, Charlie walked up to Stella and petted her on the head. Angela turned to Tam with joy. "Look, he's not scared anymore! She can stay home now, right?"

Tam nodded, a big smile breaking over her face as some of her worry melted off her. It would be wonderful to have Stella home again. She hadn't realized how much she'd missed the dachshund, and now their family was complete.

Except they were without Tony. When she took Charlie to tour the preschool they'd picked, she had to pause at the front door before entering, remembering Tony's hand on the small of her back the last time she'd been here. She held tight to Charlie's hand as they entered the preschool, his eyes round as he took in all the hooks with names over them, the children's artwork hung on the walls, and the cheerful mural of animals and flowers against the back wall. Tony's absence from their side was like a giant hole in her heart.

After their preschool visit, she took him to the park. He ran toward a group of children but didn't join in; he just watched as they played and talked. A little girl fell and started crying. "Daddy!" she wailed when her father picked her up.

Charlie turned to Tam and patted her on the cheek. "Daddy."

Tears sprang to Tam's eyes that "daddy" was Charlie's second word. "No, I'm Mommy. Daddy's not with us anymore."

Charlie tilted his head to one side and studied her, then said again, "Daddy."

"I know, Charlie." Tam pulled him close and breathed in the little-boy scent of him that was becoming as familiar to her as Tony's had been once. "I miss Daddy too."

HER MOM CAME to New York again at the beginning of May, this time bringing her father. Tam almost cried in relief. Her parents stayed for two weeks, and having full-time help gave Tam the chance to finally deal with all the paperwork to officially adopt Angela and apply for Charlie's passport and social security number once she got his Certificate of Citizenship.

"Have you thought more about moving to California?" her mom asked one night as Tam sat at the dining table like a zombie. "I'm worried about you. You're too thin and you're so pale. This is too much for one person."

Tam was mechanically eating the wontons her mom had made. While a part of her brain registered how nice it was to eat food she didn't make, the rest of her was so exhausted from the past two months that she couldn't seem to focus. Her dad was helping Charlie eat, and it felt so good to sit still and not be responsible for anyone but herself.

"Tam. Wake up." Her mom snapped her fingers at her.

"What?" Tam brushed her hair off her face. She blinked and tried to remember what her mom had just said.

"Don't you want to be closer to us? You need help."

"I know. This is so much harder than I thought. Bee and Abby are doing everything they can, and Adam has been stopping by and bringing us food, but I don't know if I can keep doing this by myself."

Her mom clicked her tongue again. "I don't like how that Adam is hanging around here. He has a girlfriend. And what doctor makes house calls these days?"

"Mom." Tam gave a tired sigh. "He's just a friend, and he's helping me. The kids love him."

Her mom wrinkled her nose. "I don't like it. Smells fishy. He wants something. And he's not Taiwanese. Or even Asian."

Tam took the elastic off her wrist and tied her hair in a ponytail. "There's nothing fishy. You don't understand."

Her mom muttered in English loud enough for Tam to hear, "She always say I don't understand. Bah! I understand much more than she knows. But she never wants to hear what mother says. She knows best."

Tam swallowed a grunt of frustration and tried to change the subject. "Anyways, I just can't see uprooting us. Angela is finally at home here and Charlie is getting used to everything. It might be better to stay put."

"Well, I can't move here. Our whole life is back there."

"I know." Tam's voice softened. "I don't expect you to move here. I just wish there was a way for us to be closer." She got up and put an arm around her mom. "I do need you." Her mom sniffed, but there was a pleased smile on her face.

Tam managed to keep the truce with her mom until they left, so much so that she was actually sorry to see them go.

Two days after her parents went home, a social worker from the child welfare agency came to do their home inspection, which was part of the process to legally adopt Angela. That night, the little girl came up to Tam after she'd put Charlie to bed. Angela usually stayed up for another half hour after Charlie went to sleep, and this had become their special time together, the only time when Angela had Tam's undivided attention.

"I was thinking," Angela said. "Mama will always be my mama. But it makes me feel funny to call you Tam or even Auntie or Ayi when Charlie is calling you Mommy." Charlie had finally learned to say "mommy." Tam would never forget the burst of joy that radiated through her body when he first called her that. "Do you think my mama will mind if I call you Mommy too?"

"Oh, Angela." She gathered the little girl to her and hugged her close, wondering if Angela could feel how fast her heart was beating. "Your mama will always be your mother. Even with all that happened between us, she trusted me enough to take care of you. I don't think she'd mind if you called me Mommy. And I'd be honored."

Angela smiled and blew out a breath. "Then I'm lucky, aren't I? I have a mama and a mommy." She thought a minute and then frowned. "But what did you mean when you said things that happened between you? What happened?"

Tam hesitated and looked down at Angela's innocent face. Could she ever tell her the truth about how she'd told Mia to leave and take Angela with her, knowing that Tony was her father? Angela wasn't even six yet, and she wasn't old enough to understand. But Tam hated having this secret between them. Secrets were the cause of all her problems with Tony. She didn't like to think that her new, fragile family was starting out with yet another secret. But she couldn't imagine telling a child the truth.

"You don't need to worry about that now," Tam finally said. "Your mama wrote you a journal explaining everything. You can read it when you're older and we'll talk about it then."

"Promise?"

Tam nodded.

51

AT THE END of June, to celebrate the beginning of summer, Adam offered to take Tam and the kids to Long Beach for the day.

"Be careful, Tam." Abby had stopped over as Tam was packing food for the outing. "He's engaged, or almost. Don't go falling in love with him. You'll get your heart broken."

"I know what I'm doing." Tam was washing grapes and strawberries at the sink. "We're just friends. It's nice being friends with the kids' doctor. When Angela woke up that day covered in spots or when Charlie caught his first cold and coughed so hard he threw up all over me, I was able to call Adam for advice."

"But he doesn't just call. He's been stopping by your place and stays for dinner sometimes, doesn't he?"

Tam turned and made a face at Abby. How did she know that? He *had* stayed for dinner a few times. She'd asked Adam if he had to get home to Jessie and he'd said, "She's working late in the city again." She had felt bad about Jessie, but they were just friends after all. There was nothing going on between them, even if she was attracted to him. But on some level, she must have thought it was wrong, because she hadn't wanted to share that fact with anyone.

"Angela," Abby answered before Tam could ask. "She tells me everything. She's in love with Dr. Adam."

Tam laughed. "Right. But don't worry." She placed the fruit in a container and opened the fridge to look for the baby carrots. "I know there's no way he's interested in me. Jessie's gorgeous. Plus, she's an attorney, and from what Adam says, she's really smart and driven. How can I possibly compete with that? And anyways, I never want to get in the middle of a relationship."

Abby shot Tam a look, and Tam knew Abby knew she was talking about Tony and Mia. Abby shook her head. "Don't underestimate yourself, Tam. I know men. They don't hang around a woman unless they're interested on a sexual level."

Tam raised her eyebrows as she grabbed the carrots. "Yeah, and I'm so sexy these days. I only wear workout clothes because it's easier, and my hair is always dirty. I never have time to put makeup on. I'm chasing after two kids by myself and trying to toilet train one, who seems to think it's a game and absolutely refuses to pee or poop in a toilet. The one time I took him out to lunch at Cheesecake Factory with Adam and Angela, he pooped so much in his diaper that it came up over his pants. I had to use one of the restaurant's cloth napkins to hold over his bottom to take him to the bathroom. I had poop all over my hands and had to throw out the shirt and pants he was wearing. Good thing I always keep an extra set of clothes in his bag, or he'd have been naked for the rest of lunch. Yeah, I have to say, I'm sure Adam found that really sexy."

Abby laughed but then narrowed her eyes. "He took you out to lunch?"

"Abby." Tam turned her back to her friend and put the carrots in a separate container. "It's not like that."

"Fine, but just be careful. I think there's more to it than you think."

"I'm grateful for his friendship," Tam said. "He's been so helpful with Charlie. And I think part of what makes me so comfortable with him is that I know I can't have him."

"You mean because he has a girlfriend he's about to propose to?"

"Yes. I know what we have could never go beyond friendship. I would never do that to another woman. And I'm okay with it. I worry enough about the kids and I don't need to add unrequited love to my stress."

"If you say so."

"I say so. Adam and I are just friends."

Abby threw up her hands in defeat. "Whatever you say."

Tam turned and caught Abby's eye. "Thanks, though, for your concern. It means a lot." She looked away, embarrassed. It was still so hard for her to tell someone how she really felt. But she had vowed to be more honest and to just say what she was feeling, rather than keeping everything inside like she'd done all her life.

Abby walked up to her and touched her arm. "Of course I'm concerned. You're my friend."

Tam smiled as she looked down at the vegetables in her hand. Abby was right. They were friends, and friends watched out for each other. She blew out a breath, realizing she trusted Abby's judgment. She'd thought she'd never trust another female friend again after Mia.

52

Almost two years after Tony married Tam, it finally happened. Xiao Cici was able to get my visa application approved at the American embassy, and Tony agreed to let me stay with them. When I talked to Tam on the phone, I could tell she wasn't thrilled at the idea of me living with them. She said all the right things, but it was in the hitch in her voice and her hesitation before saying she was looking forward to my arrival. I didn't blame her. If she knew how I really felt about Tony, I'm sure she would have put her foot down and said no.

And to top it all off, Madame Zheng said she had a friend whose sister's neighbor's daughter lived in Flushing, Queens, and owned a nail salon. Can you guess who that was, Angela? Jenny, of course. I couldn't believe my good fortune. I was going to America and even had a job!

The only problem was that I had a visitor's visa, so I'd have to go back to China after six months. But I felt sure that Tony and Xiao Cici would find a way for me to stay in America. I had no idea then how hard it was to get a green card.

I told Yao I was leaving. He didn't want me to go. He told me he loved me and wanted me to marry him, that he'd take care of me. Even though I liked him and would be forever grateful to him, I didn't want him to take care of me. My focus was on Tony.

When I told Yao I didn't love him, I saw the hurt in his eyes. I wasn't sorry to be leaving him, but I suddenly felt bad for hurting him. He hugged me to him as if he never wanted to let go. But I pulled away and left him standing on the corner, turning my back so I didn't have to see the tears in his eyes or watch them fall.

Xing Xing Ayi and Shushu were also sad when I told them the news. Xing Xing had been listening to me talk about going to New York for two years, but I knew she didn't think I would ever go. She'd already lost her son to America, and she'd told me she didn't want to lose me too. She held out her arms and I went into them, holding her tight. She was the only mother I'd ever known, but I felt like my destiny was in America. I had to go and try.

She understood. She patted me on the back and told me she knew all these years that my heart had been in America with Li Qiang. I couldn't believe it. Could she possibly have known all along about my love for Tony? I thought I had hid it well.

Apparently, I didn't do that good a job, because she said Shushu knew too. But they said they'd keep my secret. Shushu made a zipping gesture over his mouth. I was so embarrassed because I had no idea my love for Tony was so transparent.

But I'll never forget what Xing Xing said to me next. She told me I could find a new life in America. No one there knew I was an orphan except Li Qiang. She bought me a statue of Guan Yin to take with me and to watch over me. Xing Xing had prayed to her to protect the souls of her lost babies and to protect Li Qiang, so far away in America. Guan Yin had been a comfort to Xing Xing all these years, and now she would guide me in my new life. Hopefully a happy and prosperous one.

I was stunned but I realized she was right. I could start over. Even though I would have to take along the last name—Guo—that the orphanage had given me, since it was on all my paperwork, no one in America would know it was a name usually given to orphans.

I would tell everyone I was Tony's cousin who'd lived with his parents when my own parents passed away. I could start over, remove the stigma of being an orphan, and just be Mia Guo. I'd do everything in my power to convince Tony he belonged with me and finally have the family I'd dreamed of all my life. No one in America had to know I was an orphan. That would be my little secret.

53

THE WEEK AFTER the beach trip, Adam called Tam in the afternoon and asked if he could stop by.

"Abby took the kids to the pool, and then they're all going to Bee's house for dinner. I needed some alone time before I go crazy." Tam let out a self-deprecating laugh. "I know the kids will be sorry to miss you."

Adam was quiet for a moment, and then he asked, "Want some company? I'm getting out early today."

Tam's heart skipped a beat. They'd never spent time together without the kids. She'd come to expect that he visited them because of Angela and Charlie. The thought of seeing him alone suddenly made her palms sweaty and her breath quicken.

"That'd be nice." She tried to make her voice nonchalant, but inside she was dying.

When he arrived, she went to hug him at the same time he tried to kiss her cheek, and they ended up headbutting. She clutched her forehead and Adam laughed, breaking the tension. "I guess we're not used to being together without the kids." His laugh was rich, soothing Tam's nerves. "Do you want to go for a walk on the trail? It's not too hot out."

She nodded. *Yes, please. Let's get out of here before I start having inappropriate thoughts.* Oh, why hadn't she listened to Abby and had a meaningless one-night stand? Then she wouldn't be lusting after a man she couldn't have.

As they walked though, she relaxed. This was Adam, her friend. Not someone to have a one-night stand with.

But he's got such a beautiful body, an impish voice said in her head. *Don't you just want to do him?*

Get your mind out of the gutter, Tam. He has a girlfriend. You are never going to be the cause of another woman's pain, she scolded herself.

"What did you say?" he asked.

Oh, no, had she said that out loud? "Nothing." She shrugged and could feel the heat in her face.

"So, how are things?" he asked after giving her a quizzical look.

"Better. I didn't think I was going to make it those first few months. But I finally have a good routine with the kids." She looked at him. "Thanks for all your help."

"Anytime," he said. "Those kids are really special." His gaze was steady on her face, making her wonder if he thought she was special too. She blushed again and looked away. They walked in silence until they got to a clearing. This was one of her favorite spots. There was a large tree stump a ways from the trail, and she liked to stand on it and look around. The only thing she could see was land and trees, and it felt like she was the only person for miles. She'd shown Adam and the kids the spot before, and now he gestured toward it with a question in his eyes. As they made their way off the trail and toward the stump, he asked, "Do you still miss your husband?"

"I don't know. Before I went to China, I felt as if the worst of the grief and regrets were over. But then I came home with Charlie and it all came back."

"Regrets?" Adam asked. "I understand about the grief, but what do you mean by regrets?"

Tam shrugged and sat down on the stump.

"Does this have anything to do with Angela being your husband's daughter?"

She nodded, staring at the peaceful scene around them. "Yes."

"I know I told you this once, but I really am a good listener if you want to talk about it."

She turned her head and studied his face, those kind light brown eyes that shone with compassion, and the little scar above his lip that he'd told her was from a fall off the monkey bars when he was eight. He was nothing like Tony, but she realized he'd become as familiar. She wanted to tell him the truth. She was tired of keeping secrets from the people she cared about.

"Yes," she said. "I do want to talk about it." And Tam told Adam everything. How Mia and Tony told her Mia was his cousin, and how she'd lived with them when she came from China. She told him everything, up until the part where Tam suspected the baby was Tony's and confronted Mia, who confirmed her suspicions.

At this point she paused, not sure if she could go on. Her mouth was burning to let the truth out, but she cared what Adam thought of her. He seemed to sense her struggle because he said, "It's okay. You can tell me."

She took a breath and finished her story. "I didn't tell Tony that

I knew Angela was his. I gave him an ultimatum instead. I said Mia and Angela had to move out or I would. He agreed. I let him kick his own daughter out of his house and I never said a word about it. And I never saw or talked to Mia again."

She lowered her head, the shame of what she'd done still as fresh as the day it happened. "Mia promised she wouldn't contact us, but she called Tony a few months before the accident and told him the truth. That's when Tony started visiting Angela. That's also when he started lying to me. He told me he had an afternoon class and office hours on Thursdays, but he was visiting her every week. He never told me Angela was his daughter. And Mia never told him that I already knew."

"How did you find all this out if Tony and Mia were killed?"

"Jenny found Mia's journal. My brother translated it for me." Tam paused. She hadn't finished reading it though. She had gotten to the part where Mia had written about what happened with Tony and just couldn't bring herself to read about their affair. She looked at Adam out of the corner of her eye. "Are you shocked?"

"No," Adam said. "I don't shock easily. And by the way, he didn't start lying to you when he visited Angela. He lied to you from the very beginning when he told you Mia was his cousin."

She stared at him. "That's what my mom said."

"She's right."

"I know this is all going to come out one day. I'm sick of keeping all these secrets, and I want to tell Angela the truth, but she's not even six yet. That's too young for her to really understand. I want to tell her before she reads her mother's journal, but when's the right time?"

"You'll know when that time comes." Adam reached out and squeezed her hand. "I hate that you're beating yourself up over this.

You didn't do anything wrong, Tam. No one would blame you for how you reacted. I don't want to speak badly of the dead, especially because I didn't know them, but your husband and Mia had just as much responsibility in all this."

Tam sighed. Adam sat down next to her on the stump and they stared out at the woods. They stayed that way for a while, not speaking, shoulders touching. From the trail, they could hear the sounds of dogs barking and children laughing, a girl's voice raised in an excited pitch as she yelled out, "No, you didn't!" But Tam and Adam stayed still on their stump, both lost in their own thoughts, until Tam felt Adam shift slightly.

She looked up and found him staring down at her. Her breath caught. The look in his eyes made her stomach flutter, and in that moment, she wanted nothing more than for him to kiss her. He didn't break their gaze, and she found herself leaning toward him, and then suddenly, she was kissing him and he was kissing her back. The world fell away, and all she could feel was his mouth on hers as they deepened their kiss. Tam moved closer until it felt like her entire body was touching his. She could feel his erection against her thigh and it sent a chill down her spine. Her body awakened as if from a long sleep. She lost herself in him, in the smell and feel and touch of him. She never wanted this moment to end.

But all too soon, she came up for air, and that was when reality hit. She was kissing and touching another woman's man. She, who had felt so betrayed because her husband had slept with another woman, had kissed this man first. She pulled away and wiped a hand over her mouth as if she could erase the kiss. She turned and ran toward the trail, with Adam following after her.

"Tam, wait," he said. She kept going, hoping he would leave her alone, but he followed her all the way back to the entrance to her town house complex. It was there that he took her by the arm and said again, "Wait."

She looked at him. "I'm so sorry. I don't know what came over me. I know you have a fiancée and I know you think of me as a friend and I have no idea why I kissed you."

"She's not my fiancée."

"You haven't proposed yet?"

Adam gave her a look she couldn't decipher. "No. I'm not sure if I will."

"Oh, no. Did you guys break up?"

"No."

"It's so weird that we've never met her," Tam blurted out when he didn't elaborate. "I mean, I know I saw her that first time in yoga class, but we've never formally met."

Adam laughed, but it wasn't a happy sound. "Well, I don't see much of her these days. In fact, I think I see you more than I do her."

"Is everything okay between you?"

He shrugged. "Everything is exactly the same as it's always been with us."

"I'm sorry. I shouldn't have kissed you like that. She's still your girlfriend and it was wrong of me. Plus, I'm not sure I'm over what happened with my husband."

Adam tried to interject, but Tam plowed on. "Please, let's just forget this happened. It was a mistake. I'm so embarrassed."

"But it did happen," Adam said. "Tam—"

She interrupted him. "I can't. I hate myself for kissing another woman's boyfriend. I'm sorry. I have to go."

And with that, she broke free from Adam and ran away from him toward home, leaving him to stare after her.

54

MIA'S JOURNAL

I know you've probably been wondering what happened with Tony and how you came to be. I'm not proud of what I did, but at the same time, if I hadn't done it, I wouldn't have you. So how can I regret it? You are the best thing I've ever done. Please don't hate me as you read the following words. I could have sugarcoated it, but I never want to lie to you, Angel. So here is the ugly truth of how you were conceived.

The day it happened, I was still technically with Kenny, but I'd been trying to break up with him for months. Tam was with her friend Abby at a concert, and I knew she'd be home late. She'd just had her third miscarriage a few weeks before, and Abby was trying to cheer her up. I was down the hall in my tiny room in the Astoria apartment, alone and restless. Tony was working in the kitchen. As much as I'd come to love Tam like a sister, I still couldn't let go of my infatuation with Tony. I wanted to feel what it would be like to have him hold me in his arms and kiss me, just once. I wanted him to look at me like a woman, not his little sister. My longing for him had been building the past few months. I'd lived with Tony and Tam for over a year at that point, and being so close to him yet unable to have him was driving me crazy.

I called out and told Tony to come and take a break. I had a bottle of Johnnie Walker Blue that a customer had given me for the holidays on my table. Tony doesn't drink much, but I knew he liked scotch. He'd been just as upset as Tam about the miscarriages, but since Tam wasn't talking to him about it, I wanted to console him.

I let him talk and kept his glass filled. I knew he was getting drunk when his face turned red and he started to slur his words. I went to sit next to him on the bed and told him to take off his shirt, that I'd give him a massage. I'd often practiced on him in China when he came home for winter break, so there was nothing unusual about this. He talked about his worry for Tam as my fingers went to work on the knots in his back and shoulders. All of a sudden, he stopped talking and I realized he was asleep. I should have left him on my bed and gone out to the living room to wait for Tam. But I didn't. I stayed, watching him sleep, and then I couldn't help myself. I kissed him, and it felt so good and he smelled so good that I did it again. He stirred in his sleep but didn't wake. I know what I did next was wrong, but I couldn't help myself. Here was my Tony, asleep in my bed, and I wasn't thinking about Tam or Kenny at all. I wanted Tony, and all my longing for him over the years overrode any common sense. I kissed him all over and took off his pants, seeing he was aroused. I was so happy, thinking, He wants me! But he called out, "Tam!" and when he opened his eyes and saw it wasn't Tam beside him, confusion clouded his eyes. I kissed him and got on top of him, thinking he'd stop me if he didn't want this. I knew the moment he surrendered because he started moving with me until he came.

I guess I was stupid to think this would change everything, that he loved me now. But he pushed me off and was asleep in minutes. I got dressed and lay next to him, listening to his familiar breathing. I heard Tam come home, and moments later, I heard her outside my door. I held my breath, not sure what I would say if she opened it and found her husband naked in my bed. But she didn't come in; I heard her leave and go into their bedroom.

Tony was upset when he woke up a few hours later. My eyes opened to see him getting dressed, and he turned to me when he heard me stir. He had the most devastated look on his face, as if someone had died. I'll never forget what he said. "Mei, this never happened. I love Tam and you're like my sister. Tam must never know."

I knew then he would never love me like he loves Tam. There was no red thread between Tony and me. The red thread was between Tony and Tam. How could I have been so wrong all my life? I didn't answer and only stared as he rushed out my door and back to his wife. I put a hand on my belly, where, unbeknownst to me, you had already started to form, and I felt sick to my stomach. And then a few weeks later, I realized I was pregnant.

I knew the baby was Tony's, since I hadn't had sex with Kenny for a while. But I let everyone think it was Kenny's, and when Kenny found out, he told me he wanted to marry me and raise our baby together. He didn't know how far along I was at the time. I should have said yes and married him, but I couldn't take the thought of being stuck with him for the rest of my life. Instead, I told him I had cheated on him and the baby wasn't his. Kenny was so angry he threw a chair at me.

That was the only time he'd ever been violent with me. He demanded to know who the father was, but I refused to tell him. I didn't hear from him for a week, and then he came back, saying he was sorry and that he'd decided to forgive me. I told Kenny it was over between us, that I didn't want to be with him. And that's when he started following me.

55

"OH, NO!" TAM slammed her laptop shut and covered her mouth with one hand. She was beyond stunned by how wrong she'd been about what had happened between Mia and Tony. She'd thought he'd had a willing affair with Mia. But he hadn't. Truth be told, Mia had violated him.

After that kiss with Adam, Tam knew she had to finish reading Mia's journal. She needed to find out once and for all what had happened between Tony and Mia. She'd been putting it off like a dreaded dentist appointment, but she'd finally made herself read it.

And she'd been so wrong. Boy, had she gotten everything so, so wrong. She moaned and clutched her stomach, doubling over as if in physical pain. "What have I done?" she said out loud to the room. She was filled with regret at the way she'd treated Tony these last few years. She'd been so angry with him and repulsed that he would sleep with his cousin, and even after Mia and Angela moved out, she couldn't get past it and forgive him in her heart. She held him at arm's length, refusing to let him close, punishing him for what she believed was a willing affair with Mia.

"But it wasn't," Tam whispered. "Mia took advantage of him." If only she'd let Mia explain the day she confronted her, all of this would have come out then. If she'd just spoken up and told Tony that Angela was his, Angela wouldn't have been brought into their web of secrets and would have had at least her first five years with her father.

She should have talked to Tony, trusted in his loyalty to her. She should have talked to Mia, whom she had thought of as a sister and hadn't thought would betray her. Instead, she'd nursed her anger, and look what she'd done. She'd kept Angela from her father and wasted all that time with Tony. And now they were gone.

Tam buried her face in her hands. She'd never be able to talk to Tony, hear his side of the story, and tell him she was sorry for her part. She'd never be able to talk to Mia again. She wondered, if they hadn't died, would she have forgiven Mia like Mia wanted and become a part of her life again? Or would Tam have kept Mia away, never sure if she should trust her again?

She curled up into a ball on her bed, her laptop thrown carelessly to the foot of the bed. Thank goodness Bee had the kids. She cried into her pillow, the tears soaking the cotton until it was as wet and sodden as her face. She'd been such a fool. She berated herself, drowning in regret and sorrow until she was so spent she couldn't even lift her hand to get a tissue. She lay on the bed and thought of Tony and Mia until it grew dark and she knew she had to go get the kids.

A few days later, on the Fourth of July, Tam took the kids down by the Hudson River to meet Abby, Jeff, and Steven to see the fireworks. Adam joined them, and when the kids were occupied with

Abby and Jeff, Adam pulled her aside. "We should talk about what happened."

Tam shook her head. "Nothing happened, Adam. It was a mistake. I don't want to get in the middle of you and Jessie."

"About that—" Adam started to say, but they were interrupted when someone called out, "Hi, Tam."

Tam looked up to see Marcus walking toward her, holding the hand of a tall blond woman. His parents, the Hoopers, trailed behind the couple and raised their hands in greeting.

"Hey, Marcus." Tam wished the ground would open up and swallow her. She'd run into Marcus after their failed date, but always at a distance and so could get away with a wave. She didn't need this now, coming face-to-face with Marcus and what appeared to be his new girlfriend while having a difficult conversation with Adam.

"This is Kim." Marcus introduced them, and then Tam had no choice but to introduce Adam. After an awkward pause, Marcus waved and said, "Well, catch you later."

Tam turned to Adam, speaking fast to cover up her unease. "I need your friendship, Adam. Please. You've become so important to the kids, and I don't want to lose you because of one stupid kiss. Can we just forget what happened and put it behind us?"

Adam regarded her for a moment and then nodded. "Okay. The kids mean a lot to me too." He turned and went to where Angela and Steven were trying to teach Charlie how to run. He swooped down and picked Charlie up when he tripped and almost face-planted, throwing him up in the air so he screamed with laughter. Tam stared at them, her mind swirling with conflicting thoughts.

"Shit, shit, shitballs!" she whispered, the frustration building inside her. She'd made such a mess of the relationships in her life, and she was still screwing up. She'd made a big mistake with Tony and Mia and now with Adam. What was wrong with her? Why couldn't she have a normal relationship with someone without fucking it all up? "Fucking shit!"

"What did you say?" Abby spoke from behind her, and Tam jumped.

"Nothing."

"What's going on with you and Adam?" Abby plopped down on the grass next to Tam. "Did something happen between you?"

Tam sat too and wrapped her arms around her legs. "What's going on with you and Jeff?" Tam gazed at the handsome father as he leaned down to say something to Steven. "You guys are still together."

"Yeah." Abby shrugged. "I like him and he likes me. I'm trying not to read too much into it. But what about you and Adam?"

"I kissed him," Tam mumbled into her knees, almost hoping Abby couldn't hear her.

But Abby had ears like a hawk. "I knew it!" she crowed, as if she were responsible for the kiss. "I still don't think it's a good idea, but hey, I'm glad you stood up for something you wanted and made the move."

Tam smacked Abby on the shoulder and her lips twitched.

Abby smirked. "Did he kiss you back?"

Tam nodded, unable to suppress a smile.

"And it was good?"

"Oh, so good," Tam drawled, and the two of them burst into laughter. But when the laughter died, melancholy settled on Tam like a heavy blanket. She gazed at Adam playing with the kids. He made things easier for her. Just when she felt as if she'd reached the end of her rope with the kids, he'd show up like he did today and distract them, giving Tam a moment to collect herself. When she'd lose her temper and yell because Charlie wouldn't eat or Angela wouldn't stop talking and asking "Why?" about everything or Stella barked incessantly at the squirrels in the backyard until Tam thought she'd lose her mind, Adam was always the first person she thought to call to calm her down. And now she'd gone and ruined their relationship.

"You were right." Tam didn't look at Abby as she spoke.

"About what?"

"About falling in love with him."

"Oh, Tam." Abby touched her on the arm.

Tam turned her head so that her cheek rested on her knees and looked at Abby. "Yeah." She let out a long sigh. She'd really messed things up with Adam.

56

ON A HUMID, muggy day in the middle of July, Tam sat across from Kenny and his father in a teahouse in Flushing. The police had called her a few weeks ago to tell her no charges were being made against Kenny or Joe for Tony's and Mia's deaths. Kenny had begged them to give Tam his contact info, saying he needed to speak to Tam in person.

She hadn't wanted to see him, the man who had inadvertently caused their deaths. But Abby had convinced her maybe it would give Tam closure, and Jenny had insisted on accompanying Tam. Jenny was now parked at a different table, her eyes boring into Kenny's back as if daring him to make one wrong step with Tam.

"I had to see you," Kenny said, bringing Tam's focus back on his face. "I'm so sorry for what happened. I never meant for them to be killed. And Joe is just so broken up about it. His wife finally convinced him to see a therapist." His eyes pleaded out of a face like carved stone. She'd be afraid if not for the pain in his eyes. Pain and regret for his part in their deaths.

Kenny's father, an old Chinese man with stooped shoulders, spoke. "I sorry too." He twisted his hat in his gnarled hands. "For you loss. But my boy, he is torn up. He needs you forgiveness." Then he sat there helplessly, his fingers worrying the bill of his cap.

"I loved her," Kenny said, his voice breaking. "I will never forgive myself for what happened."

Tam sat for a moment, remembering everything Mia had told her about Kenny. Mia had loved him once. And Mia had always said how much she'd liked Kenny's father. Tam's heart went out to him. He was suffering too, another casualty of this whole mess.

Tam turned to Kenny. "I don't blame you. I know you loved Mia. Maybe a bit too much, but I know you didn't mean for the truck to run over her and Tony." And as she said the words, something in her chest loosened, and she realized she needed to say those words to Kenny. "Please tell Joe not to blame himself. It was an accident. I don't blame either one of you." She reached out and touched Kenny's father's arm and turned away to give Kenny a moment of privacy when she saw the tears rolling down his cheeks.

She walked back to Jenny's apartment with Jenny afterward, relief coursing through her body. Angela had stayed with Lily while they went to meet Kenny, and Charlie had stayed home in Dobbs Ferry with Tam's mom, who was visiting from California. Tam was glad she'd agreed to see Kenny. Abby was correct. It had been the right thing for her.

Angela was unusually quiet on the train ride home. When Tam asked her what was wrong, she shrugged.

"Nothing. I'm just tired," Angela said.

Tam looked at her closely, but Angela shut her eyes and pretended to sleep. Tam let it go and didn't think anything of it until a few days later, when Lily called to speak to Angela. Tam was sitting on the living room floor doing a puzzle with Charlie when Angela yelled into the phone, "You're a liar, Lily, a big fat liar! I never want to speak to you again!"

Angela threw the phone on the couch and ran upstairs to her room. Tam turned the DVR on to an episode of *Sesame Street* and said to Charlie, "Can you stay here with Bear and Stella and watch Elmo while I talk to Angela?" Her mom had run to the store to pick up milk.

"O-tay," he said, flashing his dimple. He walked over to the couch where Stella was curled up and climbed on with Bear, the teddy bear she'd given him when they first met and which he was never without.

Tam walked upstairs to Angela's room and found the little girl facedown on the bed.

"Angela, what happened?"

Angela flipped over and stared at the ceiling. "Lily is a big fat liar. I hate her!"

"Why? What did she lie about?"

Angela turned toward Tam. "You."

Tam chewed on her bottom lip. What could Lily have possibly said to get Angela so mad? She watched Angela take a few angry breaths before the girl suddenly sat up.

"She said you threw me and my mama out of your house when I was a baby!" She looked at Tam. "You didn't, right? You wouldn't do that. Lily was lying, right?"

Oh, no. Tam felt her heart drop into her stomach. How did Lily find out about this? And what had she told Angela?

"Mommy?" Angela's voice was pleading now.

She couldn't lie to her. She'd been dreading this moment for so long, and she still thought Angela was too young to understand, but she wouldn't lie to her. She had made a vow not to keep secrets from her loved ones anymore. Whatever Lily had said, Tam owed it to Angela to tell her the truth.

"Yes, I did tell Tony that I wanted you and Mia to move out of our house. But there were reasons for it. You once asked me if your mama and Tony had done something wrong. I told you grown-ups sometimes do things that aren't right but that it had nothing to do with you and we all love you very much. That's still true."

Angela stared at Tam, her brows furrowed. "I don't understand."

"I know you don't, and I don't know how to tell you so that you understand. These are things you might not understand until you get older. What exactly did Lily tell you? And how did she find out?"

"She said she heard her mom and dad talking. They said you let Uncle Tony throw me out of his home when you knew he was my daddy, and you didn't tell him, and that's why they wanted to take me away from you. I told Lily she was a big fat liar because I knew you would never do that." She swiped a hand over her eyes. "But you did!"

"Angela, there's so much more to the story than that. And it doesn't mean I didn't love you. I do. I love you with all my heart." Tam could feel the tears building behind her own eyes as she watched Angela struggle not to cry. She heard the front door open and her mom asking Charlie where they were.

Angela swiped again at her eyes and took a big breath. "But you did tell Uncle Tony that we had to leave? Lily didn't lie about that."

"No, she didn't lie about that. But there's so much more to it. I was hoping when you were old enough to understand, we would sit down together and I'd tell you the whole story."

Angela stood up and turned her back to Tam. "Me and Stella don't want to live here anymore. We're going to go live with Bee."

Tam's heart broke. She looked at Angela's back, and she ached for the pain the little girl was feeling. She wanted to explain to her so that she would understand and not feel so betrayed. But how did she tell her the truth without making her mother look bad? How did she explain sex and betrayal and Mia's obsession with Tony to a child?

"I don't want you to go, Angela. I love you so much, and I want you with me." She tried to hug her, but Angela pulled away and ran downstairs. Tam followed and heard Angela telling her mom what had happened. She stood on the last step and Angela looked at her and said, "I'm going to Bee's now."

"Angela, no. You can't leave like this. Let's talk about it." She stepped down and was reaching a hand out to Angela when she felt her mother behind her.

Zhong-Ying said quietly into Tam's ear, "Let her go. I'll walk her over there with Charlie. Call Bee and tell her."

She watched helplessly as Angela put Stella's harness on and then called Bee.

"Of course she can come over. I'm so sorry this all came out. I could just wring that Jenny's neck. She's always the cause of some big catastrophe or bad news. What was she thinking, talking about it where Lily could overhear?"

"It's not her fault," Tam said. "In a way, I'm glad this all came out. I've wanted to tell Angela, but I thought she was too young to understand."

She knew she loved the little girl, but how could she show her when the words describing what she'd done sounded so harsh? She sank onto the couch and covered her face. How was she going to fix things with Angela?

57

MIA'S JOURNAL

You have no idea how much I regretted hurting Tam. Despite myself, I did become close to her, and even though I hated her for being married to Tony, I also loved her. When she had all those miscarriages, I felt bad and tried to help her, but I was secretly glad. Glad that she wasn't able to give Tony the children I knew he wanted. But then I started to care about Tam and I no longer gloated. I felt sorry for her. I was conflicted; on the one hand, I treasured the friendship between us and I wanted to be loyal to Tam, but on the other, I loved Tony so much that I couldn't help myself when the opportunity came up.

I have never seen Tam stick up for herself except for the day she confronted me. Tam is usually so quiet that a lot of people think she's aloof and distant. Only people who know her well know that she's not stuck-up. She's shy and insecure and tends to hold things in. I was always telling her to let go and stop worrying about what other people think. If you don't stick up for yourself and go after what you want in this life, no one is going to do it for you. I knew she had a hard time opening up to her friend Abby, and even with Tony she held a lot back. But she let me in, and I was proud that she trusted me enough to tell me things she'd never tell anyone else.

I was wrong to try to come between a husband and wife, wrong to think Tony belonged to me. I see that now, but back then, all I saw was Tony. From the age of six, I always thought he'd be my knight in shining armor and rescue me from my life as an orphan. I thought he only married Tam because he got tired of waiting for me to grow up. But anyone can see how much he loves Tam. Anyone, that is, except Tam herself. She'd confessed to me more than once that she thought she loved Tony more than he loved her. I knew differently, but I never tried to reassure her. Instead, I fed on her insecurities and told her stories that weren't exactly true, hoping that, eventually, she would feel she didn't deserve Tony and walk away. All I wanted was Tony. And yet, I grew to love and respect Tam, but not enough to stop plotting to get her husband from behind her back. I know I'm not a bad person, but looking back, I am ashamed of my behavior.

How can I ever explain to you where you came from? How can I possibly tell you that your mother slept with a married man and you are the result? That one day, out of desperation, your mother got your father really drunk and then had sex with him? That's why I wanted to write this journal for you. I need you to understand, even the bad parts, and know that no matter what I did to get you, I love you more than my life. You may not condone what I did, but you need to know I did it out of a terribly misguided love for a man I couldn't have. I have no right to ask for your forgiveness, but I hope you will one day be able to forgive me for how you came into the world.

58

WHEN ZHONG-YING CAME back, she said to Tam, "I left Charlie with Bee for a bit so we can talk."

Tam shook her head. She didn't want to talk. She went to the sink and started washing the dishes, hoping her mom would leave her alone. But she could feel her mother standing behind her.

"What?" Tam asked without turning around.

"You never want to talk to me. Even the whole business with Tony and Mia, you never told me the whole story. I only know what Wei told me."

Tam shut off the water. "You wouldn't understand," she said. "You didn't grow up here."

Her mom slapped a palm down on the counter, making Tam jump. "You always say that. Why you think I not understand, 'cause my English so bad?" she asked in mock broken English.

Tam watched her mother walk to the couch, her back tense, bristling with indignation. She followed her.

"My English not good, but I understand. More than you know." Her mom switched back to Taiwanese. "I was married to a man who wanted to bring home mistresses, concubines, he called them." She said "concubines" in English.

Tam stared at her in shock. "Dad wanted concubines?"

"No, no." Zhong-Ying waved her hand. "Not your father, before him. I was married to a very bad man when I lived in Taiwan. He thought he was still living back in the old days when it was okay to have more than one wife. Everyone knew he had mistresses, but the only person who told me was my oldest sister. But what could I do? I already married him, and in those days in my family, there was no divorce."

"You were married before Dad? Why didn't you ever tell me?"

Her mom shrugged. "I tried. You were never interested. When I try to tell you stories from before, you never want to hear."

Tam started to protest and then realized her mom was right. She'd never been interested in her mom's stories about the past. She was too busy living life as an American, worrying about the prom, what college to go to, or whether to stay in New York or go back to California. She didn't have time for old stories. But how was it possible that she didn't know her own mother had been married before?

She sat next to her mother. "I'm sorry." It had always been hard for her to say sorry to her mom, even when she knew she was wrong. "Does Wei know?"

"Yes, I told him years ago."

"Oh." Tam felt a flash of hurt that her brother knew and hadn't told her. "I do want to hear your stories."

Her mom shook her head. "There's not much to tell. We were only married for a year, and then he died of a heart attack. He was a young man, not even thirty. My mother always said he must have had such a bad heart that it killed him. And then my oldest sister, the one who told me about the mistresses, introduced me to your father. He'd started working with my siblings on the software they were developing. We got married and then decided to move to California when my brothers and sisters started the company there, and that was that."

Tam stared at her mom. "I know there's more to the story. I can't believe I never knew."

"You were never interested in the past, like Wei was. You always say, 'You don't understand!' But I do." She paused. "I understand more than you know."

The doorbell rang and Tam jumped up, thinking Angela had come back. She opened the door, and the smile dropped from her face.

"Oh, it's you."

Adam laughed. "I've never felt more welcome."

Tam gestured for him to come in. "I'm sorry, it's not you."

"I know," he said. "Angela called me. That's why I'm here. I wanted to see if you're okay."

He came in and greeted Tam's mom. "I'll let you two talk," her mom said, and went down to the basement, leaving the door open.

Tam and Adam stood in the kitchen and looked at each other. Things had been so uncomfortable between them. That kiss was always there between them, even though they didn't talk about it.

"Are you okay?" he asked.

"I knew this day was going to come. I just didn't think it was going to come so fast. I thought we had more time."

"Tam, that little girl loves you very much and she knows you love her. Once she's had a chance to think it over, she's going to realize that."

"I thought things were going so well. And even finding out the truth that Mia was the one who seduced Tony . . ." She broke off, realizing she hadn't told Adam this part yet.

"What?" Adam took a step closer to her. "Mia seduced Tony?"

Tam nodded. "He wasn't having an affair with Mia. He loved me the whole time." She lowered her eyes to the floor, unable to meet his gaze. "Mia got him drunk one night and had sex with him while he was practically passed out."

Adam reached for her and gathered Tam to him. She stiffened at first, but when he started stroking her back, she relaxed into him. She felt the vibrations in his body as he talked. "My God, Tam. That must have been a shock to you."

She nodded against his chest. She didn't realize she was crying until Adam's shirt was wet. Why was she ruining this man's shirt with her tears?

"I thought I was handling everything so well, but then I find out I'd been so wrong to punish Tony all these years. And I thought I could raise Angela and Charlie by myself, but now I see I can't. How do I deal with things like this? Maybe I should move to California. My mom and I have been talking and I think I need her. I can't do this."

"No," Adam said, running a hand down her back. "I don't want you to move to California."

"I don't either, but I can't do this alone. I need help. I think Angela might need counseling or someone besides me to talk to. Who's going to help me if something bad happens? Who's going to help me make important decisions for our lives?"

"I will," Adam said.

"I was kidding myself when I thought I could be a single mom. I can't!"

"I'll be here for you. Let me be the one to help you and be your family."

"Wait, what?" She pulled away and looked at him in confusion. "What are you talking about? I don't think Jessie would like that very much."

"Jessie no longer has a say in what I do. We broke up the day you and I kissed."

"What?" She stared at him, her mouth open in horror. "What do you mean? Why didn't you tell me?"

"I tried, but you didn't want to talk about it. You seemed to regret our kiss so much. I didn't want to put any pressure on you."

"What happened? Was it my fault? I can explain to Jessie that it was my fault." She looked around frantically for her phone, as if she really meant to call Jessie right then.

"No, Tam. It wasn't you." Adam stilled her movements by placing a hand on her arm. "We'd been drifting apart for a long time. I just didn't want to admit it." Adam smiled, but it didn't reach his eyes. "After we kissed, I realized I'd changed. Jessie is still the same woman she was when I met her, driven, moving up in the world. But I changed when I met you and the kids. It wasn't all about the career for me anymore. I wanted a family, and to come home to the kids every day. And not just any kids—your kids. And I wanted to come home to you. I realized I was in love with you and not with Jessie."

Tam felt her mouth drop open. She'd just found out her mother had been married to someone else, and now Adam was telling her he was in love with her. Had the whole world gone insane?

"Are you crazy? What kind of man wants someone else's kids, and they're not even my own?" She said the first thing that came to her mind.

"I do. Maybe it's crazy, but I love those two kids like my own. And I love you. I told myself I would wait. I knew you weren't ready, and I wanted you to be at peace with your husband's death and everything that happened. But I don't want you to leave."

He picked up one of her hands in both of his. "I don't want you to ever feel like you have to handle anything alone again. I want to be there for you, to get through this with you, to help Angela understand what happened. I want all of you."

"I don't know what to say," she said. They stared at each other, and then Adam leaned in and kissed her. Nothing had felt so right in so long as this kiss and being in Adam's arms. It was like coming home and being welcomed, and she kept her eyes closed, even when he drew away.

"I want to marry you. That's how much I love you."

Tam's eyes flew open. "We haven't even had sex yet. How do you know it'll work between us?"

He took her hand and put it over his growing crotch. "Oh, I think it will work just fine. Do you want to test that out now?"

"No!" Tam snatched her hand back. "My mother is downstairs. She's probably listening to every word." Adam smiled at her, and she couldn't help but smile back. "I need to talk to her. She just told me she was married before she married my dad, to a bad man who had mistresses. I never knew this. I didn't think she'd understand what happened with Tony, but I think she understands more than I gave her credit for."

Adam took her hand back and interlaced his fingers in hers. "Okay."

She looked at him. "I think I have feelings for you too. I might even love you. But so much just happened that I can't process it right now. I always thought you were off-limits, so to suddenly find out you broke up with Jessie a couple of weeks ago because you love me and the kids, well, I need to figure out how I feel about that."

"I'll give you time. I'm not going anywhere." Adam squeezed her hand. "I'll go talk to Angela. It might help her to talk with someone who's not involved."

She nodded, and he pulled her into his arms for another kiss and was gone. She took a deep breath and then turned to go find her mother.

59

ZHONG-YING WAS WAITING at the bottom of the stairs. Tam knew she had heard every word. She prepared herself for words spoken against Adam.

But her mom surprised her. "It is fate and *yuanfen* that bring two people together. Value an encounter and treasure a relationship."

Tam started to roll her eyes but then caught herself. Why did she always get impatient when her mom talked about the old days or Chinese customs? She should want to hear what her mom was willing to share with her.

"What is *yuanfen*?" she made herself ask.

"Fate or chance that brings people together. Kind of like karma, as you say in English."

"Oh."

"Sometimes fate brings you together with someone who may not seem suitable. Or your family may not approve of. But if it is fateful coincidence for your two lives to come together, then you need to recognize it and treasure it."

"Are you saying it's okay for me to love Adam even though he's white and you and Dad might not approve?" Tam asked.

"I'm saying that sometimes life doesn't happen exactly the way we plan it, for ourselves or for our daughters. The smart woman learns to let go and let what is predestined and what good luck has brought together be." Her mom sat on the couch. "Tam, I know we've had our differences, and I know you have no patience to hear about my past or my thoughts, but I know you. You keep things inside, not wanting to share with people who can help you. You let thoughts fester in your mind until it becomes unhealthy for you. Don't make that mistake with Adam. He is a good man. I know I didn't approve before because I thought he had a fiancée. But my opinion of him just went up a hundred percent when he said he broke up with her because he realized he loves you and the children."

Tam went to sit next to her mom. She knew her mom was right. Instead of talking to Adam about it the day they'd kissed by the tree stump, she'd kept everything in and refused to talk about it. Just like she'd done with Tony.

"I try to come as much as I can because I know you need the support even if you think you don't need your mother. Angela is going to need help to come to terms with how she came into this world and what her father and mother and you did. Even when I thought he had a fiancée, that man loved those kids with all his heart. He was the first person Angela called when she was hurting."

"I always thought you wanted me to marry a Taiwanese man," Tam said.

"He's white, but he's got good energy," her mom said. Then she laughed. "A mother can hope though, can't she? We are Taiwanese and you should be proud, yet all your life, you've been ashamed of your roots. You weren't like Wei. You were always itching to break free and be like the American girls. Your father and I were surprised when you married a Chinese man." She paused. "What happened with Tony?"

"Wei already told you."

"I want to hear it from you. In your words."

And so Tam told her. She was embarrassed and ashamed to tell her mother about her relationship with Tony, so the story came out slowly. But she told her everything, just like she'd told Adam. She told her how angry she was when she thought Tony was having an affair with his cousin, how tormented she was by what she did, and how confused she was when Tony and Mia died. And with each re-telling, Tam felt as if she were shedding a skin, ridding herself of the heavy mantle of guilt and hurt. Her mom took her in her arms and hugged her, like she used to do many years ago, before Tam became too old to want hugs from her mother.

"You have to stop blaming yourself. If you figured it out, why didn't Tony? He only saw what he wanted to believe."

Tam pulled back. She'd never thought of that, that maybe Tony knew deep down that Angela was his but had taken the easy way out and chosen to believe Mia.

"But I lied to him by not telling him the truth."

"And he lied to you from the very beginning. He wasn't perfect. He was weak; he didn't stand up for you, his wife. He brought another woman into your home without telling you the truth."

"I was so ashamed of everything."

"You shouldn't be. I know you don't like to hear bad things about Tony and Mia, but they were the ones who lied to you. They took the decision out of your hands," her mom said.

"I didn't want to tell you about our relationship because I knew you'd say, 'I told you so. Their kind is different from us.'"

"I'm sorry." Her mom let her arms fall away from Tam. "I know I always go on about that. But you have to forgive yourself and forgive Tony. He might have been wrong, but in the end, he was trying to do the right thing with Angela."

Tam nodded slowly. Her mother was right. She needed to remember Tony as a husband, a father, a flawed man who was trying to make things right. She had loved him, but he was gone. "Oh, Mom. I've been such an idiot."

"No. You're human," her mom said. "This is why family is so important. Without my family, I wouldn't have wanted to get married again. But my sisters and brothers stood by my side and they introduced me to your father."

She looked at her mother, really looked at her, and realized she'd lived a whole life before Tam was born. And in all of her thirty-eight years, Tam had not been interested enough to ask about her mother's past. Was this what Wei had been trying to tell her before she left for China? He'd said their mom understood more than Tam thought, and now she knew he was right. She'd been so involved in the drama of her own life and thought her mother couldn't possibly understand.

She reached out a hand and laid it on top of one of her mother's. "Tell me," she said. "I'm ready to listen."

Her mother's eyelids fluttered closed, and for a second, Tam thought she'd lost her chance. But then her mom opened her eyes, and in them, Tam could see the heartaches, the pain and betrayals, but also the joy and happiness of her mother's life. She nodded at Tam and began to speak.

60

MIA'S JOURNAL

When I left for America, Xing Xing Ayi told me an old Chinese proverb: "Fate brings people together no matter how far apart they may be."

If fate should be so cruel as to separate us, my dear Angela, know that I will always be with you even if I'm no longer physically on this earth.

I hope I will be around to see my little girl grow up, to see you live the childhood I didn't have and become someone better than I became. But I trust in fate and know that whatever happens, things will turn out the way they are meant to.

All I want is for you to be happy. If it's with me, then my heart will burst out of my chest with gratitude and happiness that I get to see my little girl grow up. But if that is not to be, I know you will be happy with Tam and Tony, growing up in a complete family. Maybe you'll even be able to get a dog like you've always longed for. And when Tam and Tony bring home their little boy from China, from the same or-phanage I grew up in, you'll have the little brother you've always wanted. I want that for you, Angel. I want you to have a complete family like I always yearned for.

If I am gone, I know there will be rough times. I know when you are old enough to understand and read my words, you'll be hurting over what we all did to your life. You will probably have doubts as you grow up, and questions, so many questions. But I am comforted knowing you will have your father and Tam to help you. They are the best people I know, and they will stand by you and get you the help you need as you grow up and come to accept how you came to be on this earth.

But the one thing you won't ever have to doubt is that you are wanted. You are so loved, by Tam and by your mama and baba. If I am no longer on earth to watch you grow up, you will feel my presence when you need it. A breeze in your hair when you're feeling lonely, a leaf fluttering gently down in front of you when you need answers, or a familiar scent wafting through the air when you have doubts. You will see me in your dreams and be soothed, knowing I am watching over you from above.

You may hate me when you become a teenager and fully understand my actions. But one day, I know you will reach out to me in your dreams and say, "I forgive you, Mama." And the red thread of fate will bring our hearts together again.

Author's Note

RED THREAD OF FATE was inspired by my family's journey when we adopted our son. My husband and I discovered a new definition for family during the process and how a family can be formed not just by blood, but by fate bringing people together. The term "red thread of fate," originated in Chinese mythology where it was believed that the gods tied together an invisible red thread between lovers who are destined to be together. This thread can never be broken; it might be tangled or stretched but will never break.

In more recent years, this term has been embraced by the adoption community to include adopted children and their new families. There is controversy over this use, as its critics say adoptions are not destined to happen. With this line of thinking, the birth parents are then thought to be "destined" to lose their children because of devastating circumstances in their home country. We need to understand the political and economic conditions that lead to birth parents having to give up their children.

I wrote *Red Thread of Fate* because I wanted to show the human side of Chinese orphanages, of the many ayis (nannies) who took care of the children. These ayis care for the children despite often grim circumstances, especially in Guangdong Province where few government resources could meet the needs of the flood of children being abandoned as a result of the one-child policy (note: this policy has since been lifted).

Pam Thomas (the China Program Director at Hand in Hand International Adoptions, whose tireless work with children from China for more than twenty-five years has brought many families together) shared with me her own experiences of visiting the social welfare institutes. She told me it was not uncommon for orphanage workers to become attached to certain children they care for. The affection is real, and often a source of pain for the caregivers who have to say good-bye to a child who is being adopted. I hope I have accurately portrayed this bond between a child and her ayi in *Red Thread of Fate*. Thank you to Pam for everything you did for our family, but also for reading parts of this book and making sure I got the most accurate descriptions of what orphanages were like in the 1990s. I am thankful that there are now continual improvements in the facilities and resources that are available, especially for children with special needs.

This book explores the red threads that bind a family together, not just of lovers, but of biological parent to child, adoptive parent to child, and everything in between. It is not meant to perpetuate the thinking that adoptions are acts of destiny; rather, my family, with deep roots in Taiwan, truly believe that our family was brought together by fate in some way. We never forget about our son's biological parents. I wonder about them, who they are, and wish they knew what an amazing little person their son is. There is a light within him that should have been dimmed by the circumstances of his earlier years but only makes him shine brighter, and many have dubbed him the happiest little boy they know.

If you'd like to learn more about the books I read while I was researching Chinese orphanages in the 1990s, here is the list:

The Lost Daughters of China by Karin Evans
China's Hidden Children by Kay Ann Johnson
Silent Tears by Kay Bratt
Unseen Tears by Beau Sides

Thank you for letting me share this journey with you. Please note this is only one perspective on adoption from China. There are many, and this novel is not meant to represent all. This story is a figment of my imagination, based on my experiences with the process.

Acknowledgments

To everyone who read *The Tiger Mom's Tale* (and this book!) and spread the word, thank you from the bottom of my heart. I wouldn't be here without readers like you.

As always, my fabulous agent, Rachel Brooks, has my undying gratitude for all she does for me and my books. Never could I have imagined a more perfect working partnership and a champion of even some of my craziest ideas. When I make her snort in laughter and respond in all caps, I know I'm on the right path. Thank you, Rachel. You and BookEnds are the very best of the best.

There are not enough words to express how amazing my team at Berkley is. Cindy Hwang, you are the editor of my dreams and I still pinch myself that I get to work with you. Jin Yu and Cat Barra, I'm so grateful for the care and attention you put into getting my books out there. Angela Kim, you never cease to amaze me with all you do. Danielle Keir, Dache Rogers, and Brittanie Black, I couldn't have asked for better publicists, who work so hard to get me every opportunity. Vikki Chu, the cover is brilliant once again, and thank you also to Eileen G. Chetti, Alison Cnockaert, and Megha Jain for everything you do.

Every writer needs writing friends who read your work, cheer you on, and lift you up. Thank you to: Christine Adler, Alison Hammer, Bradeigh Godfrey, Robin Facer, Jessica Armstrong, Lainey Cameron, Anita Kushwaha, Saumya Dave, Sarah Echavarre Smith, and Delise Torres; you all inspire me so much.

To my Berkletes, you made Debut Year exceptional. Thank you especially to India Holton, Ali Hazelwood, Nekesa Afia, Eliza Jane Brazier, Lynn Painter, Olivia Blacke, Elizabeth Everett, Libby Hubsher, Mia P. Manansala, Courtney Ellis, Sarah Grunder Ruiz, Amanda Jayatissa, Sarah Zachrich Jeng, Lauren Accardo, Alanna Martin, Amy Lea, Joanna Lowell, and Freya Sampson, for not only the support but the lesser CE GIFs, knotting, and pooping (and therapy needed for all of the above).

Thank you to the members of the New York City Writers Critique Group, especially Christopher Keelty, Steven Tate, David Geshwind, and Peter Van Buren, for reading early drafts of this book.

To Melissa Danaczko, I will never forget your kindness when I queried you. Your enthusiasm for the concept of this book pushed me forward to not give up on it.

To the Heck family: Allison, Maren, Abigail, Linna, and Carey, you were part of the journey we took that inspired this book.

To Pam Thomas, thank you for your insight and willingness to share your experiences in the orphanages and for reading my passages to ensure accuracy. Any mistakes are completely my own. Also, special thanks to Penny Smith Berk, who brought Pam and my family together.

To my friend Lauren Gleicher, our friendship of over twenty years (Twenty! What?! How old ARE we?) means more than you know. You are a star, and I can't wait to see you shine.

So many thanks to my family—C. J. Liao, Hsiang-Fang Liao, and Yaw-Ting Liao—for everything (even though my parents only read one line of my book before giving up, waiting for the Mandarin translation!), and for taking care of my son so I could sneak off to write.

To my husband, Jim, who fully supported my harebrained scheme when I decided we had to live in Kauai for two months to research a book (best decision we ever made during the pandemic!). And to Lakon, our ray of sunshine. No, Lakon, this book is not *about* you, it's *inspired* by you. And to close this out in true Lyn fashion, thank you to my dogs, Lokie, Mochi, and Cash (and Pinot up in heaven). You are the ones who truly stick by my side for every word written and every anxious moment waiting to see if anyone wants to read more of my books.

RED

THREAD

OF

FATE

LYN LIAO BUTLER

Discussion Questions

1. Do you believe in fate or destiny, and that there are people you are meant to be with in your life?

2. If you were in Tam's situation, would you have taken in Angela and completed the adoption for Charlie? Are you a single parent or with a partner, and does that have any effect on what you would have done?

3. Mia did something inexcusable in Tam's eyes. After hearing Mia's story, do you feel any sympathy toward Mia, and can you understand why she did some of what she did?

4. Have you tried any of the food mentioned in this book? Which would you like to try? (Note: egg custard tarts would be a great addition to your book club meeting!)

5. What's one thing you've learned from reading this book that's made you think?

6. Mia thought the red thread was between Tam and Tony. Do you agree? And if not, who do you think Tam's red thread was really connected to? What about Mia?

7. What did you think about the men in the book: Tony, Adam, and Kenny? Was Tony weak for not figuring out the truth and telling his wife? What did you think of Adam's friendship with Tam? Did you feel any sympathy for Kenny at all?

8. Tam's mom is an important side character. How did you feel about her?

9. Abby proves to be a great friend to Tam. Do you have a friend like this, who would drop everything to help you if something catastrophic happened to you?

DAVE CROSS PHOTOGRAPHY

LYN LIAO BUTLER was born in Taiwan and moved to the States when she was seven. Before becoming an author, she was a professional ballet and modern dancer, and is still a personal trainer, fitness instructor, and RYT 200-hour yoga instructor. She is an avid animal lover and fosters dogs as well as volunteers with rescues.

When she is not torturing clients or talking to imaginary characters, Lyn enjoys spending time with her FDNY husband, son (the happiest little boy in the world), their three stubborn dachshunds, and trying crazy yoga poses on a stand-up paddleboard. She has not fallen into the water yet.

CONNECT ONLINE

LynLiaoButler.com

🄵 LynLiaoButlerAuthor

🄾 LynLiaoButler

🄽 LynLiaoButler

Ready to find
your next great read?

Let us help.

Visit prh.com/nextread

Penguin
Random
House